Misguided Lives

Misguided Lives

a novel by
Alain Elkann

Translated from the Italian by
William Weaver

THE ATLANTIC MONTHLY PRESS
NEW YORK

First published in Italy in 1988 by Arnoldo Mondadori Editore S.p.A.
First Atlantic Monthly Press edition, October 1989

Published simultaneously in Canada
Printed in the United States of America

Library of Congress Cataloging-in-Publication Data

Elkann, Alain, 1950–
    Misguided lives / by Alain Elkann.—1st Atlantic Monthly Press ed.
    "First published in Italy in 1988"—T.p. Verso
    ISBN 0-87113-295-8
    I. Title
PQ4865.L485M57   1989   853'.914—dc20   89-34782

Design by Laura Hough

The Atlantic Monthly Press
19 Union Square West
New York, NY 10003

FIRST PRINTING

To Diane
and with special thanks to Claudio

Part 1

Misguided Lives

1. The Answering Machine

Guia went out, slamming the front door behind her. Incredulous and frightened, Mario rummaged through the apartment, opening drawers and closets, searching among the papers, photographs and clothes. In the bathroom, her cosmetics and perfumes were still there. That she'd left everything behind meant she'd come back. She'd gone away other times. The year before, she'd run off to India for a month, and then they'd made up. But this morning she'd talked about separation, lawyers.

Unable to read or concentrate on what had happened, Mario picked up the phone and called Antonio. The answering machine replied, "Leave a message, I'll be back after midnight." He called Ginevra, a former girlfriend from Rome, and got her answering machine: first some Brazilian music, then Ginevra's voice, then music again.

After hanging up, he turned off the tape player. From the moment Guia left, he'd listened constantly to the same sad music. He dialed Ginevra's number again to hear the Brazilian music. Then he called a friend in Florence, whose answering machine said, "My soul is at home but my body . . ." Call after call, Mario penetrated

MISGUIDED LIVES

deeper and deeper into the world of answering machines, to which, previously, he had never paid much attention. He thought about the message and music he would record if he had a machine himself.

Throughout the evening, the phone rang constantly. In a flood of words, Mario told everyone who called the same story, with different details. Nobody seemed to regret the end of his marriage. They were all affectionate, inviting him to lunch, to dinner, to a country weekend. He talked as if it were all over, but it could be just a threat. God only knew where she'd holed up.

Mario and Guia had met when they were children living in the same building in Milan. They exchanged their first kiss at fourteen, during a party. Much later Mario heard that Guia had married. Then they met again in Turin and spent the entire night walking and talking. Both of them were separated, and they agreed they would never leave each other. For almost three years they lived in Paris and Milan, and when their divorces came through they married, despite the disapproval of their families. "You're living together!" everybody said. "Why get married?" From that day on, things between them started deteriorating. There was no plan to their existence, and the amorous spell faded, leaving only misunderstanding and quarrels. In Paris they stayed home constantly and spent sleepless nights taking drugs, drinking and talking. When Guia's eyes started turning glassy, her sensuality wakened. Mario said obscene things to her and treated her like a prostitute. The sexual act was transformed into a long masturbation that went on till morning. Guia read many picture magazines, and she followed, as if they were serialized novels, the lives of certain famous women. One of these, a French actress, had been photographed for all the papers holding a magnificent Irish wolfhound, and Guia bought the same breed, a puppy they called Mandarin. Once the enthusiasm of the first days was past, they stopped looking after him. During the lazy weekends, they let him roam about the apartment and bark and shit everywhere. At most they dragged themselves into the

4

kitchen to open a can of meat for him. On Monday mornings the maid would find the house a wreck, but she didn't say anything. She had a sick husband; they paid her twice the normal wage.

When they ran out of drugs and the Duchess didn't have any more, they felt a deep sense of guilt. Their bedroom, they realized, had become a pigsty: empty bottles, butts everywhere, burns and stains on the carpet, dirty sheets, foul smells. Ashamed, Mario would launch into speeches about how to take this situation in hand and change it. As a rule, they decided to leave as soon as possible for some distant place, preferably on the sea, with a deluxe hotel, where they took refuge as if it were a sanitarium. They tried to follow a strict schedule, to eat regular meals. They swam and deceived themselves into thinking they were starting a new life. At the beach, Guia was transformed; she became tranquil, and when the time to leave approached, she would often beg Mario to stay on. They could settle right there, look for a house, open a pizzeria, keep well away from their families and from temptations. But for Mario, these attempts to escape their fate seemed capricious and feckless. So, more discontent each time, they would return to Paris. From the airport they called the Duchess to find out if she had anything. "We'll have a party to celebrate being back, and then we'll quit." They would say this then pick up where they had left off. Sleepless nights, floods of words, dissolute sex, cigarettes, alcohol—until they went off again to another seaside paradise, another deluxe hotel.

They had spent their last vacation, a disaster, on an island in Indonesia. Mario suffered from a painful ailment of the genitals, and when he complained Guia turned contemptuous, calling him impotent. In the end they were silent for entire days, shut up in their bungalow under the torrential rain. Guia would lie stretched out on the bed; she smoked, had a few drinks, took tranquilizers. Mario knew she was neurotic and eccentric, but he harbored the illusion that they could work things out. Love would heal all wounds. But it didn't. Guia was too fragile, too insecure. She knew she was beautiful, yet she couldn't stop herself from asking, "Am I ugly?" or "Do you love me?" Were all these reasons enough to explain why she'd gone off like this after three months of marriage? They hadn't been able to build a solid relationship. They'd behaved childishly until their nerves had frayed.

Their friendship with Paola and John had sprung up on the evening of Mario's birthday. Paola had generously passed out drugs, hinting that it wasn't hard for John to get more. This changed their rapport with the Duchess. Mario hated the arrogance of that woman, who spoke in a loud voice, had horrible superstitions and compelled her customers to socialize with her, even when she was sitting on the toilet. Time and again, as he climbed up the Duchess's steps, he identified with Raskolnikov, going to kill the old moneylender! But weakness always triumphed, and he would flatter her, do anything in order to procure one of her little envelopes. The best way to escape this situation would've been to prevent Guia from using her money, but he couldn't do without it. He would accept some magnificent present, only to regret it.

Though well aware of the failure of their relationship, they would talk about what would happen when they had a child and what they would call it. At times they even quarreled over the name. Then superstition would take over: if they kept talking about imaginary children, they would never have any real ones. They would start calculating the right days for making love, and psychosomatic menstrual delays would result. They blamed their failure to have children on their debauched lives and on the apartment, which was unlucky. Guia said it was essential to go and live somewhere far away. Mario didn't want to. He had friends in Paris but was forced to see them by himself because of Guia's criticisms. She couldn't accept that he had a life of his own, and she was terribly jealous of his past. The last few weeks had been violent. After many reproaches and arguments, Guia had taken refuge with Paola and John. She blackmailed them into keeping Mario away. Finally she came home, apparently wanting to make up, but there was another terrible fight, and she left with an overnight case, slamming the door behind her.

After a few days of confinement, Mario went out. The apartment smothered him in memories, and he needed a change of air. In the elevator he met Odile, Philippe's wife, and they smiled absently at each other. When he came back, around eleven, he ran into her again and they exchanged trivialities: "We don't see each other for months, then we meet twice in one morning." Once back in the house, Mario felt he couldn't stand the place any more. He called Philippe; Odile answered and explained that Philippe would be back on Sunday night.

"You're alone?" he asked her.

"No, the children are here."

"What are you doing for lunch?"

"Eating with them."

"Don't you want to come out for a pizza?"

"I don't have much time. I have to take Pauline to her gym class."

"We'll make it quick."

"I have to be back at two."

"All right, at two I'll bring you home."

"Promise?"

"Yes."

In the pizzeria Odile smoked and smiled. Thirtyish, pretty, dark, tiny, very French, she spoke and acted like a student. They talked briefly about Guia. That afternoon, they talked on the phone. Odile couldn't go out for supper, so she'd drop by later. When she came up, towards midnight, it was clear she had come to make love. To Mario this seemed disloyal to Philippe, but she explained that they had an open relationship; they could live their own lives.

Making love with Odile, Mario felt Guia's absence. With her it was different. In the beginning he hadn't been able to tell if Guia had reached orgasm or was frigid until she explained what he should do to arouse her.

MISGUIDED LIVES

One evening she let him discover her as she was leafing through some pornographic magazines; then she took him to a sex shop. Guia's favorite city was Amsterdam. The women in the windows fascinated her. She liked to say that she wanted to become one of them. When she did come, something animal-like possessed her. She couldn't stop, and she became ravenous in an embarrassing way.

When Odile left, Mario felt free again. He hadn't felt anything before, only Guia's absence. That night he could only recall the most beautiful moments of their time together, especially their first trip to Egypt. Guia was irresistibly attracted to distant places.

Mario spent that Sunday with a friend, a girl from Naples who worked at the Italian Cultural Institute, and a colleague of hers, a likable and remarkably intelligent man. That evening he thought again of Dennis's laconic voice on the telephone: "What can I say? I told you not to marry her!"

Even though Guia's departure seemed the proper consequence of a mistaken situation, Mario kept wondering why she had chosen to go back to Milan, to a mother who looked like a piece of candy and went to the hairdresser every day to maintain her impeccable appearance. Guia had never been able to rebel against her because the woman had twice attempted suicide, blaming it on her daughter. Actually, she enjoyed torturing Guia, making her suffer.

A month later, Mario learned that Guia had been hospitalized and would soon be released. He left a message on her answering machine, and then Guia left one on the machine Mario had just had installed. They exchanged messages.

"I had to do it because I couldn't stand your nastiness any more."

Mario: "Do you still love me?"

Guia: "You know perfectly well I've always loved you."

Mario: "But after what happened, what should we do?"

"That's for you to decide."

"Would you come back to me?"

"What about you?" This was Guia, a few days later.

"I don't know. I think we still love each other, but we don't know how to live together."

"Then it's useless to keep telephoning. Let's call it quits."

Mario left a message on Guia's machine: "You want a divorce?"

The answer was, "Not particularly."

Then the messages stopped.

2. The Boy in the Red Shirt

Sitting in the museum café, Paola saw a man arrive, sweating, a briefcase stuffed with documents and a bundle of newspapers under his arm.

He had the sallow complexion of someone who has a bad liver and drinks too much coffee. There were deep, purplish hollows under his eyes. Though he carried his forty years badly, Paola noticed that he combined a lighthearted manner with a disturbing gaze.

The way he sat down at the table showed a sense of satisfaction, almost happiness. When the waiter came over, with a slightly hypocritical smile, he ordered a gin and tonic then undid a button of his shirt, which was too tight, before lighting a cigarette. Smug, he looked around and massaged the rolls of fat on his stomach. Watching him, Paola was seized with desire. She studied him, enchanted, as he gripped his glass and raised it slowly to his mouth, as he shelled a hard-boiled egg, dipped it in the salt and ate it in two bites.

She felt something vibrate inside her and had an irresistible yearning to suck this man's tongue into her mouth. She would taste that mixture of cigarette, gin and hard-boiled egg. Marziano's receding hairline made him comb his scant, too-long hair into a messy, unfortunate arrangement. He had hazel eyes, deep-set, small, vaguely satanic.

Unable to restrain herself, Paola moved to Marziano's table and asked bluntly, "You're Italian, aren't you?"

"Is it so obvious, immediately?"

"I don't know. I wanted you to speak Italian."

"I see. Can I offer you something to drink?"

"Thank you, no."

Marziano had a singsong voice that left a strong impression. His manner of speaking held a hint of irony. His gaze concealed an overpowering ambition that kept him in a state of constant tension. Because he was consumed with anxiety, his digestion was bad. More than anything else, he would have liked to be handsome, tall and slim.

Marziano and Paola had dinner together. They set off along the empty Rue de Varenne, where they saw only a few young policemen, sweating in their bulletproof vests, standing guard at the barricaded entrances of ministries and embassies. At the restaurant they had felt like lovers even before they touched. Marziano talked about Marina and how she had gone away without a qualm, after fifteen years of marriage, to follow a boy to California. He and Marina had a daughter, Tatiana, who was studying in a boarding school near Oxford. On late spring mornings, Marina used to go and sunbathe in the Luxembourg Gardens, and there she had met a blond boy who always wore the same red shirt. Paola, in reply, told him about John, the boy she lived with. He had no possessions, hated to work and moved like a cat. While Paola was talking,

Marziano started thinking about Tatiana. Maybe he should have rejected the boarding-school idea and kept her with him in Paris. She was such an intelligent girl, but irritable and unhappy. Unlike Marina, she wasn't beautiful: too fat, terribly nearsighted. She had blond hair, like her mother's, but hers was dry, strawlike.

Once out in the street, Paola and Marziano looked for a dark, secluded place. Behind a stairway they made love violently. His hands under her clothes, Marziano touched her hips, her legs, and he kissed her with passion. In Marziano's arms, Paola felt reassured. Suddenly he seemed impatient to go away. Marziano was one of those men who, having reached orgasm, become indifferent and start thinking of other things. But it was this animalism that had first attracted Paola, back in the café.

3. The Woman of My Life

The first thing you felt about Donna Ada was her determination to control and dominate others. With the passage of time she had overcome her anxiety about not being beautiful. Rich, tight-fisted, she moved hecticly between her estate in Tuscany, the rice plantations in Lomellina, a farm in the Veneto and an apartment in Rome's Parioli district. She had never married, had always had more than one lover at a time and had never revealed to her son Dennis the identity of his father. The only subjects she would talk about involved money, power and gossip.

When she was with certain men she enjoyed behaving like a dimwit. During the early days of a love affair she would pretend to be servile, then she would tire of that and liberate herself.

MISGUIDED LIVES

Dennis had been born delicate, and his mother considered him of little interest, too elusive, taciturn and stubborn. He made her nervous because he was interested in things as if they were all equally important. As a child he refused to wash or to change his clothes until they were filthy. By the age of nine, he could already express himself so articulately that Donna Ada suspected he was precocious, perhaps worthy of attention. Blond, with pale blue, nearsighted eyes, Dennis read complicated books or amused himself by playing with dogs and cats or by taking long walks.

At fourteen, fed up with school, Dennis dropped out and began to travel in search of teachers and encounters that would satisfy his hunger for learning. When he came home, he was ill for a long time. Once he was well again, Donna Ada decided to send him to a sanitarium in the mountains to convalesce. There he met Max, who was being treated for drug addiction. He and Max talked about films, women, German literature, cooking, Chinese philosophy, some special studies pursued in Dutch universities. Their favorite subject was the search for the dwelling place of happiness. Both were very interested in happiness. When Dennis ended his stay in the mountains, it seemed natural for him to go back to Rome, where Max also lived. There he met his first lover, Marcella, a stage actress. After Marcella, Dennis, who was seventeen, did nothing but search for the woman of his life. Whenever he told Max he had found her, Max would answer, almost laughing, "For the moment it seems to me that the woman of your life is Marziano."

Max had succeeded in making the two boys inseparable. In the morning they would go to the Borghese Gardens, each with a pile of books; sitting on a bench, they would start reading and arguing. When it was cold or raining, they would take refuge in cafés. Vanessa Muller, if she was in Rome, would join them in the evenings in some restaurant.

Since meeting Marziano and Dennis, Max smoked and drank less, and he felt better. He used to say to the boys that the most desirable thing in life was what had happened to him, to be born rich and to become poor with age. To tell the truth, Vanessa Muller saw to it that Max's impoverishment wasn't too painful. Though he made an effort to be frugal, his frugality was luxurious. He worked only if he wasn't paid, he bought rare books, he invited everybody to dinner.

When Max died, Dennis realized that situations can't be inherited and, after his eccentric and extraordinary studies with Marziano and their master, it was time for him to change his way of life. That's why he went to Turin and started a publishing firm. While it was easy for him to decide how to organize his work, for years he continued the exhausting search for the woman of his life. When the affair with Florence came to an end, he began living with Clara, but this was chiefly to irk his mother, who was against it.

4. The Heirs

From childhood Max had been obsessed by thoughts of death. He always tried to understate life's importance, because to him it seemed unfair that you could die at any moment, without warning. How could anyone plan serious, constructive studies when death could interrupt everything? So he led an oblique, provisional life, satisfying his curiosities and his whims. When he learned he was gravely ill, he went off alone to New York, where he died a few months later, in a hotel, on a Sunday afternoon.

Max thought that human beings, since they don't have roots like plants, should be nomads. The study of Oriental philosophies had taught him to display a great calm, but hidden within him was an impatient and sentimental nature. With Vanessa Muller he acted cold in public, but privately they were very affectionate. Their life together was based on rules: they woke early, took a walk, spent the day separately, meeting for dinner then retiring.

Vanessa Muller had never been fond of Marziano and Dennis. After Max's death their encounters with her became less frequent. The boys felt that their master, in escaping to New York, had turned his back on them. He had taught them the foundation of everything and then had vanished without a word or message. And he'd left his papers and books to Vanessa, who saw to it that nobody got near them.

Marziano tried to justify his behavior, arguing that Max probably didn't want to burden them with the weight of an inheritance. But Dennis recognized Max's decision that certain things would not be studied by others. Max, however, had failed to take into consideration Dennis's eye and his prodigious memory; he knew by heart the titles and authors of all of Max's books.

The boys' real loneliness came from their master's absence. He had been a snake charmer in whose presence things became easy, more amusing. If you made a mistake or changed an opinion, you were never judged; you studied, after all, only for the pleasure of knowing. It was necessary to repress sad thoughts to keep from thinking about death.

Max and his pupils were fond of idiots because without them it wouldn't be possible to say nasty things about anybody, and life without some malevolence becomes insipid.

For them there were "to ourselves" days and days when they were forced to see "somebody else."

Marziano had always been curious about Max's life. He would've liked to know who Max really was, if he had secret lives apart from the one they knew. What mattered to Dennis was the intellectual aspect of their relationship. After his friend's death, he was very sorry about Annibale's going to England. He was saddened to think he wouldn't see Max's café-au-lait bulldog again, who was going to live with Vanessa. He adored that animal because of its melancholy gaze, its awkward, lazy walk.

After Max's death, they discovered he wasn't circumcised. That jest of fate had made him a Jew in his mind, but not in his body. This could have been the source of much of his insecurity. Dennis insisted Marziano come with him to Turin and join him in the publishing house, but Marziano refused. The commercial aspect upset him. He couldn't understand why Dennis thought it was so interesting to translate and disseminate the esoteric books that had absorbed Max. Marziano, who had studied seriously, now allowed himself to be drawn into applying for government posts. The bureaucracy, slow and functioning badly, like a large intestine, seemed to him an austere and mysterious labyrinth. Since he had to work—because, unlike Max, he was neither rich nor helped by a rich woman—he would feel safer in a bureaucratic job. Certain aristocratic attitudes about the futility of work had died with Max's generation. Furthermore, Marziano found it ethically preferable to work for the state rather than for a private individual.

Part 2

The Two Roads

1. Marina

Costanza Scipioni and Vanessa Muller became childhood friends at a boarding school in Florence. When Vanessa met Max, the two girls stopped seeing each other. Max couldn't stand Costanza. To him she seemed pathetic in her role as devoted custodian of her father's memory. Professor Scipioni had been a fool, he insisted, who had had a career thanks only to skillfully exploited political connections. Marziano, who liked Costanza, often went to visit her, and they would talk for hours about Vanessa and Max. Constanza considered Max a snob who had taken up with Vanessa out of self-interest. Marziano also liked to hear Costanza talk about Marina, a young friend of hers. "It's a shame Marina fell in love with Jim," she would say. "She'd be the perfect woman for you. In any case, one of these days I must introduce you to her. She's very sweet, you'll see, and curious about everything. Unfortunately, her nerves are bad. Her mother's second husband is to blame, a silly man who told her—when she was nineteen—that he was her real father. Ever since she's felt like a living lie, the product of a family deceit. She would look sadly at the man who brought her up, who she'd always thought was her father, and then look contemptuously at her new, real father. In her family, marriages have always been made for money. Marina studied too much. A girl should be beautiful, ignorant and find a rich nobleman for a husband. Then, as you can see, knowing me, Marina has some women friends who are ugly and not rich, while her sister runs around with the daughters of family friends."

At Costanza's house, Marziano met Jim and Marina for the first time. Jim was in love with another girl, and he talked about her to Marina as if to a confidante. Speaking of the girl he loved, he'd call her only "she" or "a friend of mine." Marina didn't suffer, she was happy when he came to see her around noon; he would sit on the edge of her bed, smoking a joint, and talk to her for hours about politics or the woman he was in love with. Marziano could understand why Marina loved Jim. He was young and very handsome, spoke Italian with a strong English accent and had a fascinating smile. The three of them met other times at Costanza's house or in some restaurant, and they became friends.

When Costanza died of a heart attack, Marina was distraught, and instinctively she drew close to Marziano. Meanwhile, she had quarreled with her family, had left home and was living with Enrica, a friend who had a big apartment in Via del Governo Vecchio. Enrica was a violent woman with definite opinions. At her house you could encounter radical students, rebels and political refugees; with Marina's arrival came the intellectuals, the film crowd and socialites. Late into the night they talked about politics and especially about travel. Their favorite subject was the Third World. For them only these countries counted. The house was simple, with unvarnished furniture, much white linen and cushions covered with Indian fabrics. They listened to music from morning till night, and the tone was intransigent: "friends or enemies." Posters were pinned on the walls, along with maps and a large conceptual piece by a friend. Marziano didn't really belong to this world, but he was curious about it. They were all kids, a bit younger, and were living like gypsies. He felt comfortable among them. He knew he was regarded as a good cook, and he often made dinner. At the beginning, Enrica respected Marziano and acted shy in his presence. Out of friendship towards Marina she never tried to go to bed with him. Marina wasn't very erotic, and Marziano didn't find her absolutely beautiful, but he was touched by her insecure expression and by the fact that there were little gaps between her teeth. It was the first time he'd had an affair with a girl from a good family; before meeting Marina he'd loved only sexy, vulgar women.

Marina went off on long journeys to Morocco, India and South America with Enrica. The two of them were friends, rivals in their work, traveling companions, lovers. For years they were a couple. Marina's great love remained Jim, partly because it was a dream, and she fell in love only with what could never be fulfilled. But Marina was also happy with Marziano; they had a real relationship and many things to talk about.

When Marziano talked about moving to Milan, Marina felt that this was a danger, a profound change. And so they decided to get married.

It was a church wedding, with parents, relatives and friends. Marina's parents, though they considered Marziano a bad bargain, nevertheless paid for the traditional reception with wedding cake and champagne.

After the honeymoon in Greece, Marziano moved to Milan and Marina returned temporarily to Rome, but she knew that her relationship with Enrica was petering out. Marziano's strength, which had won Marina over, was his calm and his gift for taking things with good humor, never indicating that anything bothered him.

In Milan, Marziano frequently visited the Eberardts, close friends of Max and Vanessa. Arnaldo was a prominent lawyer, Alice a doctor. At their house everyone talked about literature and music. Alice prided herself on having an intellectual salon. Culture, for them, was an amusement, an essential way of enriching the spirit. What Arnaldo Eberardt liked about Marziano was that, while

MISGUIDED LIVES

remaining an intellectual, he was pursuing a career in government service. Arnaldo was a saver and believed firmly in the work ethic. Alice was a beautiful woman who, in addition to her cultural interests, made no secret of her spontaneous inclination towards amorous play and flirtation. She was very much attracted to younger boys, with whom she enjoyed a great success. She made her daughter Trixi jealous.

Marziano represented an exception. Alice considered him ugly and pedantic, and she disapproved when her daughter fell desperately in love with him. She thought that Trixi shouldn't fling herself headlong into this passion and be so expansive with that Roman intellectual, who took advantage of her and of her acquaintances in order to be introduced into Milanese society. She considered Marziano a dubious and dangerous man, and on this subject mother and daughter quarreled furiously. Trixi paid no heed and went everywhere with Marziano, even to the football game on Sunday afternoon, but her attempts at seduction proved useless. Humiliated by Marziano's absent and passive attitude, Trixi started becoming aggressive. When Marina moved to Milan, Trixi realized that Marziano was married, and the discovery made her ill. The only Eberardt who found Marina adorable was Alice. Arnaldo became furious with Marziano and Marina. "That's the very kind of mentality that's ruining this country!" he told his wife.

Thus began a complicated machination on Trixi's part; with her father's complicity she managed to get rid of Marziano. After much maneuvering, they had him transferred to the Italian Cultural Institute in Paris.

During that time of uncertainty, Marziano and Marina drew closer and soon realized they had become adults. Threatened by external forces, their marriage became something real, something worth defending.

2. The Good-bye When Marzi-
ano received
the notice of his transfer, he felt lost and endangered by Trixi's
malice. He went to Turin to see Dennis.

"I had to come and talk to you, I'm in trouble. You remember
Trixi Eberardt?"

"You mean Alice's daughter?"

"That's the one."

"Sort of plain? With none of her mother's charm."

"Trixi wanted to get something going, and when she found out
I was married, she started turning her father against me. She asked
him to investigate Marina, and some unpleasant things emerged
about a girlfriend she used to live with in Rome. Now, to make a
long story short, they've transferred me to the cultural institute in
Paris, at a lower level."

"What are you complaining about? You'll have plenty of time
to do your own research, and at last you can write a book. You can't
imagine how happy I'd be to go to Paris in your place."

"But you're in a wonderful position here. The firm's growing and
you're doing an important job. The truth is that I should quit my
career, regain my freedom and screw the Eberardts, who think they
can play with my life. I should stay in Turin and work with you."

"You're too ambitious; you couldn't stand living in Turin. In
Paris—just wait and see—you'll find a way to show your worth,
and soon you'll be promoted. It's a prestigious place. Anyway, a
few years abroad always adds to your résumé. But tell me about
Marina—I'd like to meet her. You've never spoken to me about
her."

"She's Roman, blond, comes from a good family. She's been studying philosophy; she's interested in films, politics. She's traveled a lot."

"Are you very much in love?"

"I think so. The circumstances have brought us together. And I hear you're with a beautiful French girl. Is this the woman of your life?"

"I don't know if I'll ever find her. I don't think it's Florence because we don't love each other enough. We're afraid of love. The fact that she won't leave her husband and come to live with me proves that it's not something overwhelming—don't you agree?"

"Not necessarily. Maybe she's just undecided."

"You want to know why she's undecided? Because I don't have much money. To have a woman all for yourself, you have to be making plenty. She's used to a comfortable life."

"Is she here in Turin?"

"No, she's on vacation with her husband and her kids."

"That's why she won't live with you—she has kids!"

Marziano left Turin, convinced that Dennis had hidden Florence from him.

3. Florence

Florence's husband was an important businessman, and their children studied in the United States. To pass the time she rode, played cards and spent the summer holidays in a villa in Saint-Tropez. In the autumn she spent a week in New York; between Christmas and New Year's she and her husband set off for some tropical island. In February she went to Switzerland to ski. She couldn't decide to leave her husband for Dennis because she knew he would never tolerate permanence and she was afraid it would be all over between them the moment she moved to Turin. Since Florence wouldn't give in, Dennis did everything in his power to make her nervous and insecure. When she visited he would speak with feverish enthusiasm about plants, butterflies or insects, and on Sundays he would take her up into the hills for a picnic or to gather wildflowers. Dennis was proud and would never let Florence pay for anything. For this reason he made her cook and wouldn't allow her to invite him to a restaurant. She complained because they never left Turin. She didn't dare tell her women friends what really went on with Dennis; instead, she boasted of staying in the best hotels in Tuscany and the Veneto, which she had read about in the guidebooks. Dennis enjoyed the idea that the woman who bought food for him at the Porta Palazzo market and then cooked his meal had a cook and a maid at her own home. When Florence went back to Paris, Dennis fell ill and spent whole days in bed until he went out to get drunk and play cards. He was a lucky gambler and regularly won. He invested his winnings in the publishing house.

Florence wouldn't leave her husband, but the truth of the matter was that Dennis did everything he could to make sure she didn't. If she told Dennis she would come and live with him, he would reply, "What about your children? What would your children say?"

4. Vera

In the days when he was still living in Milan, Mario often left town and went to Bologna or Venice, where he was involved in politics and an underground radio station. In Venice he met Vera, and they became lovers. She was a magnificent woman whose long blond hair framed a face with near-perfect features. She had big eyes, blue and deep, and she spoke with a distinct Venetian accent of which she was proud. She was an aggressive woman, convinced of her choices and accustomed to her independence. She traveled frequently, and she had been to the most remote Pacific islands before they became regular tourist attractions. She spent much of the winter in the mountains, and she was better friends with the mountaineers and the ski instructors than with the vacationers. She drove an old Fiat station wagon at top speed and enjoyed expressing herself in truck-drivers' language.

But she got over her taste for natives and mountain guides when she met Mario. Through him she discovered politics. For a long time they were convinced that it was really possible to change things, that they were living at an important moment in history. Intellectuals had shifted from abstract ideas to direct, armed action. Real problems should be debated in the streets, not in drawing rooms. At one time Mario and Vera lived together three or four days out of the week, and their relationship was heightened by the potential passions. Vera saw in Mario a hero, her companion, and she would've liked to share everything with him. Mario, however, was incapable of abandoning himself so drastically; he chose to confide in Dennis about his political activities. He took his friend to Venice, where he introduced him to Vera. Dennis aroused some doubts in Vera when he asserted that it was impossible to achieve a better world through the use of arms and violence.

As months went by, things became more difficult. Mario was away more and more, and a special friendship grew up between Dennis and Vera. When the situation turned more dangerous, Dennis suggested to Mario that he go abroad. If he didn't leave soon, he would be arrested. At that time Mario met Guia, and they decided to go live in Paris.

In Paris, Mario felt alone, despised. He was homesick for Italy and was ashamed of having run away with Guia. His affair with Vera had cooled; it had been too impassioned to adjust to everyday life. Dennis fell in love with Vera, but unlike what Mario imagined in his moments of dark pessimism, there was only friendship between them. Vera had been disappointed by the way things had turned out with Mario, but something really strong remained for them both. Perhaps Vera didn't go to Paris with Mario because she had a presentiment. A short time later she died, after horrible suffering, of a dreadful disease. The shared memory of Vera made Mario and Dennis accomplices forever.

5. Duilio

When Duilio joined the publishing house, things began in earnest. It was the end of the era of financing the company with gambling profits and subsidies from Donna Ada. She was the one who was convinced that this young man from the Piedmont, with experience at Fiat and in an accountant's office, could become Dennis's perfect alter ego. Duilio couldn't understand the intellectual pattern in Dennis's decisions, but he soon realized that those decisions brought the firm prestige and, at the same time, appealed to the taste of the reading public. Dennis, though he found Duilio pompous and tried to talk with him as little as possible, respected his business ability. Where they disagreed was over the choice of Mario as their consultant in France. Duilio had a special respect for the French because they were lucky enough to belong to a serious country and not a nation of windbags; he was ashamed that in Paris of all places their firm was represented by a character like Mario. Duilio despised him because of his way of speaking ex cathedra. Mario, in his opinion, was not intellectually honest.

But Dennis was very fond of Mario and considered him, of all his friends, the closest to a literary figure.

Mario tried hard. He wasn't a man to spare himself, but he was easily seduced by fads and enthusiasms. With Duilio he talked of computers, electronics or audiovisuals, but Duilio was only interested in the job. His friends were Fiat executives, with whom he played tennis or went skiing. It was said that he had had a youthful affair with a girl from Alessándria, but it had ended badly. His whole purpose in life soon became the publishing house, where he felt he was indispensable. He had great respect for Dennis, who trusted him completely and didn't interfere with his decisions. Donna Ada hoped Duilio wouldn't tire of his job and decide he wanted to work for a big company again.

Part 3

Paris

1. Rue de Varenne

Married life in Paris was hard for Marina and Marziano. It was the first time they had had to face material responsibilities. There were no shopkeepers who would extend them credit, no little neighborhood restaurant where they could charge meals. They had to pay cash for everything. Since they were unknown, the bank wouldn't allow any overdrafts. If they ate in a Chinese place or a pizzeria, they had to watch what they ordered and bear in mind that afterwards they might have to postpone having their shoes resoled or forego buying the Italian newspapers. When Tatiana was born, things became even more complicated. Their life till then had been easy, privileged, concerned with great theories; now it became exclusively practical.

Circumstances brought them closer to the masses they had talked about in the abstract. Conversations in cafés and lazy mornings of lovemaking became rare. On Sunday mornings Marziano would take Tatiana to the park, no matter what the weather was like. Their friends were less willing to come and visit them. Any conversation was interrupted because the baby cried or they had to go to bed early so that they could get up at six. Their apartment was dark, with a cramped bathroom and an antiquated kitchen; to reach his office, Marziano had to change trains on the Metro twice. The contrast between their sad, outlying apartment and the Italian Cultural Institute was enormous. Marziano felt guilty about spending his days in rooms with high ceilings and gigantic windows while Marina worked in the kitchen on her translations, interrupted by Tatiana, who whimpered a lot.

As a rule Marina did the cleaning and washing. Once a week Marziano went to the market for groceries; he cooked and took out the garbage. The chores didn't create problems. On the contrary, real life kept them together. Of course, they were still blackmailed by Trixi and Enrica, who couldn't stand their conjugal peace.

"You're an idiot, a filthy traitor," Enrica said to Marina on the telephone. "You were a free woman, a companion, and now you've turned into a wife, a mother. How can you think of a personal destiny after you've embraced a cause? You rich people are all alike! Spoiled, capricious opportunists. As long as the toy amused you and suited your needs, everything was fine. Poor Marziano, he doesn't know who he's married! Now you enjoy playing wife and mother—but what will happen later? I know you only got married because you were jealous. And now, because they've sent you to Paris, you think you can wash your hands of Via del Governo Vecchio? Well, you're wrong."

"What do you mean? I'm a free woman, and you have no right to talk to me like this. I'd like to see you in my place, living in this shit. Don't mention Rome to me! Here the weather's freezing, the sky is always gray, the people are dirty and rude, we don't have any friends and Marziano and I do nothing but work from morning to night. You think that's amusing?"

"Maybe not, but you embraced a private cause at a moment when you were needed. Maybe your life is difficult, but it's no use to our cause. Get this straight: the moment you became part of what was happening in Via del Governo Vecchio, you became one of us. Is that clear? Somebody will contact you, and you'll be told what you have to do."

And so, in addition to the problems they already had, their apartment in Paris became a refuge for strangers who slept on the floor, drank cases of beer, used up all the hot water, smoked constantly and left without saying a word. It was all taken for granted. These impositions didn't help things, and Marziano was annoyed that his meager salary had to support these freeloaders as well as his family. Besides, these suspicious guests made him uneasy because he still felt threatened by Trixi. She had come to Paris, and they'd met in a brasserie. "You're throwing yourself away," she had said. "This isn't the life for you."

"What do you know about my life? And, another thing, you're forgetting about my child. Marina and I have a daughter. Leave us in peace. I don't know what I've done to you or what gives you the right to judge me."

"It's because I know you, Marziano. I'm your real friend, and I know your worth. It isn't right for you to be wasted." They parted on the worst possible terms, and another act of revenge could be expected soon from Trixi.

Just then Marina learned about Enrica's arrest. Gianni, a mutual friend, telephoned to say that the apartment in Via del Governo Vecchio had been searched and Enrica taken away. She was suspected of complicity with some fugitive members of the Red Brigades. Marina immediately put on her red coat and went to the park with Tatiana. Her daughter played with some other children while Marina pictured her friend's arrest. Perhaps at that very moment a judge was questioning Enrica. She would keep silent. She was proud and wouldn't want to go down in history as an informer. Marina imagined Enrica with a pack of cigarettes in her hand, her faded blue jeans, a black sweater, cropped hair, one earring, face pale, circles under her eyes.

While Tatiana played, Marina remembered the time when she and Enrica crossed the United States then went through Central America and down to Brazil. A long journey, by bus, with only a little metal attaché case and her camera. That was when she acquired the habit of wearing sunglasses. She was wearing them now, in Paris, on this milky, shapeless morning. For Tatiana things would be different. She knew who her real father was, and for her generation the barriers between parents and children had weakened. With Enrica there could be no talk of children; to her, private life counted for nothing. Ending up in prison was only one episode in a long war.

That morning, in the public gardens, Marina couldn't shake off homesickness. After she thought about Enrica, some Mediterranean landscapes came into her mind: great blue skies, the light of the desert, Rome. She missed her city very much; she missed its narrow streets, her friends, her habits. She couldn't stand the French cuisine, which she thought was ruining Marziano's liver. It was too bad that an intelligent man like her husband was forced to live in exile because of a blackmailing bitch.

The first years in Paris had been calm. Marziano had worked diligently at the institute and had still made time to go to the library and do research for his book. He had also found a way of eking out his salary by doing some little jobs for the Soviet secret service. Marziano's secluded life was interrupted when it was decided to hold a conference on Max in Paris. Marziano was considered the most suitable person to organize it. He was flattered, but it seemed a bit early to stir up the too-recent past. As soon as Trixi heard about the conference and Marziano's appointment she tried to prod Dennis's jealousy, suggesting that both men should have organized the event. Dennis, however, considered Marziano an excellent choice. He wrote him a letter of encouragement, commending him for taking on this thankless task and also asking a favor. His old friend Mario was living in Paris, unhappy and cut off, Dennis said. Could Marziano see something of him and invite him to things at the institute?

Receiving Dennis's letter, Marziano was pleased to realize that he had been appointed Max's official heir.

2. The Conference

The evening before the conference, Marziano and Marina invited Vanessa Muller to dinner; at the last moment they added Daniel, a friend of Marina's. She and Daniel had met at Cortina, as kids, and while Marina's world and her way of living had changed, Daniel had remained the same: conservative and bourgeois, but witty. He always tried to keep the conversation light and pleasant. That evening, Daniel was surprised to find himself dining with an elderly, distinguished English lady. During dinner, Marina asked Daniel if he remembered Virginia Dolmann. He said no, but she went on. She felt a need to tell how her friend had killed herself with an overdose a few days earlier. This news upset Vanessa, who couldn't understand the things that happened to the young. But the conversation, thanks to Daniel and Marziano, who was making an effort to entertain, soon shifted to travel, music and happy memories. It was after two by the time Daniel escorted Vanessa back to her hotel.

MISGUIDED LIVES

* * *

The conference opened with speeches in praise of Max's achievements. Everyone underlined the originality of his work and his unassuming, withdrawn life outside the official world of culture. He was a man ahead of his time.

Vanessa, still reluctant to discuss personal matters, spoke in a brusque and somewhat awkward way. She said that in order to understand Max's penchant for intellectual provocation one had to bear in mind his youthful and incontrollable passion for gambling. He had completely ruined himself at the gaming table. Marziano briefly recalled his years as Max's student. Encouraged by Vanessa's declarations, Marziano then mentioned the libertine aspect of Max's life. Max had lived dissolutely, as if he wanted to defy death. Because he considered life temporary and ephemeral, he sought pleasure above all. Marziano added that Max's passion for gambling was a symbol of his scorn for money. If he had preserved his inheritance, Max would've spent his life defending his privileges. By losing his money and, with it, his privileges, he had set himself free.

The conference properly assigned Max and his work their real value. Vanessa considered herself satisfied, and before leaving she went to say good-bye to Marina. After Costanza's death, a friendship had developed between them.

3. Life Day by Day

How can you narrate whole years of life day by day?

In Paris, Marziano and Marina lived out the everyday events of their marriage. Mario witnessed the end of both his ideals and his love for Guia. Dennis, with Duilio's help, created a publishing firm headed for success, and he stayed in Turin with Clara, of whom his mother disapproved; she would've preferred a woman of prestige.

Those were the years that brought them all into their forties. Years in which the errors of their youth were beginning to make their weight felt. Years that decided their destinies, years in which their ambitions should have been achieved. But they didn't really arrive at what they'd wanted. Marziano had betrayed the ideal of pure intellect by becoming a bureaucrat and a spy. Marina, Enrica, Guia, Trixi and Clara had been unable to find emancipation. Dennis continued looking for the woman of his life. Mario could find no direction.

Vanessa Muller was the only one among them who possessed the secret of wisdom. She led a pleasant and withdrawn existence, strolling in the parks of London with Max's aging bulldog. She belonged to a different generation.

Perhaps it was the world that kept changing, at increasing speed. In all of them a sad laziness had gradually settled, and they lived without knowing what to hope for. None of them was religious, and nothing seemed significant. It was as if they had lost any desire to act seriously or to accept the fact that they were no longer adolescents. Marziano would've liked to be a seducer but couldn't summon up the determination to go on a diet. Marina let herself go. The only one who didn't feel defeated was Enrica. In one of her letters to Marina she had written:

You bitch,

I don't understand how, after all these years, you can still screw with that loser, that professor, who has bad breath and liver trouble. How can you be attracted to a normal, overfed individual? When I let someone penetrate me, I want my partner to smell of human flesh, not of a library. I can only stand those people who come and fling themselves on my bed as they might flop on a sidewalk or in a subway station. People who screw you only because, at a certain point, you meet them in a bed and you want that other flesh that most of the time has no name. Families turn my stomach; they're like a cupboard full of jars of homemade jam and preserved vegetables. I don't give a shit about domestic problems. These last few years I've been in and out of jail and the sacrosanct freedom to form a family gives me gooseflesh. Similarly, it seems absurd to me that you should be living in exile.

You still need the reassurance of the intelligent man who brings home a salary and supports you. The two of you, up there in Paris, think about friends, conversation, music; you go to look at pictures in museums. You're shocked by people who live at night and shoot up in order to keep going. You wrote me about our friend who OD'd as if it were the end of the world. That's the life of someone who isn't protected by vitamins, by the doctor, by long walks, good books. You hope that the coming years will be better, with more material privileges. That stuff makes me vomit. When I come out of jail the only thing that still gives me life is going to the beach and, if it's summer, having a swim: swimming reminds me of childhood, and the sea, the horizon. Write me.

Enrica

Every time Marina received a letter from Enrica she felt so guilty that she practically became ill. She would have nothing to do with Marziano, and for days she would lose all interest in the house and in Tatiana. Marziano, by now, was used to this. In these circumstances he would come home late in the evening and play the piano. He found Enrica's rhetoric stupid, dated.

Mario wanted Guia to be poor, but he couldn't have put up with her if she hadn't been rich; he wanted her to be independent but without too much freedom. He hoped she would shed her bad habits, but he would've tired of her quickly if she had.

Their quarrels exploded in restaurants after the first glass of white wine. Their conversations were always more or less the same.

"Imagine what your life would have been if you hadn't inherited money." Mario would say.

"If I follow you, you want me to give it all to you. Ok, it's yours—right now."

"You make me furious! How can anyone be so silly? You want to play poor?"

"If I gave everything away I'd really be poor and no longer dependant on my family, whom you despise so."

"But you can't even keep the house tidy!"

"Tell the truth: you wouldn't be attracted to me any more."

"With all the money you have, you could at least support some political movement!"

"I don't see why I should give my money to people I loathe."

"Sure, of course, people who've died, people who've gone to jail, who've fought for an ideal."

"And what have they changed? You tell me. What good did any of it do? The result of your politics is that you have to live abroad; otherwise you'd end up in jail."

"Who was talking about me?"

Dennis wanted Clara to have a change of air, to go and live for a while in New York. There she would learn English. But she considered New York an impossible place to live, and she didn't like Americans. Once they had taken a trip across America; he'd left her behind and gone back to Italy, where Florence had joined him. Clara found out, and there was a big fight. He called Florence "my love" and Clara "darling." He was happy when someone would say to Clara, "What a beautiful watch, where did you buy it?" She would have to say, "Dennis gave it to me."

Those were the years when parents began to grow old. Marina's real father often came to Paris on business trips, and he would take them out to dinner in some fashionable restaurant. Each time, Marina was irked by his excessive elegance, his frivolous talk; she hoped she didn't resemble him. Marziano, on the other hand, enjoyed talking with his father-in-law.

At forty, Dennis still suffered from his mother's opinion of him. Donna Ada was interested only in successful people or in certain tragic cases where she could take over. When congratulated on the success of the publishing firm, she would reply, "Big effort! These young people—they find their way all smoothed for them in advance. Mother puts up the money, pays the debts, hires a real businessman. My son may actually have some ability, but when I think of the man my father was!"

Those were years when nobody felt satisfied, and the days went by provisionally. Only Daniel had a stable and indestructible relationship with Paris. For him it represented a chosen way of life, and new things held scant interest. Because of his background he kept his work separate from his childhood friends. With them he recalled the past and repeated the same old conversations to show that nothing had changed.

Marziano was worried because the Soviets, pleased with his

work, wanted to give him more important assignments. He was beginning to be afraid and regretted having gotten involved in the first place. Unfortunately, he needed money, and in the end he accepted the new jobs. The Soviets moved cautiously, and the differences in his activities were very slight. That change made him aware of his role as spy. An oblique man, he'd wasted his intelligence on too many things. Some close friends were still expecting "the book" from him, but Marziano knew that he would never have the energy and the courage to write it. He was too critical, too cynical.

Trixi was right, and before all the others she had understood what even he had not understood. He was a dishonest man and he led a misguided life. He was ashamed of being a spy, underpaid, risking being arrested one day at home in front of his wife and his daughter. And so, disgusted, he went on leading a barren life, day after day, in a Paris that for him had lost all definition.

Part 4

Jean-Marie and Marie-Françoise

1. Elective Affinities

The search for pleasure was the moving force in Jean-Marie's life. He lived on the income from modest capital left him by his mother and was able to take long holidays and enjoy society.

Every October, Jean-Marie went to New York, where he stayed until Christmas, cultivating his American friendships. One Saturday evening, tired after a day filled with boring engagements, he telephoned a friend, a Chilean woman, to invite her to dinner. She asked him to come to a party at her house instead, and Jean-Marie accepted. While the young people were dancing, he sat down next to a woman, who irritated him enormously; with excessive enthusiasm she told him a dreary story, while she dipped big potato chips into a bowl filled with pureed avocado and ate them greedily. Luckily an English girl he hadn't seen for years came over and they started talking about a new nightclub where the music was supposed to be very good, and they decided to go there when the party ended. When she stepped away for a moment, a woman with short hair and a tense face asked him, "Are you from France?" She was wearing a black dress and sitting on the sofa opposite him.

Her voice and her question aroused his curiosity, and he went over to sit beside her. They talked for a long time and he soon forgot about the English girl. From that evening on, he and Marie-Françoise lived together. Their relationship was as intense as it was immediate. They had similar tastes, many friends in common, and soon his friends and hers were the same. They were much in demand. They led a life of luxury and had a genuine passion for beautiful, rich people. They went to balls, to the opera, to the most important sports events; in the summer they were invited on cruises aboard the most beautiful yachts. Every now and then they withdrew from society and went to some spa for a cure. For them it was important to feel agile and thin.

But there were minor irritations. Jean-Marie suffered when Marie-Françoise was annoyed by a certain affectation in Jean-Marie—for example, he would sometimes stay home all day, lounging about the house in a white robe, smoking menthol cigarettes with a holder and leaving behind him a wake of overpowering perfume. Marie-Françoise accused him of being luxurious about objects, clothes, conversation, but not luxurious in his spirit.

True, Jean-Marie had helped her correct some shameless habits, such as walking around the apartment naked, ignoring the servants. True, he had taught her how to travel with less luggage, how to be more sexy and more elegant. But this was not enough. Making love with him, she sometimes felt alone, insufficiently loved. Beyond any doubt, Jean-Marie was handsome; he knew how to make love slowly, and he abandoned himself to the voluptuousness of Marie-Françoise's body. But he was too polite, too sure of his success and his good looks to ever betray any passion. Something prevented him from letting go, from having the courage of his feelings. Instead, he shielded himself with a childlike smile.

It was impossible for him to desire a woman unless she was dressed in such a way that made him want to undress her. With women he talked obsessively about how to wear certain kinds of stockings and undergarments; he would accompany them to linge-rie shops. Jean-Marie and Marie-Françoise often regretted that they had met too late in life to have children. Actually, this talk was a way for them to demonstrate their tenderness, but they knew they weren't cut out for family life. They didn't feel up to it. They had both had sad childhoods and preferred not to reminisce.

It had been Jean-Marie's ability to move easily through the highest social spheres in various cities that had attracted the attention of an important official of the Soviet Union. Jean-Marie could take on important assignments without feeling he was a conventional spy. Rather, he was an informant who could contribute to a mission of peace in the hope of improving relations between the two super-powers. His work was immediately considered valuable because of the original way in which he revealed the things he'd seen and heard. As a personal advantage, in addition to a modest salary, he derived a sense of great protection. He liked to feel that he was in the position of a privileged observer. Naturally, Marie-Françoise was completely unaware of this activity.

Jean-Marie and Marziano met for the first time in the lobby of a grand hotel in Paris, where they had been summoned by an official of the Russian embassy. This charming and civil man explained that he wanted the two of them to meet. He didn't yet have a specific job for them, but it would be a good idea for them to exchange their impressions of certain French museums. Perhaps in the future the curator of a Russian museum would ask Jean-Marie to take Marziano to visit some private houses where very valuable Italian paintings were to be seen.

Marziano came away from the meeting stimulated, while Jean-Marie's reaction was the opposite. For the first time he felt humiliated by his job. How could they have thought of assigning to him such a tedious man, who actually was anything but well known in the field of art? Soviet bureaucracy, for all its supposed efficiency, probably didn't have a proper art historian among its spies in France.

The imposition of this unpleasant-looking little Italian professor—who smoked too much, had a nasal voice and a servile manner—created a crisis in Jean-Marie's relationship with espionage. They wanted to put him to the test. His reports were no longer enough; they wanted a witness, a countercheck. What had happened, hadn't he told them enough? Did they doubt what he had written in his memoranda? Clearly this apparently unimportant encounter had some deeper meaning. Seized with anxiety and irritated by what had happened, Jean-Marie decided immediately to visit the Belgioiosos in London for a few days.

2. The Belgioiosos

Nanni and Maud Belgioioso lived in London, where Maud ran a fashion business to cover her husband's debts and to support the family. The fact that Maud worked and was successful didn't make Nanni jealous; on the contrary, he was proud of his wife. For him it seemed normal not to work, to get up late, to devote his time to sport, to his looks, his tailor, to his friends and, above all, to the family. Their marriage worked because they loved and complemented each other. Maud had a tendency to become depressed over trivial difficulties or to turn irascible if she had a bit too much to drink. Nanni, who could hold his liquor, took care to see that all was jolly and that every detail was looked after properly.

Nanni's mania for details irritated Maud at times and so, for that matter, did his hypersensitivity and touchiness. But he kept their house simple and well organized, filled with bottles of champagne, many books, good music, objects and fabrics brought home from their various journeys or by their many friends, who came and went constantly. Nanni shaped Maud's tastes and indirectly influenced her decisions, even in her work.

Nanni and Jean-Marie understood each other well, though they spoke very little. Between Maud and Marie-Françoise there was great reciprocal respect. When the four of them were together it was always a party, and they saw to it that everything was affectionate, eccentric and, above all, chic. They considered it the height of chic to keep to themselves, just the four of them, even for a simple evening spent watching television, eating boiled chicken or eggs with Tabasco. Everything was guided by their determination to be seduced and amused.

Once Jean-Marie and Marie-Françoise arrived in London, the four of them decided to spend a few days in Scotland. A little holiday and some clean air would be good for them. They'd go fishing, taking with them some dry white wine and some grappa. To drink grappa in Scotland and wear bulky, hand-knit sweaters would be delightful.

Jean-Marie, getting drunk and enjoying himself with his friends and with Marie-Françoise, tried to forget his meeting with Marziano. The Belgioiosos decided to open their house in Normandy for the Easter holiday, and Jean-Marie and Marie-Françoise would go to a spa nearby, where there was an excellent hotel.

3. Everything Breaks Up and Begins Again

Marziano remained impressed by the meeting with Jean-Marie. The bureaucratic Soviet regime had put him in touch with a distinguished and frivolous gentleman who was to act as his guide to the homes of his friends. But it was odd that they had picked him, Marziano, as an expert on old Italian pictures. That summons surely concealed other plans. To keep from thinking of Jean-Marie, and of the fact that Marina had left and Tatiana was in boarding school, Marziano flung himself headlong into his affair with Paola. It wasn't clear whether there could be something serious between the two of them. At times Paola ordered him to see Mario on the pretext that he had been left alone and was about to go back to Italy. But Marziano, while he knew Mario was a friend of Dennis's, still couldn't stand him.

Paola appealed to him sexually, even though she was awkward, and she found Marziano irresistible. The more she reminded herself that he was fat, married and discontent with his life, the more she was attracted to him. In that slovenly, shabby man there was, she felt, an extraordinary poetic grace.

Dennis lacked the courage to admit that Clara was really common, and he grew used to the monotony of their evenings. After supper they smoked a joint and then made love. From time to time he would rebel against the life of Turin and set off alone for New

York. There, walking along the street, in the midst of the crowd, he felt drawn to look up at the sky, which could be either marvelously clean or stifling. In New York there were sudden changes of weather that fostered rapid changes of mood. He liked to walk aimlessly, as in Venice. Dennis understood why Max had gone to seek death among those skyscrapers, in a hotel room with the perpetual noise of television in the background and traffic and sirens.

Dennis forgot his identity in the oily skin of his Chinese girlfriend. After making love, after the woman fell asleep, he might happen to think of Max, of what a magical friend he had been. He had been brave enough to let other people think badly of him, to believe him a failure. But the truth was that Max had never managed to bow to conventions, to give in to the commonplace. He had never married, never had children, never written because of his modesty, his fear of failing. What use is a family that falls apart? What's the use of bringing children into the world when you're not sure you can give them a good education? Why write books when you're not sure of being able to write a masterpiece?

Marziano married Marina, they loved each other, they brought Tatiana into the world, they battled for years against adverse circumstances and then a mere puff of wind was enough to blow everything away. The marriage wore out in a moment, they sent the child away to school, they separated without any hesitation. Who could assure Dennis that his marriage with Clara, if it were to take place, wouldn't be yet another failure? She wanted to marry and have children because she was over thirty and because she realized that Dennis could give her a social position, a home. But after a few years of marriage she would look for a lover, Dennis would do the same, and in the end the children would pay the price.

Marziano went to England to see Tatiana, and in London he met Vanessa Muller. He wanted to talk to her about what had happened with Marina and to ask her advice.

The first thing Vanessa said to him was, "The pair of you

married too young, but it's no tragedy. You'll remain friends all your lives. It's only a sexual thing."

"What do you mean? We had a pretty good life."

"Marina was tired of a lot of things and she wanted something different. She wanted to have fun, a change of air, a younger man courting her and telling her she's beautiful. She needed to fall in love and dream."

Vanessa was right. Between him and Marina their sense of human values had grown stronger, as had their respect and friendship. But they had fallen out of love. "It's not easy to get used to the idea that it's all over."

"It's hard, I know, but that's the way life is. If I were you, I wouldn't fool myself. Unfortunately there's no going back, so I advise you to stop thinking about it. Try to start a new life."

"But how could she possibly have forgotten everything so quickly?"

"Men think differently. Anyway, I'm not Marina . . ."

Outside Harrods, where he'd gone to buy a jacket for Tatiana, Marziano saw Jean-Marie walking by, hurriedly, with a young, well-dressed man. A brief wave of greeting was inevitable.

Jean-Marie didn't reveal his discomfort to Nanni. He felt pursued by that short, dark man, who was leading a pale little girl by the hand. Jean-Marie saw something macabre in this encounter, as in certain surrealist pictures. Why was Marziano in London? Had the KGB sent him to spy on Jean-Marie, or was it just a coincidence? Marziano wasn't the sort of man who would come to London for personal reasons. For that Italian professor, in any case, nothing could be private. And what about that child, so wan. How old could she be—ten, eleven? And why did he have a little girl with him anyway? Who was she? Jean-Marie had come to London to forget Marziano, and here he was on the street. How can you resign from the secret service without being persecuted, without terrible consequences?

Marziano himself was shaken by the encounter; he was no longer listening to what Tatiana said to him. He was afraid. Jean-Marie's suspicious and disapproving expression had hurt him, had seemed like a reproach. What was Marziano doing in London, on a weekday, walking along the street with a little girl? Why wasn't he at his job in Paris? He had been affected by the contemptuous way those two young men were walking, in their elegant overcoats, giving the impression that they were looking at the world from above. After that encounter, Marziano was convinced that Jean-Marie must be a very important man. Even if Marziano felt the first faint apprehension about the dangers of this job, he also felt part of something big, as if fate had put him next to one of those international spies you read about in novels.

Jean-Marie had trouble getting to sleep: he heard the echo of Marziano's slightly unpleasant, nasal voice. Then he dreamed that he was in bed with an Oriental woman, languid, with curly hair, covered with jewels. At a certain point he woke up, sweating; a terrible vision had entered his dream, and Marie-Françoise asked him what was wrong.

"Nothing. I dreamed about a little girl falling onto the Metro tracks, pushed by a leper, and then the train passed and I woke up."

"It's nothing, obviously you can't digest this Indian food. I'm dying of thirst myself. I don't understand why everybody in London is so crazy about Indian cooking. What do you think of Maud's short hair?"

"Actually, I prefer her with long hair."

"But can't you see how much better she looks this way? It makes her younger."

53

"Maybe. But still I like her better with long hair."

"Nanni looks run down, kind of sad."

"He looks the same as always to me. I'm sorry if I woke you up. Let's try to sleep."

"It's always the same. We're supposed to talk when it suits you. Now you've waked me, your nightmare is over, and you'll roll over and fall asleep."

Marziano returned to Paris, unsure of himself. He was sorry to leave Tatiana and was afraid Jean-Marie would make a negative report that would endanger his career. If he needed to escape, to ask for asylum in the Soviet Union, they wouldn't allow it. His place was in Paris; the bureaucracy had decided that much until further notice. That's what he had read in the gaze of Jean-Marie in London: the surprise of a superior. Jean-Marie's reasons for being in London were no concern of his. Marziano didn't want to know why Jean-Marie was there, still less to see him on the street with another person belonging to his world. So Marziano felt crushed for having gone to visit his daughter, who was disappointed and revolted by the way he and Marina had behaved. What kind of father was he, unable to keep his family together?

But Vanessa had told him not to harbor any illusions. Marina had wanted to fall in love, and love isn't rational. Then why stay in Paris, the victim of the Soviets or the cultural institute? He felt claustrophobic and dreamed of vast spaces. He wanted to go to Africa, like Rimbaud, or to the United States. But not to New York, where he'd been with Marina and where he'd spent all his time with other Italians. He wanted to visit Texas and Arizona and New Mexico. Maybe he would have been better off working for the CIA.

What had been normal—a house, regular habits, a certain security—had failed and was now beyond repair. As Vanessa had said, it was useless to hope.

4. Contretemps

Jean-Marie and Marie-Françoise came back to Paris sooner than planned. Marie-Françoise had fallen ill with bronchitis. Instead of being considerate, Jean-Marie became grumpy and rode around the city on his motorcycle. Her sickness interrupted the natural flow of their life. They had to give up their trip to America, turn down the various invitations of the season, and he stayed home every evening watching television or putting his books in order. Luckily, Marie-Françoise was exhausted and dazed by her medication and wasn't aware of her husband's selfishness. During those evenings of enforced domesticity, Jean-Marie thought about how he would like to be a famous spy, like the ones in le Carré's novels, instead of a marginal figure forced to visit chateaux with an Italian professor. He realized this had happened because he lacked courage and had become accustomed to obeying, not deciding. This was why the Soviets held him in bondage.

What depressed him most during Marie-Françoise's illness was the necessary inversion of roles. As a rule she was the one who kept his courage up, who fueled his ambition.

Shortly after his return to Paris, Marziano was summoned to Rome by the ministry. An official had fallen ill and Marziano was asked to take over his research. At first he considered his stay in Rome a welcome distraction, but soon he began to miss Marina. Every street, every memory, carried him back in time. He felt a physical want, thinking of all the times they had kissed in doorways, drunk wine straight from the bottle, dipped chunks of bread in olive oil. Now Marina was living in California, running after a blond, athletic American boy who took her to boxing matches and basketball games. Then the boy would laugh or turn angry, and she would be happy. After more than ten years, she had achieved her dream of Jim, the young English man she'd been infatuated with for ages. And so, instead of calming down, at the age of forty she was chasing after a new adventure, a different place, different people, and this fed her need to move through life as if she were in a movie. From the situation of exile in Paris, from her position as companion and mother, she had shifted to a motorcycle, palm trees, cans of beer, motels.

Marina was to be irreplaceable in Marziano's life. She had an infectious smile and she transmitted joy to others.

Her gestures were always the same—when she went to bed, when she slipped on her glasses and sat down at the table to work, when she was ironing a shirt or having tea with her friends. At every moment she was intense yet tender. Marziano thought of her pale skin and the short blond hair that made her look like an adolescent. He saw her when she took Tatiana to the park, pushing the baby carriage with a cigarette in her mouth, or when she stopped to chat with their concierge, maybe to complain about a leaking pipe. She spoke in a slight drawl, and the gaps between her teeth sometimes made her lisp.

Marziano felt that Rome was no longer his city. It was like being in another place. Since he had gone away, the traffic had become chaotic, his friends from earlier days had either left or changed. They didn't know what to say to one another; each had followed a different path. Had he really become a spy? Now that Marina had left him, what did it matter? What did he care about Russia? Was he a communist? There was no point thinking about it; he couldn't go back.

After a few days, after thinking so much about Marina and the Via del Governo Vecchio days, he wanted to see Enrica. He found her prettier than usual, tanned. He knew the two of them would talk about Marina. That was why he'd looked her up, as he had done earlier with Vanessa Muller. Enrica took him to eat in a Chinese restaurant and said to him, "I'm fed up with Rome. I'd like to be free, fall in love and forget the rest."

"I don't believe you."

"It's true. I'm almost forty, and we did everything wrong. Dope that I am, I still believe in it all, but what good does that do? On the contrary, every day of my life I have to pay for what I've done. If I'm not in jail, I'm getting ready for a trial. I'd like to go and raise pigs in the Maremma or escape forever to the Far East. First, I'd spend a summer in Greece. Three whole months by the sea, certain that every morning you'll wake up and see a clear sky. I'd like the clouds in my life to scatter and disappear. Feminism and politics occupied all my thoughts as a girl, but now I'm different, I have a different body, another way of looking at things. You and Marina were right to separate. Now Marina is happy, relaxed; you're better, too."

"That's not really true. She may be happy, but for me it's been a defeat, a disappointment I wasn't expecting."

Then they looked straight into each other's eyes and everything changed. Marziano put her hands on his knees, under the table; she offered no resistance and asked him back to her house.

Marziano didn't know that Enrica had always wanted him but until now, out of loyalty to Marina, had never said anything to him.

The next day, at the ministry, Marziano felt listless. What had happened—had he become Enrica's lover? He rubbed himself under the desk, seeing again her slightly sagging breasts, warm beneath her blouse, her large, dark nipples. He thought also of her broad hips and of how her curly hair had warmed his face as the two of them made love so well. Her carelessly shaved armpits had a slightly harsh taste. He remembered her tough hands and her fingers yellow with nicotine. He would have liked to see her arrive, at this moment, here, in the ministry, to scratch his back. At her house the night before, they had lit a candle that resembled a taper in a church. Her bed was high, of wrought iron, with linen sheets.

Naked, Enrica looked like a model, the kind you see in art classes. She woke early, lit a cigarette, put on a djellabah and went to fix the coffee. The smell of coffee and smoke began to spread in the damp rooms of the apartment.

They lived outside of life, their days suspended. They knew those happy moments would soon come to an end, but they preferred to think that separating wouldn't be sad. The days went by, Sunday followed Sunday, and in Rome there was already a feeling of spring.

5. Donna Ada's Funeral

Donna Ada ended up in a ravine with her car and died intestate. Dennis became her sole heir. Marziano wasn't at the funeral, but he went to Turin to pay a condolence visit.

Dennis, who as a rule was the listener, now started talking with euphoria. "I can't stand Clara any more, and I don't feel much like going to New York any more, either. I had a Chinese girl there, but that's all over now."

"Why don't you take me to New York with you one of these days?"

"I've suggested that time and again."

While Dennis unburdened himself, Marziano thought how much he'd like to tell him about his spying and ask his advice about getting free of it. He wanted to confess but couldn't bring himself to.

Dennis went on talking. "Max did things only for his own pleasure. I know the commercial view spoils everything. Everything is reduced to buying and selling. But, unfortunately, if you have a publishing house you also have to bear in mind the real world. Today we live in anxiety; we need the broadest possible consensus. It's all mass culture. I just try to make culture and profit fit together."

Marziano wanted to change the subject, but Dennis intimidated him. He wanted to talk about Marina, about how she left him, about what happened in Rome with Enrica, his relationship with Paola in Paris, and how he missed Tatiana, and then the KGB, the encounter with Jean-Marie, his doubts. How could he ever escape?

But Dennis kept on talking. "Life is frankly absurd. Imagine, during my mother's funeral I flirted with Mario's new girl. She's a little blonde, very thin, young, not terribly beautiful, but there's something about her eyes, her manner, her mouth, that excites me. Clara, as you can imagine, played the part of the devoted wife to the orphaned son. Poor Clara, she's under the illusion that we'll get married now since my mother's no longer between us, disapproving. But it's not possible. I don't love her. I'm not saying I want to marry Mario's girl, but she appeals to me. We looked at each other all through the funeral. I was ashamed of myself, and yet I couldn't feel that I was a part of the ceremony. Mario doesn't know; he didn't even notice. She knows but acts as if she doesn't because I don't have the nerve to come out and say anything. So we meet in the evening, the four of us, and nothing happens. Mario, for that matter, has become a real bore since he's been back in Italy. All he talks about is electronics and audiovisual publishing. The very words 'electronic' and 'audiovisual' get on my nerves. Anyway, because of my love for his girl, I'm subjected to endless, tiresome speeches about the necessity of audiovisuals."

Marziano listened to Dennis and envied his frankness, the fact that he still talked like a boy, jumping from one thing to another. In this he resembled Max. They both had a natural, fascinating manner. Like Max, Dennis was close to and far from the things he talked about; he followed one line of reasoning, explained a theory, contradicted himself. In Dennis's presence, Marziano felt petty, guilty for being tangled up in so many lines, all of them now irreversible. He couldn't bring himself to ask if it was possible for him to stay on and work in the firm. Dennis was transparent, boyish; Marziano felt ambiguous, complicated. But he couldn't live any other way.

6. Marziano Returns

Marziano came back to Paris depressed because he hadn't been able to talk to Dennis. He resumed his habits and his job without enthusiasm. Despite a sleeping pill and a tranquilizer on top of it, he slept badly and had nasty dreams. Above all, he was dissatisfied with himself and the triviality of his actions. Living with Marina and Tatiana he'd never had time to reflect, but now he constantly felt the weight of his life and of his body, which he stubbornly neglected. Even though he had seduced Paola, Enrica and other women, he could hardly bear his role as the prematurely aged young man. He didn't live the events of his life in sequence, exhausting them then starting anew. His life was composed of strata, of slow sedimentations. This was precisely what prevented him from seeing clearly.

He couldn't resist his greed, couldn't stick to a diet or even settle on his own style of dressing. He couldn't tell if he had strict, traditional tastes or if he liked to follow fashion. He spent his money badly, buying gadgets. So he never had enough, and in the end he'd trapped himself in a dangerous job. It was a vicious circle, and he was so confused that he didn't even want to take a vacation, as he had no idea where to go. He allowed the forest to attract him, the mountains, the seaside and the country, but finally he wasted his free days in the city.

When he bought something new, he would change his life for a brief period and then end up forgetting about it. This happened more or less with everything. He envied those who, out of habit, always smoked the same brand of cigarette, or drank the same beer, the same mineral water, those who never drank red wine or else drank only red, those who drank cognac in winter and gin and tonic in summer. He was fickle: after buying a Chinese pot for steaming vegetables, he became a vegetarian and ate only at home. Realizing that he stared enviously at people eating steaks in restaurants, he then gave up vegetables because steaks suddenly seemed exquisite and he felt deprived. He couldn't work out a constant ethic for his behavior, a precise design for living.

He looked around himself like an adolescent, in hopes of a more adventurous tomorrow. He lived from day to day, dragging along disparate situations rather than confronting a single, confining commitment. As a boy, whenever he went to the movies, he would then relive the film as if it were his life, then he would see another picture and relive that one as well. Instead of being happy because his daughter came to stay with him for the holidays, he could think only that he didn't know where to take her.

When he was alone, he would stretch out on the bed and look into the air, his mouth open; he would ask himself, who am I anyway? Was he a sponge, a mirror, a scrawl? Was he unlucky or lucky? What about his family? They didn't matter at all to him now, he neither loved nor respected them. He admired only very intelligent and selfless people, those who lived their lives with a sense of humor.

7. The Old Man

"Needle thread, thread spin, spin wool, wool sheep, sheep grass, grass flower, those yellow flowers, less bright than sunflowers but a brighter yellow than lemon. Those trees obviously weren't jacarandas, because they had yellow flowers. It must have been a neighborhood in Athens, but an Athens that doesn't exist. Before, I dreamed of arcades, like a Paris *passage*, a gallery, then an immense café where some waiters were shuffling around in stained threadbare uniforms, their faces haggard, their pale eyes drunken, their hair greasy with brilliantine. These waiters were pushing trolleys of pastries that dripped cream, chocolate, sweets soaked in rum, chantilly, honey. But on a little white marble table there was a roll beside a jar of strawberry preserves, and at the next table a respectable-looking gentleman was greedily plucking the raisins from a thick slice of cake. Afterwards, climbing a circular staircase with a rusty railing, I came to a dark corridor and then an attic where a friend of mine was living, a painter I had met in Mexico City in the thirties. I had gone to Mexico to find a bit of warmth, the New York winter was too much for me. Afterwards, in that same dream, my second wife appeared, dressed in a flowing, electric-blue tunic, almost like Rossetti's *Beata Beatrix*. She smiled at me with unusual sweetness, and, instead of talking about the children, we talked first about Plato, then about Capri at Christmas. We had had a swim at the Marina Piccola on Christmas morning with an engineer from Naples. After that we ate a dish of spaghetti with clam sauce, then we went back to the pension for a siesta under our blanket of rough white wool. In '40, when the Germans arrived at our house, we were already in America. She had been the friend of many German officers, but she preferred to come with me. In the United States we bought a banana-colored Pontiac convertible. We made a long trip, from New York to California and back. After the war, we brought the Pontiac to Europe, and we used it in the summertime, in the country. Once, I don't know how, perhaps because of a gust of wind, a door came off on the Col de Tende. In America I could have joined the Liberation army, but I didn't. I hated Stalin, Hitler, Mussolini, Churchill with the same violence. Most of all I hated the war. I felt total contempt for those men who had ruled the world. Heroes and villains don't exist in wars, there are no profound reasons. When I was still a boy, during the First World War, I had been impressed by man's absolute helplessness against the course of history. I think that during the war I reacted stupidly. My wife and I wanted only to have fun. Who had decided to have a war? Did they have the right to spoil the first years of our marriage? I was weak in dealing with a young and very beautiful wife who wanted to go out and dance in the evening. It was only after Hiroshima that I realized how much that frivolous life disgusted me. Over the bodies of millions of innocent dead, history would narrate the vicissitudes of a few tyrants.

"That diabolical, shameful war would be studied by the children of future generations like a great novel, an epic rich in anecdotes and characters, a grand movie with all the ingredients required for a huge success.

"With the explosion of the bomb, my marriage ended, and I went off by myself to a Greek island. After I'd been living there a while, I met a beautiful, intelligent Englishwoman, and we became lovers. She revealed to me the importance of sex. She thought of nothing else and spent her days in total idleness. Very rarely she would write some verses in pencil, in a copybook. I worked every day, to a cast-iron schedule. I justified my life on the island by saying that at least I would write an important book. That didn't happen. The failure of my first marriage and the horror of the war affected me

MISGUIDED LIVES

too deeply; the story I was writing seemed hollow. The woman living with me insisted that an artist cannot be responsible for a war; he must be indifferent and express himself only through art. She and I shared a frugal existence. We ate mostly bread and tomatoes. We thought of having a son and calling him Ulysses, but we quarreled and I ended up coming back to Italy with a bad novel, barely drafted. I had wasted too much time. First it was fascism, then the war, then the postwar. I was a grown man, but I couldn't find my place. And so, without any conviction, I started writing for newspapers and traveling all over the world. I pursued summer, and I moved from Africa to South America to Asia. I needed warm climates, and I had to be far from my own country. One of my books had a success with the public. It was the same novel I had written in Greece, which I had finally published despite my misgivings. I stayed a few years in Italy, I was accused of writing to advertise myself. So, in revenge, to prove to myself that I was a real writer, I went off to Canada, where I wrote a very long book, which I think is my auto-da-fé. Now the novel is finished and I'm going to meet my publisher at a spa near the sea. He's an intelligent young man who takes a great interest in my work. He used to come and see me in Canada from time to time; he would read what I had written, then offer some suggestions. Now we have to go through the manuscript together. There will be some things to cut, others to rewrite. It's a novelized history of my generation. This is more or less all I can tell you, but you can ask me questions if you like, and I'll try to answer them."

This is what he said to the journalist who had made the journey with him to do an interview. Like all elderly people, Bosco was anecdotal, and he spoke in a tone between prophesy and reminiscence. His hair was white, lank, carefully groomed; his face was sharp, with prominent cheekbones. When he wasn't telling a story, he would huff frequently to indicate that everything bored him. His deep, pale green eyes communicated a vast curiosity. He wanted to know everything, see everything. His movements were restless. He asked countless questions about the most disparate things, and often, as he listened to the answer, he was already formulating another question. He liked to converse, in the broadest sense, mixing literature, life, history, reading. His aristocratic manner, his great intelligence and his knowledge of many languages and countries had fostered only jealousy and enmity in his native country. Often he was accused of preferring the novelist's life to the task of being a novelist; according to the critics, he wrote with excessive facility. Bosco, who attached great importance to his image, had made strenuous efforts to mortify his natural tendencies, the pagan instinct that would have driven him to become a star. He yearned for success, but he wanted to be respected as a great writer.

8. Escaping One Another

It was a great relief when the doctor declared that Marie-Françoise had to go to the seaside and convalesce. Both she and Jean-Marie felt reborn; they had already planned to spend the time near the Belgioiosos in Normandy. After their long confinement, life finally seemed to be returning to normal.

Meanwhile, after long consultations with various travel agents, Marziano had decided to take Tatiana to the sea, to a magnificent hotel where they offered special holiday rates, prices he could afford. A few days before their departure, Marina came home to Paris, disappointed. Her lover was bisexual and unfaithful, interested only in money. Since she didn't have any, she had left. Disappointments seemed to follow her everywhere. The moment she was back, Enrica called to announce that she was pregnant by Marziano. Marina couldn't believe it. Marziano tried to convince her that it was an accident, that out of homesickness for the old days of their youth, and with nothing else in mind, he'd looked Enrica up. One night they had casually made love. How could he imagine a woman like Enrica wouldn't take precautions? Obviously Enrica wanted to have a child all for herself and didn't care who the father was.

Marina argued that if Enrica was all that indifferent, she wouldn't have been so eager to give her the news on the phone, as if to say, You see how fate binds us together? You leave your husband, he becomes my lover and gets me pregnant!

"I believe it's all chance," Marziano answered.

As Marziano and Marina talked things over, they realized they had remained very good friends, despite everything. Their tie was tender and enduring, and they decided it would be wrong to make Tatiana suffer any further. Marina would spend a week at the sea with Tatiana, then Marziano would join them and spend the following week alone with his daughter. It would be a beautiful surprise for the child.

Part 5

Le Palace et du Golf

1. The Hotel

Le Palace et du Golf was a big white hotel of five storys with a late–nineteenth-century facade that looked like a huge wedding cake. It was furnished in the style of the period: huge mirrors, many carpets, marble columns, potted palms, chandeliers, immense salons and long corridors. The elevators were operated by boys in livery. The rooms had been modernized, but they retained their old-fashioned feeling with their oversized furniture, high beds with many pillows and spacious closets.

Le Palace et du Golf no longer had five stars, and its millionaires, professional gamblers, former monarchs and playboys had been joined by guests who were taking various cures or by families who came for the bargain-rate weeks. Raymond Dufour, the manager, had brought about the change. Instead of letting the hotel decay and then, like many others, be turned into a condominium, he had been able to foresee its deterioration and had moved with the times. His solution was to give the impression of five-star service in a four-star hotel. The old clientele had remained loyal and continued to receive the same treatment at a slightly reduced price, though everyone had to get used to some new faces and to the presence of children.

* * *

MISGUIDED LIVES

The nerve-center of le Palace et du Golf was still the bar, where the formidable Luc held sway. It was a large room, the walls paneled in dark mahogany; it had a long counter like the bar of an ocean liner, and access to its stools was decided by Luc's mood and preferences. He favored the customers who gave him substantial tips after they had won at the casino and then stayed at the bar till dawn, telling amusing anecdotes about the past. Luc himself didn't drink. He was about fifty and had jug ears, slightly oily brown hair, an open smile and a southern-French accent. Having grown up in Toulouse, he had made a number of trips around the world when he was working on ships, and he had been a bartender in New York and in Cannes before settling down at le Palace et du Golf. He had accepted the hotel's change of tone easily and was extremely cordial even to the guests who drank only beer or Coca-Cola. Oddly enough, his favorite guests were the ones who didn't come into the bar. They were there to dry out and had tisanes and fruit juices sent up to their room. Every morning on his way to work, Luc personally went to buy the freshest fruit for them. These guests gave few tips and considered his attentions their due.

Luc's favorite customers also enjoyed the esteem of Anselmo, the daytime desk clerk, an Italian from Mantua who had emigrated to France forty years before. Those who were drying out or who didn't mingle much spent most of their time in their rooms, and for them Anselmo outdid himself, taking great pains with reservations, sending his assistants into the city to run their errands and collect their packages. Moreover, he found masseurs and doctors for them at any hour of the day or night. Naturally, Anselmo was polite and efficient with everybody, and only in nuances could one sense the difference between those he thought were entitled to merely normal treatment and those who were privileged.

That year Jean-Marie and Marie-Françoise were installed in their usual third-floor suite with a sea view. Vanessa Muller had also arrived, but she preferred a second-floor double room that overlooked the courtyard.

Vanessa had met Bosco at the station. Though they hadn't seen each other for many years, she hadn't forgotten his vanity and asked what he was writing. Considering this a natural question, he summarized the contents of his book and explained that he was here to meet his publisher. Vanessa told him about Max, and Bosco was bored. He had known Max well: an intelligent, ugly man whom only an English spinster could have loved so much. Max had been considered extraordinary, a man of great culture, versatility and intelligence, yet with a modesty that kept him from writing anything. The truth was that Max was inconclusive, spoiled as a child and, above all, not creative. He must have been a repressed sex maniac. Nobody had ever seen the photographs he boasted of making of whores in brothels; some said he was terribly stingy and never put any film in the camera. To be sure, he had died in accordance with his aesthetic principles and theatrical sense. Had he died a natural death or had he been killed? Perhaps he'd committed suicide. And this woman who had hidden all her memories of Max in her house in England and lived only to worship him! When they reached the hotel, Vanessa introduced Bosco to the manager as a famous Italian writer who needed peace and quiet and special consideration.

Jean-Marie and Marie-Françoise were indifferent to their treatment by the hotel staff. They believed that all hotels had declined since the days when one traveled with one's own domestics. But this year Marie-Françoise demanded rather more special handling from Luc and also troubled Anselmo a good deal. Despite her reading and the television the days were a bore and passed slowly. Luckily, the Belgioiosos were about to arrive, and she was sure Maud would raise her morale.

As often happens in holiday hotels, the arrivals immediately examine the other guests, who examine them back; people select one another in the drawing rooms, at the bar, in the dining room,

MISGUIDED LIVES

on the beach. Then they begin to speak, friendships are formed and soon the moment to leave has come. Bosco, waiting for Dennis and trying to avoid Vanessa, met and came to know Jean-Marie. The two men took to each other at first sight. They weren't the same age and didn't share the same interests, but there was an immediate understanding between them. After so many years of isolated life in Canada, Bosco reveled in Jean-Marie's excellent French manners. For his part Jean-Marie admired the elderly writer's lively intelligence, his culture and his way of expressing himself. At the bar, on the beach or on walks through the countryside, they talked about bygone days, literature and the future of the world. Bosco appreciated Jean-Marie's elegance, envied his youth and the fact that while he, in his room, revised his manuscript, Jean-Marie went off for long rides on his motorcycle. Both were good chess players, and both loved cognac and sunbathing. Marie-Françoise, however, loathed exposing herself to the sun and found tanning vulgar. She could hardly bear the slow pace at which she was regaining her health. She still didn't feel up to spending whole nights in the casino, as she would've liked.

After dinner, Vanessa Muller and Marina met at the bar, and Luc, who knew Vanessa's habits well, prepared a special drink for them, very strong, which helped Vanessa emerge from her great shyness and open up before going off for a good night's sleep. Luc was extraordinary in judging the right amounts of alcohol; all he needed was the customers' absolute trust. In Marina's glass, for example, he put less gin. Marina and Vanessa were happy to be together. Marina needed to unburden herself, and Vanessa was delighted to listen.

"The thing that most attracted me about that boy was his total lack of modesty. But I suffered at the thought of sharing him with other women, or men. Often he would ask me for money. Small amounts, and I gave them to him regularly. Then I had the idea of punishing him. The result was that he asked someone else."

"Was he an interesting lover?" Vanessa asked.

"How do you mean?"

Vanessa blushed slightly. "How do I mean? Why does a married woman look for a lover? Is it just a need to be amused, to hear some fresh ideas . . . or are there more intimate reasons? I mean . . ."

"You mean, was it sexual?"

"Well, yes, perhaps."

"No, not in this case. With Marziano I make love better: it's stronger, dirtier, more sensual. What I liked about Martin was his clean smell, the illusion of belonging to another generation, of being carefree. However, I soon realized it was all just appearances. Marziano is not as young or as handsome, but he's much more fun. With Martin, after a while, I never knew what to talk about. It was fascinating not to understand each other, just to be in love."

"Are you still in love?"

"Maybe, but it's not my life. And the sports, all those games . . . the constant talk about sports or movies or drugs. After a while, I couldn't stand it any more."

"But why did you leave Marziano? I believe it made Tatiana suffer terribly."

"You think I don't know? But it was too much for me. When I met Martin it was summer. The Luxembourg Gardens were hot, and everything about him seemed pure, light. I looked at his delicate movements, the way he stroked a dog or drank a glass of wine, and I was enchanted. I listened to him tell stories for hours. When he entered a hotel, he would ask for a room, then go upstairs, look around, stretch out on the bed, smoke a cigarette. I was sensitive to his grace, his manners, the way he invited me to lunch or to dinner. While we sat at the table there were long silences, then he would give me a conspiratorial smile and say, 'Want to go to the hotel for a while?' It was his innocent look that fascinated me, his smile. I didn't have to leave Marziano and Tatiana, but he wanted to go back to California, and I thought I couldn't live without him. He'd been promised a job back there, doing some photographs for a calendar. He'd make money without much effort. There was something sensual about his desire to work as little as possible and only earn a little money. He wasn't afraid of living from day to day."

"Have you really separated for good, or have you just quarreled?"

"I don't know. Sometimes I think it's all over and I feel sad, and if I think too much about it, I want to go back. But I have sordid memories of California. We rented a furnished place, all plastic. He did nothing but smoke joints and drink beer. He spent hours on the phone with other women. He'd say stupid, hypocritical things in a smooth, false voice, then he'd laugh. He used a language that made me self-conscious about being a foreigner. We went to his friends' houses for endless parties where everybody was drunk. They talked vaguely about absurd projects and about money, lots of money. When we came home, any excuse was enough to start a quarrel. He always wanted to be right and to make me feel small. Most of the time our quarrels ended in bouts of passionate lovemaking; other times I would sleep on the sofa.

"As I lay on that ugly sofa in that house with its synthetic smell, I thought about my apartment in Paris, about Tatiana, who'd been sent to boarding school because of me, and about Marziano playing the piano. I felt homesick for Marziano because, to make love well, culture matters, and feelings and what you say to each other. Sport depletes sexual energy. A lover has to expend all his physical energy in sex, don't you think?"

"You know how it is. I'm an elderly woman; my memories are hazy. But if the boy is American, it's normal for him to be more desperate, less cultivated, more cruel. If it were a question of literature, and not of your life, I would say that cruelty naturally comes after lightness. But it seems to me that American cruelty is different."

"For Tatiana's sake I ought to go back to Marziano, I know that. Children always hope their parents will get together again."

"Children are right."

"Yes, maybe so, but I don't think it's possible any more."

"Times have changed, but luckily children's feelings haven't."

2. Further Arrivals

Coming out of the hotel, Bosco ran into Jean-Marie and Marie-Françoise, who were going off to Honfleur to have lunch with the Belgioiosos. He walked on towards the beach and sat at a table of the Bar Solarium, where he was to meet Dennis. As he was looking at the sea, immersed in his own thoughts, he recognized Vanessa's voice. "Good morning, Bosco. May I introduce my friend Marina and her daughter Tatiana? Marina's read all your books; she's an admirer of yours."

"Thank you, I'm glad she's interested in my work."

"We don't want to intrude, we were just walking down to the pier. Enjoy your morning."

"Thank you."

A little later Dennis arrived, accompanied by Clara, Mario and Ines, the girl who had attracted Dennis during the funeral. Because of her insecurity, Ines had an ambiguous way of looking at men. For Dennis it was enough to have her near, and he was happy that

MISGUIDED LIVES

Clara had agreed to come along. After Guia left him, Mario divided his time between Turin and Milan, and he'd become a great friend of Clara's. She knew that Ines was only a passing fancy, a girl who kept him company.

Mario was still thinking about Guia, at present in a hospital outside Florence. Dennis was less fond of Mario now that he had become closer to Clara and had created the audiovisual department of the publishing house. Dennis couldn't stand a strictly entrepreneurial mentality, but he kept his mouth shut to avoid quarreling with Mario or Duilio.

Bosco felt ill at ease among Dennis's Turin friends, but then he noticed that Ines was looking at him with feline, seductive eyes. Meanwhile Mario was gossiping with Clara. Dennis felt left out and decided to interrupt these games, so he turned to Bosco. "Shall we leave the table and go off by ourselves for a bit to talk about work?"

"No, I'd rather we met tomorrow morning. At seven, if that's not too early. At that time of day I can concentrate best."

As soon as they finished their ices, Bosco excused himself and rose from the table. "Tomorrow at seven, then. In my room. Thank you for lunch."

Dennis felt that the elderly writer had put him in his place. On their way back to the hotel, Clara began complaining, asking why Ines had been seated next to Bosco at the table. She made a furious scene, claiming that Dennis was ashamed of her; then she slammed the door of the room in his face. Dennis, irritated with himself, left the hotel and went for a walk along the beach. Only Mario and Ines remained quietly in their room.

Many times Dennis would have liked to trade women with Mario, but he was no seducer. Mario knew how to handle women, and for this reason Dennis had always admired him. He was manly, tormented, but very human. He also knew how to be funny. Dennis, on the other hand, was paralyzed by his shyness. Women didn't understand him. He was attracted to them, but his behavior was clumsy and could even seem hostile. He asked too many questions or talked too much about himself. He didn't know how to listen and was always afraid of saying the wrong thing.

Being a publisher wasn't easy, especially if you didn't follow the fashion. He had imposed a certain taste, which was more or less Max's. Ancient texts, classic authors, esoteric or odd books. But now, with Bosco's book, he wanted to go into contemporary fiction. This novel had a special ear, a great sense of language. Bosco had often been accused of moral indifference, of superficiality and lack of culture. On the contrary, he was an implacable critic of his time and was capable of being hugely comic.

It was said that he had been a Fascist, then a Communist, then a Maoist and finally a Socialist; it was these very contradictions, his shifts of mood, that allowed him to slip into the place of others, to grasp the essence of his characters. Dennis was tired of standing on this beach, stupidly watching the sea gulls pass. He headed for a café, wanting to drink a Calvados and forget the Turin bunch. He would've liked not to see Clara again, but he couldn't muster the courage to tell her it was all over. It seemed inhuman to erase a person from his life after so many years. Still, it wasn't fair to drag things out, either, to make Clara suffer even more by giving her false hopes. Things between them could never be patched up, and the fact that she'd shut him out of the room could perhaps be an excuse not to go back. But he was here to work, not to make scenes.

Bosco returned to the hotel weary and disappointed. Dennis had arrived with three strangers and he was less open than when Bosco had first met him. Dennis seemed worried, nervous, and wouldn't be able to concentrate properly on the book. In the distance Bosco saw Mario and Ines, but he didn't bother to say hello. She was a frivolous girl, with no intellectual interests, and he was a quarrelsome, violent character. Over lunch, Mario had said he hated novels, "stuff for maids," and that in his opinion too much importance was attached to the figure of the novelist. The truly great writers were poets and philosophers.

Back in his room Bosco ordered tea and biscuits. He didn't like Dennis's friends, who made him feel old. The young took drugs, and he couldn't stand that. Drugs clouded the brain; a fortune-teller in Canada had warned him never to try them.

3. Husbands and Wives

Nanni and Jean-Marie tried saunas, massages and Turkish baths in their attempts to lose weight. They were vain but greedy, accustomed to eating exquisite food and drinking fine wines. Giving all that up would be difficult and tiresome. The elegance of Maud and Marie-Françoise was downright challenging. The two women wanted to be noticed immediately, to provoke, to inspire uneasiness. Always well-groomed and made up, they exuded sensuality, as if they wanted anyone at any moment to lay hands on them. They wore heavy African bracelets, large rings and many necklaces. They walked along the beach as perfumed and bejeweled as they would've been in London or Paris. Maud had the greatest respect for Marie-Françoise, the only person in whom she could confide.

"You see, Nanni can't understand, he can't grow up. So in the end I become angry with myself, because I know that in some ways he's right. Only the real values in life mean anything to him, but he's not ambitious. As for me, I've allowed myself to become completely caught up in the system, and I justify everything by saying that I'm doing it for the sake of the children. Nanni respects the fact that I work hard, and he's not jealous of my success. It's just that at this point he gets bored with me and so, sooner or later, I'll lose him. You'll see."

"Darling, what are you talking about? How can you lose him? What would Nanni do without you and the children?"

"He's put me on a pedestal, I'm his wife, the mother of his children, an able woman, but he needs other women. He needs to take them out to lunch and make them his accomplices, to talk about sophisticated things. He can't bear anything ordinary. For himself he'll always be able to satisfy his needs, which for that matter are fairly simple."

"Are you in love?"

"Yes, I am, unfortunately, but it's hard, very hard, to have to take everything with a smile, always. At times I hate him, I despise him, but he frightens me because he dominates me."

Maud and Marie-Françoise, conversing about their lives, looked at some red starfish on the beach, limp as flowers; they stopped for a while to collect them.

4. Dennis's Walk

Dennis was disgusted by the smell in the café, but it was too cold to go outside. He ordered some tea and asked if they had a couple of aspirin.

Everybody was talking in loud voices and the television was on. His nose and his ears were frozen, and there was sand in his shoes. Dazed by the atmosphere, he began to stare at a table, off to one side, where three women were seated.

They were drinking Calvados and hot chocolate. The disorder of the café didn't disturb them; on the contrary, they seemed entirely at ease. The little girl was bored and didn't listen to the intense conversation between her mother and her mother's friend. She seemed to be watching a blue kite on the beach, but perhaps she was thinking that her mother had not been a sincere person and had not led her life intelligently. She gave the impression of knowing Russian literature and the poetry of Novalis. She was greedy, you could tell from the way she licked the spoon after she stirred the whipped cream into the chocolate. Perhaps she was already a woman, with unfulfilled sexual desires. For the moment she confined herself to licking the spoon and letting her blue eyes dream.

That table with three women of three different generations had fascinated Dennis, but then his attention shifted to two young men at the pinball machine, chewing gum and toying with their genitals, too tightly imprisoned in their jeans. Both had long, dirty hair, and they moved carelessly, like people not accustomed to much thinking. Dennis would've liked to guide the blond girl's nearsighted gaze toward these two. Suddenly he realized that the elderly lady seated at the table was Vanessa Muller. She was too intent on talking with her friend to recognize him. What was Vanessa doing here, in this season, and who was she with? Dennis didn't feel like going over and saying hello. If she was here on holiday, they'd run into each other eventually.

Outside, a strong, cold wind was blowing; it struck him full in the face, though he tried to shield himself with the collar of his jacket. He walked with some effort in the direction of the hotel, where Clara would be waiting for him, wanting to make peace. But he didn't want to make peace any more and, above all, he didn't want to make love to her. He didn't even want to see Mario again, or the girl Ines. What a mad idea to work in Turin, to be confined for years in that hard city, sealed in itself.

He was no longer interested in the firm. He wanted to enjoy himself, wanted to take his life in hand without feeling guilty. Why not go to the Carnival in Rio? Why not set out to travel the world?

At the hotel he could simply pay the bill and leave. And Bosco—
what if he were to take refuge in Bosco's room and tell him everything? This was the second time Dennis had felt this temptation,
but it wasn't possible. An elderly man, so accustomed to solving
his own problems. You never know what people think; thoughts are
a mystery and a privilege.

Dennis was glad his mother had died without suffering. How
often he'd dreamed of killing her. But providence had taken care
of it for him. Donna Ada was now only a memory arrested in time.
She was nothing now, she no longer existed. Now she could even
be canonized, but there would be no more stormy encounters,
threats, mood swings, phone calls or rifts. Only albums of photographs and memories. He had been spared the tragic moments, the
need for pity and the slow physical deterioration. Dignified and
authoritarian as always, Donna Ada had broken her neck in an
accident made to order for her personality. For her it had been
better not to know what growing old meant.

Meanwhile, Dennis had arrived at the hotel. He would have to
go up to the room and see Clara, languid in a sexy nightgown. Then
they would eat dinner with Mario and his girl. Why did he have
to support Mario, because of Vera's memory? Since Vera's death,
Mario had become another man. So why had he brought Mario,
Ines and Clara along? Thoughtlessness. He would've been better
off coming here alone to be with Bosco and their work . . . He had
to change, he couldn't always let life get the upper hand. The key
wasn't at the desk, so Clara must be in the room. He could go up
to Bosco's room and, without explaining his moods, tell him they
would go somewhere else to work, the two of them, so they could
concentrate better.

"Are you Dennis?" asked a woman who was wearing a raincoat
that came down to her ankles.

"Yes, I am. Why?"

"Could you come outside for a moment?"

"But it's so cold out there!"

5. Pistol Shot

The woman's face was hidden by her silk scarf and large sunglasses. Despite the raincoat, Dennis could see that she had thick ankles. From her tone of voice he realized this was going to be unpleasant. He remained silent, not moving, hoping to exorcize the situation.

"Come on!" she insisted.

"Can you tell me what this is about?"

She smiled and headed for the revolving front door of the hotel. Dennis went towards the elevator but then remembered that Clara was up in the room. He turned and retraced his steps. Perhaps this woman was a sign from providence, come to take him away from his troubles. So he went out into the street, where she was waiting for him. When she saw him she stamped out her cigarette.

Without speaking, they walked towards a dark side road. She fired on him at once, using a pistol with a silencer. She ran off without being seen. A few minutes later, a porter from the hotel, passing on his bicycle, saw Dennis lying in the road. He rushed to the hotel and reported to the desk clerk. Anselmo reacted promptly. He knew that Dr. Leon was examining a guest in 116, and he called him urgently. With some others, the doctor went to the spot and Dennis was carried back to le Palace et du Golf. The wound was shallow and the bullet had passed through his side. Dennis was put in a secluded room on the fourth floor. The doctor considered him out of danger; he could spend a quiet night with a nurse looking after him. If he took a turn for the worse, they would move him to the hospital.

* * *

The only thing Dennis recalled clearly was the sight, like a vision or a dream, of three children dressed in blue, playing in the hotel lobby. One of them had cried, "He's dead!" The governess scolded him and hurried them away.

In the days that followed, the manager and staff did everything to reassure the guests, saying that the wounded man was fine and steadily getting better. Dennis was fed intravenously, and in the daze induced by the tranquilizers he seemed to recall the face of a nearsighted girl with a braid, exactly like the little girl he had seen in the café with Vanessa Muller. Was she the one who had shot him?

Part 6

Sedimentation

1. Hotel Rumors

At le Palace et du Golf they tried to play down what had happened. It required the greatest discretion to keep from alarming the other guests. The police were conducting an investigation, without any result. In the hotel, the people who knew Dennis fell into two categories: those who claimed to be much closer to him than they actually were and those who gave evasive answers. Vanessa Muller was among the latter. Bosco, on the contrary, did not conceal his agitation and was constantly questioning the hotel staff, the nurses, the doctor, the police. He even overcame his initial irritation with Clara and Mario and asked them questions as well. He wanted to know if Dennis was out of danger and how long would it be before he had regained sufficient strength to go back to work. Most of the time he confided in Jean-Marie, who insisted that the shooting had been either a mistake or part of some amorous vendetta.

The Belgioiosos were among the most curious, whereas Marie-Françoise seemed nearly indifferent. What annoyed her was the bad weather, which made walks on the beach less enjoyable; when she went to the casino in the afternoon, she didn't have as much fun as usual.

Jean-Marie asked Bosco, "Forget for a moment the complications this has created for you. Isn't having been close to an unsuccessful murder attempt useful raw material? The novelist has an inner eye, he sees things the others don't see. A bit like a spy."

"You're mistaken. A thing like this prevents me from working. All I do is think about it. My suspect would be that Clara who was clinging to him so, but she has a perfect alibi. She's so jealous! And besides, that very day, it seems, they had argued, partly on my account. But she didn't do it."

One afternoon Vanessa, Marina, Bosco and Jean-Marie had tea together. Vanessa declared that the attempted murder had to be political. Bosco replied that this seemed impossible. As a publisher, Dennis had never taken a political position. Marina insisted that Marziano would be able to interpret the story. He and Dennis were childhood friends, and for years they'd had the same teacher.

The governess of the children Dennis had remembered was worried. The little girl had nightmares, one of the boys threw up everything he ate and the other made a disturbing show of high spirits. She tried to calm them as best she could, and the local pediatrician had suggested she give them a few drops of valerian. The children's mother was traveling and had left no forwarding addresses; no one knew when she would arrive.

2. Meanwhile, Marziano

Marziano did nothing but gnaw his fingernails, smoke and grow more and more desperate. He was convinced someone had put a jinx on him. Was Trixi still at it? Why had Marina come back? Enrica was in jail again. Why had he gotten her pregnant? With Paola things had changed; they no longer loved each other as they had at the beginning. He had stayed in Paris, letting Marina go off on vacation with Tatiana. During these past few days, two men from the Soviet embassy had come to see him. With excellent manners, one of them advised him not to do anything foolish and asked if he could, on his own initiative, perform some useful errands from time to time.

Frightened, not knowing if this visit was due to the Jean-Marie episode in London or to his private life, Marziano quickly did a little voluntary job. At the institute he gained possession of some documents, photocopied them and delivered them to someone who would know how to make use of them. The gesture was immediately rewarded. Enrica came out of jail, her passport was returned to her and she was handed a prepaid ticket to Paris. When Marziano learned of Enrica's arrival, he went out and gorged himself on potato salad and beer then shut himself up in the house with a whore. As if all this weren't enough, he heard what had happened to Dennis and he was plunged into despair.

Why had somebody shot him? Dennis wasn't a spy or involved in any criminal matters. What would Marziano do now with Enrica, who was arriving in Paris?

As soon as he saw her, he felt there was still something between them. Pregnancy gave her a serene, sweet look and allowed her feminine nature, which she'd hidden for years behind her aggressive manner, to show through. Marziano desired her and thought of taking her to the sea, introducing her to Tatiana. But it wasn't a good idea to involve the girl. In any case, Enrica was happy to stay in Paris, and she understood why Marziano had to go away for a while.

While alone in the train, on his way to visit his daughter and Marina, Marziano was wondering why the members of his generation, for one reason or another, were constantly caught up in legal or criminal trouble. It was incredible that someone had shot his best friend at the same hotel where his wife and daughter were spending their holiday. That morning he put on a yellow and red silk tie that Max had given him for Christmas many years ago, hoping it would act as a talisman and ward off further troubles. Marina was waiting for him at the station with Tatiana. Both were excited and happy to see him. The child was very affectionate. She didn't say a word, but she hugged her father tight then held his hand all the way to the hotel. Marina told him that Vanessa Muller was also staying there. This further coincidence irked him. What was she doing in this place?

3. The Secret of Henry IV

Marziano waited in Dennis's room until an elderly gentleman, seated beside the bed, got up and left. As Bosco went out, the nurse asked Marziano to be quick. He approached the bed and saw that Dennis was very pale. In a low voice, he said, "It's Marziano."

After a long silence, Dennis whispered, "No one must know I'm not unconscious. I'll explain later. I talk only with Bosco, about his novel. I know the manuscript well, so we can discuss some changes, a few cuts that have to be made."

"Do you have any idea who shot you?"

"I know it was a young woman, but her face was hidden by a silk scarf and dark glasses."

"Would you recognize her?"

"I don't know."

"Why are you pretending to be unconscious?"

"Please, find a way to get Clara away from here. I don't want to live with her any more. Or even see her. Sometimes I have nightmares, and I think she's coming to kill me in my sleep."

"Have you had much pain?"

"There was a flash of heat, a flame inside. Like a fire-eater, you know?"

Coming out of the room, Marziano put on an appropriately sad face. He thanked the nurse for having allowed him to enter then joined Marina and Tatiana.

"Well?" Marina asked impatiently.

"He hasn't regained consciousness."

Marziano felt great tenderness towards Marina, but he noticed with displeasure that Tatiana was constantly munching sweets and had put on a lot of weight. He didn't dare scold her, realizing the child's problem stemmed from her frustration and profound unhappiness at seeing her family break up.

It was odd that Dennis had decided to speak only with Bosco, to exploit the situation to play Pirandello's Henry IV. Max had been the first to discover Bosco's writings and had gotten them published. But Bosco had become dominated by the desire for success, and Max had lost interest, asserting that he was a minor writer.

Marziano observed the subtle games that had developed around Dennis's shooting. Who knows? Maybe the whole incident had been premeditated, organized by Dennis himself. A bogus murderer had given him a superficial wound. In the first place there was something suspicious about the fact that a man supposed to be seriously wounded had been left in a hotel room and more or less ignored by the police. Perhaps the manager was also involved in the business.

From time to time Marziano excused himself and went off to his room to call Enrica. Since she wasn't there with him, and he felt guilty, he assumed the syrupy tone of a lover. "You can't imagine how much I miss you. Sometimes I want to take the train and rush straight to you, but for the moment it's not possible."

"How's Marina? Are you sleeping in the same room? Have you made up?"

"What an idea! I'm worried about Tatiana. She's eating too much. I believe she's very unhappy, but she's so reserved, there's no talking to her. What are you doing right now?"

"I'm stretched out on the bed."

"Are you naked? Are you beautiful? Tell me the truth. A woman's more sensual when she's pregnant."

"How do you know?"

"I can tell."

"I'm stretched out on your bed, and if somebody were here I'd have myself licked like an ice-cream cone."

"When are you coming here?"

"I don't know. I don't see why I should. Sooner or later your friend will get well, won't he?"

Marziano went into the bathroom to wash. He was more and more misshapen and ugly, the hollows under his eyes as deep as furrows.

He should watch his health, but he didn't feel like it. Instead, he wanted to make love with Marina, with Paola and with Enrica. They all aroused him.

ALAIN ELKANN

4. The Dining Room

The dining room of le Palace et du Golf was vast, with pastel stucco decorations everywhere, many mirrors, chandeliers and wool carpet in a pattern of blue and pink flowers. Two expert maîtres d'hôtel directed an impressive swarm of *chefs de rang* and waiters, and there was even a Moroccan in traditional costume who did nothing but prepare and serve the coffee. In the evening the room was lighted by candles. Guests could follow the regime advised by the spa's physician or try the gastronomic menu.

That evening Bosco came in later than usual, wearing a purple shirt. He was accompanied by a very pretty young girl. It was obvious that the writer was proud of his somewhat theatrical entrance. Everyone noticed him, and whispers were heard from the table of Marziano, Marina, Tatiana and Vanessa and from the table of Jean-Marie and Marie-Françoise, who were dining with the Belgioiosos, and from the table of Mario, Clara and Ines.

Turning to Marziano, Vanessa said, "Poor Max was right—Bosco's not to be taken seriously. What's he doing here with that girl? During the day, hypocrite that he is, he dutifully goes and sits with Dennis, as if he were his only friend. And it's all because Dennis is going to publish his new novel. He's afraid nobody else will publish it. It's odd Dennis has let himself be so bewitched. But even Max fell into that trap."

Marina asked, "Why all this talk of Bosco? What does it matter if he's a great writer or not?"

93

MISGUIDED LIVES

"He's stolen, copied, patched together texts that weren't his and then passed them off as his own," Vanessa replied. "I can't say more than that."

"But those are old rumors," Marziano added.

"I wouldn't want to bring up the circumstances of Max's death," Vanessa replied.

"Surely you don't think there's a conspiracy surrounding the novel," Marziano said, "or that somebody shot Dennis to prevent the publication of Bosco's book, which might contain things about Max? Why, one of us could be the guilty party."

"Why not?" asked Vanessa.

"But we know it was a young woman who shot him!" Marziano said.

"How can you say that with such certainty, since no trace of the person has been found?"

Marziano tried to cover up his embarrassment. "Perhaps I'm mistaken. You're surely right; the guilty party could be anyone here in the hotel."

"Let's suppose something, just for fun. For example, before Dennis arrived, Bosco spent a lot of time with that man in the bottle-green velvet suit sitting at that corner table. There are four people there, gamblers, socially prominent. Well, that man in the velvet suit . . ."

Marziano felt an unexpected uneasiness when he realized that Vanessa was suggesting that Jean-Marie had shot Dennis.

"Papa's right. You remember, Mamma, the evening they shot at that gentleman, as we were coming into the hotel we saw a woman with a raincoat and a scarf. She was smoking a cigarette and waiting outside the door. You remember? He came out, and they walked off in the dark," Tatiana said to her mother.

"To tell the truth, I didn't see anything, but why are you mentioning it now?"

94

"I don't know."

Vanessa spoke up, "Then Marziano knew it was a young woman because his daughter had told him!"

"We wouldn't want to start fighting among ourselves and suspecting one another, would we." Marziano answered.

At Jean-Marie and Marie-Françoise's table they were also talking about Dennis and Bosco. Nanni Belgioioso said, "It could easily be some kind of Mafia intimidation. I wonder what's in Bosco's book."

Marie-Françoise said, in an acid tone, "And what if the guilty party was at that table of women, who have that louche man with them who looks like he's from the south?"

Jean-Marie concealed his surprise at seeing Marziano. What was he doing here, seated at table with that elderly English woman friend of Bosco's? Meanwhile, turning to Jean-Marie, Marie-Françoise said, "But you spent a lot of time with Bosco before Maud and Nanni arrived, when I was staying in my room. You and he took long walks and, if I'm not mistaken, you even ate meals together."

"Yes. He's a fantastic man, a dying breed. I adore talking with older people, especially if they're talented. You can learn a great deal."

"But he's so frivolous!"

"No, no, the purple shirt and the girl are little acts of vanity. He likes to arouse some amazement around himself, and he tries to find some distraction. He came here to work with his publisher on the novel he's been writing for ten years. The publisher was shot the very day he arrived, and he's been unconscious ever since."

Marie-Françoise said again, "I wonder who that louche man is? You know, Jean-Marie, I had the impression he was smiling at you, trying to greet you somehow."

"Oh, really, Marie-Françoise!"

MISGUIDED LIVES

"Marie-Françoise is right," Nanni said, "that character does look like a mafioso."

"Why?" Jean-Marie asked, annoyed.

"Oh, you can tell by the look in his eyes, and that Levantine manner, the shifty way he eats. He's someone I'd be on guard against if I ran into him, but I'm sure he didn't do the shooting. If I had to suspect someone here, I'd study that table of Italians at the end of the room. The dark man with the two girls. They're always together, and they hang around the wounded man's room."

Jean-Marie was amused. "We're being too nasty. Poor things, they look so innocent and lost, as if they'd never been in a grand hotel in their lives."

Unexpectedly, Marie-Françoise rose from the table. Something had waked in her. Some numbers were swirling in her mind: she saw them reflected in a mirror. She ostentatiously left the dining room, went to the bar and ordered a double vodka. Luc made no attempt at conversation. Marie-Françoise was the sort of woman who decided for herself whether or not to talk to the bartender. She gazed at the bottles lined up neatly behind the bar and began thinking about her childhood. This big hotel, old and silent, was the same as many other hotels in the many other spas where she had spent holidays as a little girl with her Sarajevo grandparents.

The Sarajevos, as she remembered them, had always lived in grand hotels at spas where they went to gamble at the casino and take the cure. What seemed to have changed since then was society. The Sarajevos were people of luxury, who lived in luxury and thought of nothing else. They talked only about good restaurants, good tailors, splendid flowers, choice wines, journeys, books, and they gossiped. After the ritual comments on the previous night's gambling, their conversations revolved around great memories of their travels. Political and practical matters were barely mentioned. They talked instead about their correspondence, letters from loved ones, friends who wrote from distant places.

On meeting Jean-Marie, Marie-Françoise had thought that this was a man of her generation who had inherited the values and the code of behavior of that past world, but there was something affected in him, something not entirely sincere.

Still staring at the bottles behind the bar, Marie-Françoise felt a desire to see the man who was shot, even though she didn't know him.

"What floor is the wounded man on?"

Luc pretended he hadn't understood the question; Marie-Françoise gave him a big tip. He smiled and said, "You needn't have troubled. I've heard there's a great deal of bustle on the fourth floor, a lot of coming and going. These things can do harm in a hotel like ours, where even the children are screened."

A few moments later Marie-Françoise was in the corridor on the third floor. Towards the end, a gentleman dressed in gray was pacing back and forth. She moved closer, realized he was a policeman and sensed that she was arousing his suspicion and risking trouble. So she took the elevator, and, going to the casino, she decided she would bet on 3, 17, 13 and 31.

She thought that Bosco had frequented the same world as the Sarajevos. Even though he was younger, he had surely known the places and the scents that she also remembered. She wanted him to caress her with his bony, veined fingers covered with dark liver spots. She wanted to know if his body still held traces of the odor she had been seeking all evening.

When she entered the big hall she looked around, as was her habit, for a table where there were fat, badly dressed men, smoking. Hardened gamblers who risked everything and whose only insurance was their round-trip train ticket. Addicted gamblers, who thought of nothing but luck and recouping their losses. As soon as Marie-Françoise approached the table she felt a renewed desire to use coarse language; she lowered her décolletage slightly and sat down in a pose that showed off her legs. It was exciting to feel beautiful and sexy among men who preferred *fiches* to sex, who cared only for the sound of the little ball spinning in the roulette wheel. They would notice her and would sink to anything in order to be able to buy more chips and try to recoup. As always, after she had been sitting at the table for a while, Marie-Françoise felt a desire not to go back to her hotel, not to rejoin her husband. She would make a promise to a gambler desperate for money and, in return, she would have him take her to an anonymous hotel near the station. There he would make love to her as best he could in order to get as much money as possible from her. In these situations, she became difficult to satisfy, demanding virtuoso performances.

Nothing could arouse her more than seeing a man become her slave in order to procure what he needed to satisfy his addiction. Her greatest pleasure, however, was to force them to become infatuated with her and distract them for a little while from their obsession. She invested an enormous passion in those lovemaking dawns, in those unknown lovers. The next morning it all vanished from her memory, and she would be happy to see Jean-Marie again and to have breakfast with him. The nights of gambling and sex put her in high spirits and made her excellent company.

5. Many Little Secrets

Tatiana, when she had finished telling her story about the woman in the scarf, felt her father's stern gaze. First she blushed, then she felt sick. How many times had she been told not to interfere in grownups' business! But she wasn't a baby any longer, and she had thought she was doing the right thing. It wasn't her fault if she was always among grownups and didn't have any friends of her own. Tatiana felt guilty for having betrayed and endangered her father.

She started to cry, and Marina had to take her up to their room.

"What's wrong? Did you eat something that's disagreed with you?"

"No, Papa scared me. When I talked about that woman in the raincoat he looked at me in a way that frightened me. Now he'll think I'm silly as well as ugly. Ever since I went off to school he doesn't love me any more. I was only trying to help."

"Don't you think you're exaggerating a bit? Your father adores you, and he's not the least bit angry with you."

"It's no fault of mine if that woman shot somebody. If children aren't supposed to speak, parents shouldn't leave them or send them to another country to live. Why did you leave me?"

"What are you saying, Tatiana!"

"You think children shouldn't see anything or know anything. Now you've come back, and you want to be with Papa again, but he doesn't want you any more."

"What are you talking about?"

"I know Poppy had another girl, Enrica, and they're going to have a baby."

"Tatiana!"

"I know Enrica's your friend from Rome, and now you're jealous of her."

"That's enough, Tatiana!"

"We won't have our house any more. And what if Papa has other children?"

"But you're not the only one in the world such things happen to. Think how many children have divorced or separated parents."

"Poppy knows why they shot that man, and he doesn't want anybody else to know. That's why he looked at me like that!"

"Now, Tatiana, stop exaggerating!"

"Did you love that man a lot, the one who took you to America?"

"Yes."

"Is he very handsome?"

"Yes."

"Do you think you'll go back to America after the holidays?"

"No."

"Do you think Poppy loves her? Enrica, I mean."

"Yes, I think so."

"But why? If he used to love you and had a little girl with you, why does he love someone else and want to have a little girl with her?"

"These things happen."

"I want to get married only once and have lots of babies. When Papa has another child he'll forget all about me. In the old days, on Sunday, we used to go to the park together to have ice cream and afterwards, at home, he'd play the piano. He used to say that a person must always tell the truth. Now does he think I shouldn't tell the truth?"

In another room, Marziano was lying on his bed, leafing through a magazine. Many things were upsetting him, but most of all he was worried about money. Because of the Dennis business, they had gone beyond the bargain deal with the hotel. They had two rooms, there were three of them at meals.

Marziano was depressed by the fact that he couldn't concentrate on just one woman. Every woman aroused in him a yearning for another. At that moment he felt listless because he wanted to go to Marina's room. He remembered her heavy slumber, her warm smell. She was the woman he had slept with most often in his life. Instead he telephoned Enrica. The conversation was tense, and her arrival was postponed. Enrica made him nervous by talking about a friend of hers, a political refugee from Guatemala she hadn't seen for years. Marziano was allergic to political refugees from the Third World and felt he was listening to the Marina of ten years ago. Suddenly, he wanted to ask Paola to come and see him. With her it was different: she was his girl. Curiously, all his women had one thing in common: the palms of their hands were very sensual, soft. Looking at those hands, he thought every time of his mother, who wore on her little finger an emerald in a loose setting.

Marziano came out of his room and felt like going to Marina's, but because of Tatiana it wasn't possible. Marina had trouble accepting the idea of being forty. For that reason she had rebelled and decided to go off with a boy to a place where there was sunshine, neon lights, clean air. But she soon realized that there were also roaches, drugs, emptiness and, beyond the Pacific, an ancient, incomprehensible world. Defeated, frightened by the diseases that were going around, convinced she had ruined her life and the lives of the people she loved, she had come back to Paris, only to discover that her husband had gotten her best friend pregnant.

In the elevator Marziano ran into Jean-Marie, who was with the Belgioiosos. They made a brief gesture of greeting, and Marziano recognized Nanni. But where had he seen him before? In the lobby, he asked the desk clerk to put him through to Bosco's room. He asked if he could come up for a moment. Bosco said yes.

He was sitting in a bathrobe in the freezing room, the window wide open. "I'm sorry, but before going to sleep I need to breathe the strong sea air. In Canada, on that island where I lived for many years, the sea became an integral part of my life, and I can't do without it. For days and days, the sea and the gulls would be my only companions."

"But wasn't it very hard? Didn't you feel you were wasting your life, staying so far away?"

"No, I needed absolute silence in order to give all possible time to my work. I wanted to try thinking only of my book, without any excuses."

"Is the book finished?"

"I'd say yes, but it would be helpful for me to check some parts of it with Dennis. Even if we do manage to speak to each other, I'm afraid it's not enough. For that matter, there's one part of the book that Dennis suggests I look over with you. It's the part that concerns Max."

"Let me ask you an indiscreet question. I'd like to know if there's something so explosive in your book that it might endanger the publisher."

"Listen, Marziano—if I may call you by your first name—you were sent to Paris because some injustices were committed against you. Dennis told me that. Well, as you know, the end of poor Max was never very clear. At that time I was in America and, as chance would have it, I had access to his room. I was lucky enough to find some manuscript pages of his. Some Swiss notebooks, like a child's copybook. In those little notebooks, which I took so they wouldn't be lost, some fundamental thoughts were noted down, thoughts with which I fully agree. You're close to the diplomatic world, you know better than anyone else how certain things cannot be said in Italy. At times, when someone dares to disseminate facts that others want silenced, there can be incidents. Sometimes they capture the agent, but not the mind that sent him. You understand me?"

"When would you like me to look at those pages?"

"As soon as possible. But now, to avoid arousing suspicion, I'd suggest you ignore me, perhaps pay a few more visits to Dennis, then change hotels. It's not a bad idea for Dennis to prolong his convalescense a little while. He'd like us to help him get Mario and Clara away from here. I don't know if he talked to you about it, but he'd like to see the business manager of his firm. He wants you and Duilio—that's the man's name—to find a way to send these friends away."

"All right, I'll talk to Dennis about it."

"Good-bye, my friend. It's been helpful, this meeting. Thank you for the visit. But we have to see each other less frequently; the others mustn't realize we're acquainted."

6. Things Decided Early in the Morning

Marziano sat down at Dennis's bedside, as had now become ritual. "I've talked with Bosco and we agree. I'll go over the part of the novel that deals with Max. But what about you? How do you feel?"

"Better. I'd like Duilio to come, and I wish Clara and Mario would go away and I want to know why Vanessa Muller's here. I also wish you'd do me a huge favor: go to Rome and contact the lawyer Danesi, Raimondo Danesi. He was my mother's lawyer. You want to know something? Now and then I have the feeling that somewhere, sometime in the past, I've seen the person who shot me. Every now and then the tone of her voice comes back to me."

"Do you think it has anything to do with Bosco's book?"

"Anything's possible; it could even have been a mistake."

Marziano went off to find a fairly secluded hotel that would do for Enrica. In a café near the port he ran into Jean-Marie, who was flushed and shivering.

They greeted each other, and Marziano approached him without any shyness. "Odd coincidence, our being here together!"

"How about a cognac?"

"At this time of morning?"

"Afterwards we could take a walk on the beach. We have to leave in a few days. Marie-Françoise's convalescence is over, but if we rushed away it could arouse silly suspicions, which in our case are best avoided."

Marziano wondered if these last words were spontaneous or an indirect warning. Even when he uttered banalities, Jean-Marie had a special way of expressing himself. For the first time, in that café, there was a sense of complicity between the two men. They felt equally undecided and insecure about a choice they'd made, for different reasons, which for some time had been frightening them. That murder attempt had been a warning to them both. A third person, an outsider, had been struck to intimidate them and recall them to order. These thoughts, and others, crossed the minds of both men, and they decided to meet soon in Paris and visit some private collections, then draw up a report.

When Jean-Marie went off, Marziano felt that the whole world was falling down around him. Everybody demanded something different of him; it seemed he'd become a chameleon who accepted any role, forgetting his own identity in the process.

In his frustration, he was seized by the desire to find release with the first woman he met. Most of all, he desired a miracle that would change the course of events.

As he walked along pensively, he ran into Marie-Françoise, still in evening dress and disheveled. In his present mood he couldn't resist the desire to court this women with her smeared makeup. The fact that she was the wife of Jean-Marie, whom he'd just left, made the idea all the more alluring. When they reached the hotel, he took the elevator with her and looked at her shamelessly. She blushed only slightly, and they got out at the same floor. Immediately, he asked her, "Does your room have a view of the sea?"

"Yes."

"Mine doesn't, and I'll have to change hotels. I don't have enough money to stay on here."

As Marziano said these words, he put his arm around Marie-Françoise's waist, undid a hook of her bra and took her breasts in his hands, stroking the nipples, first gently, then squeezing them hard. Furtively they entered Marziano's room. They tore off each other's clothes and without another word behaved like animals.

After Marziano's first orgasm they felt reciprocal disgust: they hadn't even looked into each other's faces. Marie-Françoise slipped on Marziano's shirt, which was too big for her. Without a word, Marziano put his hand between her thighs. He was attracted by Marie-Françoise's odor; there was a coolness in it. She liked the way Marziano manipulated her, as if she were a big mass of putty. When Marie-Françoise left, Marziano remained stretched out on the bed, at peace. He had seduced another woman, whose perfume still lingered on him. He had seduced the wife of Jean-Marie. He missed her the moment she left. Between them it had been a matter of skin, impelling, natural.

Still warm from the encounter, Marziano went to Marina's room. "Go down to the lobby for a moment." he told Tatiana." I have to talk with your mother. We'll join you right away."

"But, Papa, what have I done? You've been mad at me ever since you got here."

"What on earth are you talking about, Tatiana?"

"The minute you came into our room you looked at me as if I were a monster, and now you say, 'Get out, I have to talk to your mother.' "

Marziano went over and took Tatiana in his arms and held her for a long time. He felt that his daughter was the only woman with whom he had a pure, inviolable relationship. "Tatiana," he said softly, "I must talk to your mother about things that aren't for children's ears."

"The same old business about children! When it suits you, you say children mustn't hear this or that. But children always know everything, and if you send me out, I'll listen at the door."

"Come on, Tatiana. Don't misbehave. Be a good girl and wait for us downstairs. We'll be there soon."

Huffing, Tatiana went out. Marziano looked at Marina; she appeared beautiful, calm, a statue. He wanted to draw her to him, but he was intimidated by her. He didn't dare do anything, but then desire overcame his shyness, and he clasped her to him. She started laughing and thrust him away.

"You must forgive me, but I can't take any more. Just think how degenerate I've become. First I was a lesbian, then I fell in love with you and now I like very young faggots, thin, practically beardless. You know, the ones whose chests still aren't developed. I've let myself go, and that's why I'm attracted to skinny men. Tatiana's a big girl now, and soon I'll be a grandmother. You're with Enrica. By the way, congratulations. She told me it's going to be a boy."

"When did you talk to her?"

"We talk to each other every day. Just because she's expecting your son doesn't mean we can't go on being friends. She says she's coming here today or tomorrow. If I may tell you what I think, I'd advise you not to let Enrica take over your life too much. She's absurdly possessive, she wants all the space for herself. You remember how she was with me, and how overpowered I was. Let's hope Tatiana isn't listening at the door; we sound like two girlfriends exchanging secrets."

7. Arrivals and Departures

Duilio arrived, and two days later Mario and Ines went back to Turin. Clara remained alone in the hotel. Dennis's condition was stable. Marziano and Duilio spoke several times; at first sight they felt reciprocal dislike and respect. Meanwhile, Enrica arrived. She talked a great deal with Marina and made friends with Vanessa

Muller. Relations between Enrica and Tatiana were tense but polite.

Duilio led a secluded life. He went every morning to visit Dennis then took long walks. One afternoon he found Clara on the road, wounded. She had been beaten unconscious.

Clara's conditions didn't improve in the local hospital, and Duilio arranged to have her moved to a hospital in Paris. Then he got in touch with Mario, asking him to inform her family. Someone had to deal with the problem of getting her back to Turin.

Part 7

Chinese Boxes

1. Paola

Paola had come to visit Marziano for the day. "You're immature," she told him. "You can't resist telling me all the disagreeable little things of your everyday life as if they were events of supreme importance. You don't even know how to play the role of lover. You're already in the pathetic situation of having two wives, but with me you could at least pretend, try to be seductive. Instead, you're boring!"

"If I'm so boring and you don't want to have anything to do with me, why did you come?"

"Because I wanted to discuss these things with you and tell you not to take out your frustrations on me. Is that clear? You mustn't bother me with your prying and your blackmail. I loved you, but I have my own life. In your opinion, I should be at your disposal. Look what you did to your wife! The moment she left, you went to Rome and got her best friend pregnant."

Marziano looked at Paola; she was lighting one cigarette after another and spilling out these clichés as if they were great discoveries, truths never before expressed. The truth was that his thoughts were elsewhere. He had seduced Marie-Françoise. Now she really was a beautiful woman, one who knew how to make love. He was fond of Paola, but at this moment he found her humorless. She was too honest for his taste. She accused him of talking too much about his concerns, but she was so full of the commonplace. He respected her, but he didn't desire her any more. She smoked too much, she was untidy, he didn't like the way she dressed.

When Bosco came by, Marziano introduced him to Paola and they walked on together. They ate some shellfish and drank white wine, which dispelled their gloomy thoughts. After lunch, Marziano and Bosco accompanied Paola to the station.

2. BOSCO

"Paola's pretty," Bosco said as they were returning from the station. "Now that Clara and Mario have gone, you should start seeing Dennis more."

"What do you mean?"

"You should try to throw some light on what happened and help him with the firm. Duilio and Mario bore him."

"But I have another job, as he knows very well."

"Your job is precisely what could help you get to the bottom of this business. If I may take the liberty of giving you some advice, I'd say waste less time with women, who give you nothing in the long run. I'm leaving in a few days, I have to go to Italy, but I'd like you to give Dennis a hand with my manuscript."

"Yes, of course. We'd already decided that. I'll look over the pages that concern Max."

In the distance they saw Jean-Marie, Marie-Françoise and the Belgioiosos.

"Elegant people, the happy few," Bosco said. "Once we were all like that, dilettantes, until it became a mortal sin. Nowadays being a dilettante is no longer allowed."

Marziano thought of Marie-Françoise. Only he knew that one of those elegant women, bejeweled, a dilettante as Bosco had said, was his mistress. Only he knew that the husband of this mistress was a Soviet spy.

Of the Belgioiosos it could be said that they belonged to that class of rich Italians who know how to live abroad. Italy, for them, was too provincial, too cramped.

"What do you mean, Bosco, by saying my job could help me get to the bottom of this story? I'm not a policeman," Marziano said.

"No, of course not. I only meant that it's important to find out who made the attempt on Dennis's life. If the guilty party isn't found, our friend's still in danger."

"In a few days, unfortunately, my vacation ends and I will have to return to Paris. Do you think Dennis suspects anybody?"

"He claims it was all a mistake."

3. Conversation between Dennis and Marziano

"I imagine you feel better now that Clara's gone, as well as Mario and his girl. But don't you think you're being a bit cruel?" Marziano asked.

"I don't understand what you're talking about. Cruel? Why?"

"In two days' time I have to go back to work. I wanted to know what I can do for you."

"Thanks, that's very sweet of you; it's made me feel better just knowing you were nearby at a time like this. I'm better now, but I won't go to Turin for a while. I've arranged things with Duilio so I can run the firm from a distance. I want to get well, and as soon as I've gotten my strength back, I hope I'll be able to make a trip to America. I need a change of air. I want to keep clear, I want some time to pass so my relationship with Clara will fade for good, without any further trauma."

"And I feel my life has become horrible, but I can't see any solutions. I wouldn't know where to start."

"Why don't you take up your studies again, write something? I don't dare ask you again to come and work with me. But after what's happened we should see each other more often. I'm a bit ashamed I never came to see you in all these years."

"Yes, you're right. We should see each other more often."

4. Anna

The three children and the governess were waiting at the bar for Anna to arrive. They were all dressed up and had just come from the hairdresser's. The governess was pleased that the children's mother was coming back to verify the progress they'd made, thanks to her. She wasn't jealous of her mistress, knowing that the children interested her only at a distance and for short intervals, but the governess acknowledged that Anna was an unusual mother, her eyes quick to catch every detail and pick out at once what was good and what was bad.

Anna arrived late, beautiful and pale, wearing an otter coat. First she kissed the children with great tenderness, and then she absently shook the governess's hand. Luc was struck by the overpowering and fascinating presence of this woman who asked, with a shy smile, if he could make her a margarita. She was dying of thirst. After her third drink Anna began to take on a rosy tinge and, stroking the children's heads, she listened to their rambling, affectionate talk as they tried to win her admiration. She felt hot and bored. Meanwhile she was looking around, trying to figure out who was there.

She realized that two men, Nanni and Jean-Marie, were looking at her with curiosity. This reassured her; she pretended to be indifferent to them, and she laughed at some silly remark of her older son. As if in reaction, she took off her fur and said, "I'm dreadfully hungry." Then she turned to the governess. "Is the food good in this hotel? I should think it is, the children are as fat as pigs. Luxury agrees with them."

The manager sent over a bottle of pink champagne to welcome her. Anna barely tasted it, but the governess seemed to like it, and the children asked if they could have a sip. Anna ordered some beer, ice-cold. She was dazed by the margaritas and was still thirsty. The children, happy to be with their mother, looked at her with wonder and found her very beautiful. When she wasn't with them, they talked about her all the time, about her travels, and waited for her postcards, which they saved. Anna made an effort to transform her melancholy into euphoria. She joked with the children, asked all sorts of questions about what had been happening to them and listened idly to their answers. She constantly moved her long, white neck, so that she would be reminded, by every new suitor, that she resembled a swan. When she moved her neck in that way, she would often look towards heaven, half-closing her eyes. Her hair, which already had a few white strands, was bobbed. In spite of the three children and her dissolute habits, she still had a beautiful figure.

MISGUIDED LIVES

In that great dining room, decorated in pastel shades and meringue stucco, where the waiters were alert and smiling, Anna felt a growing sense of well-being from the knowledge that she had arrived at a reassuring place.

During lunch she thought about what would happen in the afternoon, what she would do with the children. She loathed the word "children." She had no fondness for childhood, which to her seemed an ungrateful season of life, almost an illness. The only things she liked about children was their smell, their texture, their voices like background noise. In any case, she was happy to give them an image of herself composed of beauty and luxury. The theatricality of life, the proper way to appear and introduce oneself, was of the greatest importance to Anna, like good manners or fine cuisine. During the day she would never put up with anything that might seem vulgar. Vulgarity, for her, belonged only to certain moments of the night.

At first glance, the guests of the hotel didn't seem very amusing. But the place had an old, padded quality that attracted her and made her feel that this had been a good choice for the children. Her daughter didn't resemble her: she was blond, with blue eyes. She would grow into someone interesting, you could tell from the way she asserted her presence. The only one of the children who eluded her was the oldest. He had a self-willed manner, but at the same time he was ambiguous, and it wasn't clear whether his instincts were good or bad, whether he was sincere. All three were very well brought up, by English rules. The oldest looked at her timidly, while the youngest tried, whenever he could, to establish some physical contact. The precocious voluptuousness of that child did not displease Anna, who sensed in him a solid manliness.

Where would they live, now that they had no more money? But any resistance had been beyond her strength: she had had to go off with that Greek boy. Now she had lost him, like all the others. She had run away, but the moment she found her children again, all her despair passed. After lunch she would retire to her room. And after her siesta she would change and take the children for a long walk on the beach, without the governess. She wanted to be alone with them for a bit and listen to them chatter freely. Before dinner she meant to write some letters. A hotel was the ideal place for correspondence; everything was made easier by the letterhead paper found in every room and by the bowing clerks who took care of stamps and mailing. She had to write a letter to Aunt Gustava and a telegram to her cousin Freya, who would soon be leaving for Cairo. Freya had suggested le Palace et du Golf to her for the children, and she had been right. The weather at these northern European spas was healthful, invigorating for the children.

The two men Anna had seen at the bar now entered the dining room, accompanied by two women. Anna looked at Maud in particular and had the impression of having seen her before. "Who are those people?" She asked the governess.

"I know the younger couple; they have children more or less the same age as yours. We went to a party at their house, a villa away from the sea."

Anna's daughter interrupted, making a face. "They're disgusting," she said. "We like Tatiana better. She's really lucky!"

"Who is Tatiana?" Anna asked.

"She's the daughter of a friend of Miss Muller," the governess replied.

"And who is Miss Muller?"

"An English lady, very refined, here on holiday. But she's leaving tomorrow."

"And who are the parents of those children?"

"The Belgioiosos. They live in London. She's a fashion designer. She uses the name Maud professionally."

"I see."

Anna was gnawed by a nervous jealousy of Maud's beauty. They must have been the same age, but Maud was thinner, fresher. And designers, if they're successful, make all the money they want by putting their name on the widest possible range of products. The

117

two couples looked like a very congenial little group. They displayed shared tastes; they clearly attracted one another. The women were slightly mannish, with a *sportif* elegance, the men faithful, obliging.

Anna envied that harmony, feeling excluded from it. She didn't have a young, reassuring husband. She had three children, she was alone and she had ruined her life. She never knew how to get anything out of her romantic affairs. Only her Aunt Gustava exploited them. She made Anna tell her everything and then constructed great passionate romances. So Anna kept going thanks to the money her aunt gave her in exchange for the story of her life. Her aunt would've been able to put the four people who'd just entered the dining room into her next novel. But Anna wasn't seeing them as future characters for her Aunt Gustava; they were people she would like to know.

While she was thinking about these things, she mechanically answered the questions of the children and the governess and ordered stewed prunes. The desire to enter the life of those still-unknown people made the prospect of her stay here more stimulating. She thought she would go up and change as soon as possible. She wondered what she should wear in order to be most seductive in the role of mother taking her children for a walk on the beach.

5. Difficult Choice between Two Conflicting Temptations

Something unforeseen happened. Anna had taken her children for a walk in the hope of running into the group she had glimpsed in the dining room. Instead she found some other people who were speaking Italian and seemed to her seductive in a different way. She had always had a weakness for that language, familiar to her since she learned it as a child in the Trentino.

Seated on the terrace of the Café de la Mer, Marziano, Enrica, Tatiana, Bosco and Vanessa Muller were chatting and taking the sun. They gave the impression of being unhappy, of having just quarreled. The sun seemed to irk them, nobody was speaking the truth, they all felt guilty for something surviving from the past. They had one unanimous opinion: the coffee was undrinkable because it tasted of chicory. The ocean at low tide seemed alien. Carelessly dressed, they looked like poor intellectuals. They were all sensitive people homesick for the Mediterranean. From their behavior it was clear that they were exiles, probably political exiles. The only thing missing was background music played on an accordion by a blind man with an Alsatian beside him. This image

119

brought Anna back to reality. She would have liked to belong to this group, who were very different from the four snobs in the dining room.

Anna's older son broke the ice by saying hello to Tatiana, who was sitting by herself in silence, polishing some shells. This allowed Anna to bestow a smile of greeting, and immediately Bosco returned her smile. Then he politely rose from his deck chair and, after ceremoniously introducing himself, asked if she would like to join them for a cup of coffee. She allowed herself to be caught up in the game, and though she wanted to say yes, she replied instead, "Thank you, it's very kind of you, but I promised the children I'd take them for a walk. I've just arrived. Another time." She went off, playing the diva a little. Anna realized that new adventures would befall her in this place. She had arrived only a few hours before, and already she was nervous because she didn't know which group to prefer; she wasn't even certain that one would exclude the other. She appreciated Bosco's polite flirtatiousness, but on that bleak beach she missed the spicy savor of her Greek boy. He liked the radio, gambling, filter-tip Camels and friends. She had also grown used to those things, but then she ran away, leaving behind a family jewel as a souvenir.

At this spa all was different. It was a world of not very virile people who could carry on great conversations and move their hands elegantly. Her older son was a bit like this, as his father, for that matter, had been.

Walking along the beach and breathing in the air that smelled of brine, seaweed and fish, she began singing softly, gaily. As she sang, she let euphoria seize her, and she added her own words to famous arias like "La donna è mobile." Her words were often coarse. Even the children were allowed, while singing, to express themselves in naughty words, because the governess wasn't with them. In that outburst of musical obscenity, they sang their hearts out and enjoyed themselves hugely. The bracing air made them hungry, and they stopped at a café where they ate salami sandwiches and Anna drank some red wine. The children also demanded to taste the wine. Their governess would have been horrified, but that afternoon she was off-duty, she had gone to the races with a woman friend.

When Anna was alone again, in her room, she decided to send Freya a letter, not a telegram. She had too many things to tell her. She wanted to thank her for having suggested this place and this hotel. Anna didn't know that in the room next to hers Marziano and Marie-Françoise were making love. They were united by a very strong passion. Marziano could drag Marie-Françoise down to abysmal depths, and he derived his pleasure chiefly from despising her.

Meanwhile, Anna had finished writing her letter to Freya and was preparing herself for an early dinner with the children. She took pleasure in being a young and elegant mother but liked the image of herself as a widow, inconsolable. She put on a black dress.

6. The Bar

That first evening Anna learned about the Dennis business, and the story was told to her in many different versions by the people she got to know in the days that followed.

Instead of picking out one regular group, Anna assumed a butterfly attitude. She made friends and chatted more or less with everybody. One evening, in the bar, Anna was surrounded by Jean-Marie and Marie-Françoise, Bosco, Marina and Vanessa, and they talked of this and that. Later Marziano joined them, and Marie-Françoise felt strange. There was a tacit agreement to be in a good humor that evening. The bartender had been transformed into the privileged spectator of a play without a script. To Luc these people who talked easily to one another were like an excellent troupe of actors improvising.

Towards midnight, very pale, Dennis came in and sat with them. His appearance was the dramatic twist indispensable to any important theater piece. Dennis didn't interrupt the conversation, which continued with its same verve. He enjoyed himself and was grateful that no one uttered any exclamations of wonder. After a while he made his exit. They all started talking about this apparition, as if to convince themselves it had been a mirage. They stayed till the small hours, when some went to bed and others went to the casino. In any event it was a memorable evening. There was no way of knowing if Marziano and Marina spent the night together, but he saw her to her room. Bosco accompanied Anna to her room, looked at her, held her hand for a moment, kissed it and then retired; he regretted not having the courage to court her more intensely. Jean-Marie claimed to be very tired and made a vain attempt to read, but kept thinking of Anna and Dennis. Those two made him feel that his life was an absolute lie. He did nothing but try to escape from what was happening to him. And yet that evening he had a strange sense of Anna's attraction. Seeing the pallor and simple elegance of Dennis he felt like a beggar.

For her part, Anna's head was spinning lightly. She flung open the windows for some fresh air and, without taking off her makeup, undressed and lay on the bed. She felt beautiful, less bloated than when she had arrived. She had never been in love with her Greek boy. She had been captivated by him and then had left him. Now she was alone in bed, drunk. She had the ability to drink excessively without anyone noticing. She drank very slowly and never drained her glass, which was always refilled.

At this moment, stroking herself, she savored the pleasure of that big bed, with its white, properly ironed sheets. She began singing softly, running her hands over her hips. She was a bit flaccid, soft. She was hungry again. She felt like calling the waiter on duty and drawing him into the bed, but at this hour there was no more room service. If she really wanted something to eat she would have to get dressed and go to the casino.

So she made do with a beer from the mini bar. At that moment she started thinking about Dennis. To her he looked more like a murderer than a victim. But everything had happened so quickly; her thoughts were blurred. How would she pay the hotel bill? She had to get in touch with Aunt Gustava. It would be better to move to the Trentino with the children. Their father would shower insults on her and wouldn't understand yet another change. It was terrible when children were involved. You could never then be rid of a person who had only been a brief episode in your life; he remained forever the father of your children.

Dennis stretched out on his bed, weak, still dressed. Inside he felt a great joy. For many days he had really been ill and had felt removed from everything. The shooting had reduced him to the condition of a goldfish in a glass bowl. He felt like getting lost in a strange city. He wanted to see Bosco's novel printed. He also wanted to be closer to Marziano. He had to persuade him to join the firm or to write an important book. It was wrong for Marziano to squander his intelligence as if defying life. Then Dennis remembered a dark, pale woman who had been at the bar with the others. A woman with raven hair and a long neck.

And so Dennis, thinking of his first moment of renewed freedom, finally fell asleep.

Part 8

A Love Story

1. Everything
Stops
The day after Dennis's appearance in the bar, Inspector Bernard warned the manager of le Palace et du Golf, Raymond Dufour, that it would no longer be possible to keep the matter quiet. An English reporter had spent a weekend at the hotel and had learned about Dennis from an acquaintance staying there, a Miss Muller. On returning to London the reporter, Marc Blum, found himself assigned to investigate a shooting that had taken place in a spa in the Pyrenees. The coincidence of two attempted murders in spas within such a short time had made Blum suspicious, and he had gotten in touch with Inspector Bernard. Realizing this reporter could harm his career, Bernard asked his friend Dufour to let him conduct a discreet inquiry among the guests who had been there the day Dennis was shot. Nobody knew or had seen anything except Tatiana, who told the inspector about the woman with a foulard scarf around her head, sunglasses and a long raincoat. Tatiana saw her speak with Dennis in front of the hotel, and then the two had walked off together.

The inspector asked Marina, who had come with Tatiana, why she hadn't said anything. Marina apologized and admitted it had been irresponsible of her and her husband not to pay more attention to what Tatiana said. When Marziano was questioned, he said, "I didn't think it was important to report a child's tale to the police. Now I'm sorry I didn't. We should all pay more attention to what children say."

Having consulted all the other guests, Bernard had only to question Dennis before Marc Blum extended his investigation. Dennis was extremely polite and described the great sensation of heat, the sultry, stifling heat he'd felt. He remembered that he had been shot by a woman in a raincoat who had called him by name. He didn't know and couldn't figure out anything more. Dennis didn't really answer the inspector's questions, yet he gave the impression of having made an exhaustive statement. He then thanked the officer for the care and attention with which his case had been handled. Maximum discretion, excellent doctors, considerate officials; it had also been reassuring to wake up in the hotel and not in a hospital. He then expressed his heartfelt hope that Bernard would discover the identity of his assailant as soon as possible.

When Blum again phoned Inspector Bernard, the officer told him that the would-be murderer was a young woman. This fact had been confirmed both by Dennis and by a little girl who had witnessed the encounter. The hotel guests, after their interrogation, felt somewhat uneasy. Those who stayed on preferred to forget; others decided to leave sooner than anticipated. Luckily Enrica, who had stayed in a different hotel, had already gone and was now back in Paris.

ALAIN ELKANN

2. Shyness, the Development of Ties Old and New

Dennis reacted badly to the interrogation. He had already suffered enough, and he didn't feel up to facing the investigation of his case. He assumed a nihilist attitude and spent the whole day in bed, thinking about his life. He saw it unfolding before his eyes like a documentary. Despite his professional success, he had not yet resolved his personal problems. His mother, for example, had died, taking a secret with her. She had never told him who his father was. She had always put him off, saying she was waiting for the right moment. There was a rumor that Max and Donna Ada had had an affair and that Max was Dennis's father, but this was only gossip. At times, pondering his fate, Dennis became infuriated. Like a spoiled child, he had the idea of staying in bed until he had found a way to discover his origins.

Bosco was dumbfounded by the cold, precise meetings he had with Dennis. It was as if Dennis gave him homework to do each day. Dennis suggested he should revise, apply himself more, but Bosco did none of this because he had become infatuated with Anna. Jean-Marie was also taken with her. Neither of the two men dared confess his love. Both were shy, and they confined themselves to daydreaming. She was cordial to them. She realized they were paying her court, and this pleased her.

MISGUIDED LIVES

Marziano, for his part, was worried by the growth of his passion for Marie-Françoise. Though he led an untidy life, he still wasn't used to the idea that Enrica was pregnant. In some ways he had a very Italian, very bourgeois mentality. He was confounded by the thought that soon he would have two children from two different women, just when he was getting involved with a third. He and Marie-Françoise knew it was an impossible affair, without any future, but they couldn't stop. As if this weren't enough, Marziano was suffering great anxiety because of his financial situation. The bank was threatening to stop his checks, and his expenses were mounting all the time. He had had to take two rooms at le Palace et du Golf and another for Enrica at the du Port, which wasn't much cheaper.

Anna, meanwhile, though she let herself be courted by Bosco and by Jean-Marie, had another involvement. She wanted to establish a special relationship with Maud Belgioioso. Nanni had to go to London for a few days, and Anna seized the opportunity to see a lot of Maud. Anna had become a very attentive mother and encouraged the friendship between her children and the Belgioiosos'. Every day she suggested picnics, walks, snacks or excursions to the amusement park. While the children played, Anna and Maud talked about their complexes, their perversions. Maud went so far as to confess to Anna that, during certain periods of frustration, she masturbated several times a day. In their relationship the roles had become reversed. Anna had become shy, insecure and, in talking with Maud, she always used a tone of implied flattery. When she told stories about her past, she was very careful not to seem too immoral, too much of an adventuress. The desire to please Maud betrayed her need for a metamorphosis. She loathed herself, felt she was vulgar, inefficient, badly dressed; she wanted to be Maud. She wished their children were brothers and sisters, all dressed alike, attending the same schools. When Maud shyly talked to her about her frenzied masturbating, Anna felt a protective tenderness towards her friend, who saw evil in a harmless habit she had had since adolescence. Anna was ensnared in more sinister things, had let herself succumb to unforgivable excesses and weaknesses. She had always wanted to go all the way, even at the price of horrible suffering. She wanted to hurt herself and then try to recover. Until a few days ago she had been in Athens, where she had gone through a dreadful affair, something not to be told it was so humiliating.

But her life was different again. At night, in her room, she spent long hours trying to imitate her friend. She would get into bed with a book Maud had mentioned to her. Even if it bored her and she had a hard time concentrating or simply turning the pages, she forced herself to find it sublime and read it to the last word. She suffered because she wasn't a slim woman with tiny bones, thin wrists, narrow hips. It was a question of constitution, not of diet. She was feminine, languorous, while Maud was energetic, nervous. Anna considered her own sensitivity repugnant, but it was the very quality that attracted men.

Maud, not usually inclined to accept flattery, was struck by Anna's attentions, and day by day she let slip some sentence, some observation about her married life, which was not all that easy. She was profoundly tied to Nanni, however. He kept the house going, he was a man of the south, and for him the institution of the family had a value that was no longer fashionable.

Though attached to her children, to Nanni and to her work, Maud felt an unexpected tenderness for Anna growing within her. She felt Anna's fascination, her sensuality. Very often, instead of going out, the two mothers would let the children play at home, and they would stretch out on a sofa, talking, caressing each other. Maud found Anna's slightly buxom shape attractive and envied the way she could assume the pose of an odalisque. She adored listening to Anna tell stories of past loves or recount episodes from her childhood, like her parents' fatal car accident, or talk about her love-hate relationship with her cousin Freya. Aunt Gustava had never let it be known whether Anna or Freya was her favorite niece. According to her moods, she gave and took away from each the illusion of the role. Maud felt a distinct physical desire for Anna one evening while in her bath. She asked herself why it was her fate to carry things forward and to hide the truth from herself. She had never bothered about the most intimate values of her life. In the tub she felt a sharp desire for Anna, who always laughed, giving the impression she had no worries and could face things gaily. Anna felt no guilt towards her children. Seeing them or not seeing them was the same thing; they were her children, after all.

3. Movements

Marziano's departure was imminent, and Dennis felt impelled to write to him.

Dear Marziano,

We haven't written to each other for years. Thanks for coming to see me so promptly. Thanks for talking with Bosco about his book, in spite of your misgivings. Real friendship is, most of all, being close in the important or difficult moments of life. I am writing you to force myself to stop holding my breath and come to the surface. After the police inspector's interrogation, it was as if everything had fallen on top of me, and now I am seeking refuge, hiding under the blankets. Who shot me? And why? What did they want from me? Was it some question of jealousy? Was it connected with the publication of Bosco's book? Was my mother's inheritance the reason? I'm coming to the point. I am obsessed by my heritage. As you know, my mother was a rich woman, but she became rich chiefly after inheriting the wealth of someone who loved her. Now that wealth is mine. Was my father the man who left it all? She had promised me I would know one day. Poor woman, she had no idea she would die so young, and perhaps in the end she would have told me who my father was. But she didn't have time. Being wounded brings the awareness that our life is a faint breath that can stop any moment. Now I am healed, but before I pick things up again, I'd like to know who I am. Before accepting an inheritance I want to know where it comes from. I've lived for forty years, running away, hiding, first in those walks with you and Max, then in the firm, but now I want to find out who my father was.

This letter is not only a proposal but also a request for a huge favor. I know you are very much caught up in your work and that you have a very busy private life, but what I'm about to ask of you is something I can't ask anyone else. It's a matter of going to Rome and getting in touch with two people who, I believe, know the truth about my father. One is Danesi, the family lawyer, my mother's financial administrator and the executor of her will; the other is Adriana Montefiore, a young woman who was her best friend during the last years. Let me know, as quickly as possible, if you can meet these people and help shed some light on the mystery that surrounds my life. I can't trust anyone else, so I beg you to be straightforward with me. If you can't do it, our friendship will continue unchanged. I don't feel like resuming my life without knowing where I come from. It's an obsession that perhaps only someone in my condition can understand. Forgive all this frankness. Consider this letter a secret between us and a proof of friendship.

Yours,
Dennis

When he had had the letter delivered, Dennis felt the remorse of not having expressed himself well, of having asked too much. Marziano, on the other hand, was deeply moved. There was something poetic in Dennis's wish. In a world where children as a rule want to kill their fathers, Dennis yearned to discover who his father was. Strange that Donna Ada had never chosen to tell him. Perhaps

MISGUIDED LIVES

she herself didn't know and the man who had left her everything wasn't Dennis's father. How could Marziano refuse to investigate for his friend? And how could he ever manage to leave for Rome given the chaotic situation he was in? He had to invent an assignment, a pretext to make the ministry pay for his trip. If the ministry wouldn't pay for it, how could he find the courage to tell Dennis he couldn't go because he didn't have any money? The rich are embarrassing because they have no idea about the little everyday expenses of ordinary people.

Dear Dennis,

Thank you for your warm letter, which gave me great pleasure, especially as a sign of friendship. I wonder if what happened won't bring our paths together again. I'll try to make the people you mention see me, and I'll do everything in my power to figure out if they know anything. I realize this is a delicate mission. I wish that I, for my part, could tell you in this letter the tortuous circumstances of my life and ask your advice about how to deal with all the compromises and subterfuges I live with, but it is too soon. I can only say that at a certain point a man loses the courage of honesty. I'm surprised you can have faith in me because I have changed so much since the days when we were young. It's humiliating, at my age, not to have achieved real economic independence, to grow bald, to see my health breaking down, squandered in carnal passions, unable to be a proper father or husband, having reduced one's own intellectual life to wretchedness. At this point I am certain that intellectual life is useless and that what we read should be forgotten. Unable to find the right path in the labyrinth of my days, I'll confess to you that the mission you entrust to me stimulates me to rediscover the few worthwhile things I have left. I will do my best to succeed. In the meanwhile, an embrace from

Marziano

4. Alone

The ministry authorized Marziano to travel to Rome to look for some dossiers that had gone astray. They would reimburse his train fare and hotel. Bosco had turned in his manuscript, and he would go to Florence and wait there till proofs were ready. The Belgioiosos closed their house and went back to London. Jean-Marie and Marie-Françoise went to Paris.

Anna and Dennis remained at le Palace et du Golf, but they didn't know each other. They had seen each other, without speaking, that night when Dennis appeared in the bar. Feeling alone, for different reasons, they went into the salon after dinner to watch television. Anna was a bit melancholy, and she was wearing a red pullover Maud had given her. They had said they would see each other again soon, but when? As soon as the children went off to Aunt Gustava's in the Trentino, Anna would join Maud in London. After that evening in front of the television, Anna and Dennis ran into each other constantly, exchanging smiles, but they couldn't bring themselves to speak. They seemed to chase each other, seek each other, but they also seemed satisfied with their silence.

One morning there was a great wind that colored the sky an electric, disturbing blue. Anna couldn't stand wind; she was nervous, ill-tempered, and she hadn't felt like going out for the children's walk. She had received an affectionate letter from Maud on her personal blue paper.

Maud described in detail her return to London and her life. Anna felt jealous and imagined how reassuring it was to work, to have

MISGUIDED LIVES

a house and a husband. The security of living there with the children, who had been going to the same school for years, the same little bus coming by to pick them up every morning. Anna was always on the move, like a gypsy. This day had begun badly. Maud's letter, rather than bring her pleasure, had depressed her. She felt swollen, having drunk too much the night before, and her digestion was sluggish.

Instead of getting up and doing her gymnastics and then going out for a walk, she lay in bed brooding. She decided to react against this dullness, to go down to the bar, drink a double coffee and write Maud a long letter, equally rich in details, which would make her homesick for her holiday and their afternoons.

At the bar Anna ordered a Bloody Mary, didn't write the letter and fell to daydreaming. By the second drink she had forgotten both her bad humor and Maud's letter, and she was playing dice and chatting with Luc. Dennis came into the bar, chilled, and from the distance his gaze lighted on Anna, whom he saw sitting on a stool, bent over the counter.

Even before he looked into her face, he sensed that he desired her. He sat down next to her, smiled and asked what she was drinking. He ask Luc to give him the same. Then he started playing dice with her, without paying much attention. He looked at her legs and he wanted her. Anna had realized. After a little while, as she went on playing dice with one hand, indifferent to what Luc might think, she rested the other hand on Dennis's sex. They sat for a while like that and then, impatient, they went upstairs. Anna undressed as if she were freeing herself of a burden, and she flung herself on the bed. Her armpits were carelessly shaved, her hair was disheveled and she was flushed, overheated, very sensual. Dennis, frail-looking, had a possessive, guiding way of making love. He took the initiative, and she let him, passively. Anna was creamy, lazy, she barely moved and she reached orgasm many times. From the very start there was love between them. Even in their lasciviousness there was tenderness. At times Dennis stopped, caressed Anna's hair and said sweet words to her. When they finished making love they felt light and happy.

During the days that followed, Anna and Dennis seemed unable to stay apart from each other for a moment. They made love many times, day and night. Otherwise they ate in one of their rooms and talked about themselves and their memories. They slipped on their stockings and wrapped themselves in a blanket or an old sweater if they were cold. He told about the publishing house and Donna Ada; she, about Aunt Gustava and Freya, her Greek lover and her children. They dreamed of taking a trip, going together to Portugal or Istanbul. When they talked, they loved each other, the hours passed quickly. They discussed buying a dog, a fox terrier, and calling it Besuto. What would they do with Anna's children and about the legal problems that lay ahead of Dennis? Anna suggested a convalescence in the Trentino. They could take a little villa near Aunt Gustava's house. The mountain climate would be good for Dennis.

"Have you met Maud Belgioioso?" Anna asked him.

"No, why?"

"She was here until last week."

"But I was still keeping to my room."

"That's right, I'd forgotten. What I meant was that if I hadn't met you I'd have fallen in love with Maud. Life is so unpredictable. I'd never been attracted to a woman. I found her so elegant, thin. She's not really beautiful, but she has a way of moving, of moving her hands, of speaking. And she has these extraordinary eyes, very expressive. We took foam baths together, with lots of salts and perfumes. Maud has the body of a young girl. Tiny, without hips. If you see her, I'm sure you'll fall in love with her."

"You're not in love with her now, are you?"

"When we went upstairs, the first time, from the bar, I would never have thought you'd be so sweet and strong."

"What if we went to the Trentino? I want to meet your aunt. I've never read her books, but I could become her Italian publisher."

"She sells very well in Germany and Brazil. The statistics say her readers are chiefly people who work at night, are unmarried and use public transportation. Aunt Gustava has the most incredible imagination. She uses my affairs and Freya's and then she invents terribly complicated stories, very adventurous. The last few novels have had a Palestinian setting."

Anna and Dennis fell in love more deeply than they thought. They attracted each other with great innocence. Together, they felt good and free.

5. Rome

As soon as Marziano arrived in Rome, he telephoned Adriana Montefiore. Adriana had a peculiar way of speaking. She had a barely perceptible Roman accent, and here and there she dropped phrases of her own invention or slightly altered French or English expressions. Marziano introduced himself as Donna Ada's nephew, in Rome briefly to do some scholarly research. He told Adriana that his aunt had often spoken of her and he would like to invite her to lunch. Adriana was amused by this unexpected phone call and curious about a nephew of Ada's she had never heard mentioned; she suggested meeting at the Casina Valadier. With a bit of luck they could eat in the sun. Marziano realized that Adriana must be an unusual person, but this wasn't surprising, because he had known Donna Ada. The fact that she had accepted his invitation seemed a good sign. He decided to wait before calling Danesi, the lawyer. If she were to admit that she knew Dennis's father, there would be no need to make the other call.

On his way to lunch he went to the Trevi Fountain and threw

in a coin, praying that everything would work out. He lingered to look at the windows of a sporting-goods shop, then he walked on towards the Pantheon. He missed Marie-Françoise, and desire for her seized him often, suddenly. Passing Montecitorio and the Chamber of Deputies, Marziano asked himself if he was really a communist. It was incredible that a sceptic like him had allowed himself to be lured by the temptation to be a Soviet spy. For once, however, he was fortunate enough to be in Rome for personal reasons.

Adriana was waiting for him, seated in the sun. Her face was half-hidden behind huge red and black eyeglasses. Pale and tiny, she had classic, aristocratic lines and was dressed like an American college student of the sixties. She spoke in a low voice, then burst into loud, communicative laughter. She talked without any thread of logic to mask her insecurity. They talked about Ada, about Rome then about what they wanted to eat. Finally there was silence. Their first genuine conversation was about the raw artichoke salad, which she insisted was better without the chips of Parmesan and with only a hint of pepper. He preferred it with the Parmesan. They agreed on the fact that raw artichokes were particularly good in Rome.

Adriana said, "Don't you think that the beach at Fregene, especially in bad weather, looks like some of the beaches in California?"

The unexpected mention of California after the conversation about artichokes upset Marziano, who recalled Marina's flight and all the troubles it had led to. He understood, however, that the reference to Fregene might imply a second meeting, but what was he supposed to answer? In the end he said, "What you've said makes me feel strangely guilty and reminds me what an infernal life we lead nowadays. A person remembers the beach at Malibu perhaps because one way or another he spent a Sunday afternoon there at some point during the past few years, but if you haven't lived in Rome for a long time, you don't remember Fregene at all.

MISGUIDED LIVES

I wonder how Fregene has changed. The only difference is that in California there are beautiful palm trees, and at Fregene it's mostly pines."

"You're right!" Adriana said, amused by the division of the world into palms and pines. That sentence had seduced her.

Even though this man repelled her a bit physically, he had magnetic, intelligent eyes. They managed to conduct their razor's-edge conversation so well that they parted with an equally sincere desire to go out to Fregene on Sunday afternoon for a walk.

It was easy to understand why Adriana had been such a good friend of Ada's. The girl was very intelligent and quick. She grasped the nuances of what was being said and hid herself skillfully behind a veil of vagueness. To get the name of Dennis's father out of her would be no easy task; Adriana would prefer to evade the question. Marziano had better get in touch with Danesi.

He discovered that the lawyer was a very tall, thin man with shrewd blue eyes. He paid attention to his clothes, all in the English style, and he used a sandalwood cologne. Though he was very polite, he intimidated Marziano because his exquisite manners, a relic of another age, created a barrier between him and any interlocutor. It was hard to ask a direct question of such a person. He asked the questions himself, and in fact, looking straight into Marziano's eyes as he puffed on his pipe, he said, "You're Marziano? I was expecting a visit from you. Dennis wrote to me and asked me to discuss with you the most urgent aspects of his mother's bequests. These are things that can't be dealt with over the telephone."

"Yes, I came because Dennis can't travel yet."

"How is he?

"Better. He's recovering, but before resuming normal life there are certain things he wants to know."

"He would like the guilty party to be found, I imagine. That's not going to be easy. Dennis must surely have read some excellent articles by an English reporter, whose name escapes me for the moment, about a series of crimes committed at various spas. The reporter suggests they could be the work of a maniac or acts of terrorism. Dennis was right to send you here; he must be very uneasy. Tell him that as far as his mother's estate is concerned there are no urgent problems. Everything is under control, there are no bureaucratic obstacles, the will is simple and the economic situation quite healthy. He and I can meet in due course, when he's well again."

Marziano realized that if he didn't do something, Danesi would accompany him to the door and dismiss him without revealing anything. So he replied, "I came myself to see you, not only as messenger, but also to decide, with you, what should be done. Dennis is still in shock and is afraid of a conspiracy. He fears they might try again. He's hiding in the hotel, confined in his room, and doesn't want to leave it until he's heard your advice, until you've worked out a plan. Dennis trusts only you, as a strategic mind, as a tactician. I've come to ask your advice about how he should act in the near future."

Danesi didn't feel the least flattered by Marziano's words; on the contrary, he considered his visitor a despicable, slimy character, and he disliked and distrusted him. Dennis was in trouble, but why should he, Danesi, have to put up with this ill-shaven creature who stank and looked at him with sly, impertinent eyes? He didn't like the visitor's way of getting to the point only at the end of their meeting, virtually at the front door of the office. "I believe he has to decide on a line of action," Danesi said. "Would you mind coming back around seven-thirty? I have some appointments now. Later we can talk more comfortably."

Marziano came out of Danesi's office bathed in sweat, and he grinned, thinking how contemptuously that snob had looked at him. He went into a bar to unwind after the tense encounter. The effort that some bourgeois characters expended on the construction of their dignity frightened him. He, who had constructed nothing, felt how fragile life was. Man, however conformist and cautious, was still at the mercy of uncontrollable events. Marziano suffered from the difference between the abstract thoughts man was capable of and the reality of things.

The most important element in leading your own life was luck, but only a few knew how to manage it. There were no formulas. Danesi, even though he was privileged, was afraid. Afraid of losing his status. He was a man who had arrived, and people who had arrived were finished. Through these thoughts Marziano allayed the sense of inferiority caused by direct confrontation with certain individuals. The more nonchalant, scented and elegant a person was in his presence, the more insecure and envious he felt. This was what made him sweat like a pig.

Soon it was time to go back to the lawyer's office. Reassured by his reflections, Marziano opened the conversation, bringing up without any hesitation the most pressing matter. "Dennis's real suspicion is that this whole thing has been masterminded by his father."

"His father? What?" the lawyer asked, amazed by this unexpected assertion.

"Yes, he's afraid the whole thing has been set up by his father to contest the inheritance."

"Why his father? I'd advise him to forget about his father."

"I don't know what the relationship is between Dennis and his father; all I know is that he was very much attached to his mother and, to spare her pain, he avoided talking about him."

"I won't say Dennis doesn't have good reasons for suspecting his father, but I believe he is off the track here. What do you think?"

"I've no idea, I don't know Dennis's father. Dennis is reluctant to talk about him; he's a vague childhood memory. I believe he was a mean man; in any case, he abandoned them. Do you know him?"

"Who?"

"Dennis's father."

"No, I don't. Ada never spoke about him."

"He must be a cruel person."

"He may be, but let's be serious about this. Abandoning a child is one thing, having him shot by a hired killer is something else. I should think there would be a middle course."

"You see, Dennis is in doubt about accepting the inheritance. It seems that his father and his mother held everything jointly, and therefore his father would be entitled to a share, which he could see escaping him."

"But this is absurd. If I didn't know that Dennis really has been wounded, I'd say he's suffering from paranoia. The truth is that Dennis doesn't know his father, doesn't even know who he is. I suspect Ada never wanted to tell him. If you ask me, Dennis is inventing this story about the division of the estate because he's always had a complex about not knowing his father's identity. I really know nothing; I could be mistaken. Ada may have admitted other things, and Dennis may suspect a specific person. But to get back to our subject, and to be pragmatic, I'd suggest contacting that English reporter I mentioned. He could investigate for us and put us on a more plausible track."

"That's a good idea!"

"We could meet him in some remote place and work out a strategy. Naturally Dennis would also have to join us, if he's able to make it."

Danesi had deftly dismantled the business of Dennis's father and, if he did know who the man was, he would never say.

"It seems to me there are two problems. One, to convince Dennis that it's right to entrust the matter to this reporter; and two, to hear this reporter's reaction. But how can you obtain discretion from a newspaper man?" Marziano said.

"By paying him a great deal," Danesi answered.

6. Fregene

As Adriana and Marziano drove out to Fregene, the conversation was slightly hostile, prickly. But the spaghetti and white wine made them more relaxed, and after lunch the tone altered. Marziano realized that Adriana would spend her life seeking herself, going to the analyst, constantly questioning what the truth was, because she had difficulty accepting herself. Walking along the beach after their meal, Adriana reminisced about her stay in California—the enthusiasm of leaving, of arriving out there, and then the slow, creeping homesickness that had finally brought her back to Rome. Their conversation had become light, like leaves falling from the trees. Marziano would have liked to ask point-blank if she knew who Dennis's father was, but instead he said, "Did Aunt Ada work with you?"

Adriana had one of her bursts of laughter. "Ada didn't work! She didn't have time. She had too many things to do. She was very worried about her son. Dennis was in Turin, and he was having trouble finding his way. I met him in New York when I was living in America. He was sweet, didn't talk much. For Ada anyone who didn't talk was dishonest, stingy."

"Were you friends for many years?"

"Yes. Ada was sublime! It's insane, her dying so young; you've no idea how much I miss her. Since she's been gone, my life has been different, meaningless."

"It's true that things between Ada and Dennis were difficult, especially because she stubbornly refused to tell him who his father was."

"Maybe she didn't know. Ada was such an extraordinary woman. She wouldn't have refused to say if she hadn't had a reason."

"How can you refuse to tell a child who his father is and then expect him to be brilliant?"

"True, but what she reproached him for mostly was for leading what she considered a foolish private life. For years he had a drab girlfriend. And, unlike Ada, Dennis could never grasp the sense of life as a game. You understand? How can anyone remember Ada without thinking of jokes and gambling and fun?"

"All the same, it's terrible not to tell a son about his father."

"That depends on who the father was. And what if the mother suspects several men? Ada was incapable of fidelity. During the day she was calm, clearheaded, but then in the evening she would begin to drink and flirt with the first man who came along, and she had to go to bed with him; it was a habit. Ada was an extremely faithful friend. But sexual fidelity for her was death, boredom, lack of risk, of creativity."

"Being a person's child isn't the same thing as being a friend or a distant relative. It seems normal for there to be a conflict between a son and a mother who won't reveal his father's name."

"Yes, you're right. But Ada's situation wasn't easy either. Why do we have to spoil our walk with this obsessive chatting about Ada? What does it matter if she did or didn't tell her son who his father was? Poor woman, let her rest in peace. After all, what do we care? Her son's a forty-year-old man who just inherited a fortune. Let's talk about us. Would you like to come back to Rome to live?"

"I don't know. Maybe I also have too many troubles I'd rather not talk about. I have to go back to Paris. Did you think you would stay in California forever?"

"When I left here I did. The first year I didn't come back to Europe at all, but then something happened. You remember that song about home we all used to sing when we were children?"

7. Having to Face
Reality
When Anna and Dennis felt the need to telephone Bosco and tell him about themselves, they had no idea that he would react badly. Instead of feeling flattered that they'd chosen to confide in him, he considered himself betrayed. Anna had given herself to Dennis when she knew very well that Bosco was captivated by her.

For his part, Dennis was eager to emerge from the shell in which he was living. He would have liked to find the criminal at once and discover the reason for the attack on him so he could then go off and marry Anna. She appealed to him enormously, even though he could see her faults. She was a gypsy, a dangerous woman accustomed to absolute freedom. To believe that Anna was the woman of his life meant taking a huge risk, but instinctively he trusted her. It was fascinating to have, for the first time in his life, a love that wasn't protective and reassuring, a relationship where any pattern could easily be fatal. Anna was looking for protection and, at the same time, she could rebel against anyone who wanted to protect her. She longed for a family life like Maud's, but she preferred for it to remain a dream. In any case she possessed a solid family context: Aunt Gustava's house in the Trentino, her competition with Freya and the children, too. The figure of a man protecting her was chiefly a luxury, a fetish. But Dennis was quite willing to give the impression of protecting her while actually doing so as little as possible. He knew, after all, that his financial position would, in case of need, allow him to help Anna. Now he wanted to get well and be able to enjoy himself with her, take a long trip and then stay a while in the United States. The children had to go to school anyway, and it had been decided that they would go to the Trentino. Anna would be able to take an intelligent interest in his life as a publisher. She was lazy but curious and imaginative. Marrying Anna would mean a definitive liberation from Clara, a way to break with her and stop her constant calls from Turin.

Marziano returned crestfallen from his Roman trip. He hadn't found out who Dennis's father was, but luckily that search became of secondary importance. Dennis asked many questions about what Danesi suggested, about the strategy to be followed to free himself from the threat of another attack.

Marziano talked about the English reporter Danesi recommended and explained that engaging him was only a question of money. Dennis liked the idea of meeting in some other place. He could go there with Anna.

He didn't talk to Marziano about Anna, considering it premature and pointless to mix the things together. Even if the subject of the unknown father had been shifted to the background, Marziano felt he had to mention the encounter with Adriana. "Adriana is an intelligent, likable woman," he said. "There were moments when she reminded me of Marina, during the early years in Rome."

"Was she nice to you or suspicious?"

"We talked mostly about your mother and then about Adriana's life in America."

Dennis didn't want to dwell on Adriana. He thanked Marziano for the trouble he had taken. "It's really true: you can tell who your friends are when things are difficult. You went to Rome, you did some investigating for me and you came back here with an idea that will allow me to escape this dreadful situation. Thanks for seeing

MISGUIDED LIVES

Danesi in my place. The idea of the English reporter sounds good to me. I wouldn't have had the courage to go talk to Danesi, though. That self-assured manner of his irritates me. When could the meeting take place?"

"If you agree, it's just a matter of choosing the place and setting a date. Do you think they'll let you leave here?"

Part 9

The Truth

1. In England

Like many English boys of good family, Marc Blum had studied at Oxford—archaeology, Greek, philosophy and art history. Chafing at the rules of society and family obligations, he signed on as a seaman aboard a ship going around the world the moment he had taken his degree. During that voyage he had his first homosexual experience, but he realized that falling in love frightened him. He was too sensitive, and love could change his habits and his personality. After the long voyage, Blum became a war correspondent. When he was almost forty he came back to England with the intention of changing his way of life and writing a book. But he was lazy and spoiled. Instead of narrating his war adventures, he let himself be fascinated by the terrorism spreading through Germany and Italy. But that interest also faded quickly. Blum felt ill at ease in his times, and day after day he suffered the decline of his native country. By now it was the Third World that dominated the scene. His contemporaries, when their fragile revolutions had failed, had become bourgeois victims of Japanese-American marketing. In those years, talent was acknowledged only in dissident intellectuals of the Eastern countries or in South American writers. For that matter, the real reason Blum had given up being a war correspondent was that, thanks to television, wars and uprisings had become mass entertainment. People followed wars as they might watch a soap opera.

Luckily television paid scant attention to ordinary crime. So Blum became interested in why some people turn criminal.

Since he had come back to England to live, Blum would stay in bed for days on end. He smoked a cigar, munched potato chips, read the newspapers with obsessive care and made notes. Sexually, he was attracted only to Arab boys. He hated his own blue eyes, his fat cheeks and his double chin. He liked thin faces, high cheekbones, ill-shaven men who didn't wash often. When he felt like purifying himself, he would go for a few days to Belgium or Holland, to visit museums.

He felt truly happy only while walking through the streets of certain North African cities. The odors of spices and food that wafted through the markets of those cities stimulated him far more than any music. Often in his London apartment he tried to reconstruct the atmosphere and the climate of the imagined hotel where he would make love with a young Arab already toothless from excesses of kef and sugar. Among all the places he had visited he preferred Morocco and especially Fez, in the rain. The memory of that city, ill-equipped against the cold, made him shiver. Often he masturbated with the window flung wide open to recreate the sensation of damp cold he'd felt there.

When Blum discovered that Nanni Belgioioso was on the list of people questioned at le Palace et du Golf by Inspector Bernard, he invited him to lunch. He knew him only slightly, but Nanni, who was skilled in kindling the passions of a pederast, had made an impression on him. Blum remembered one very provocative detail: despite Nanni's impeccable appearance he was never properly shaven.

It was true that Nanni did everything he could to seduce homosexuals, but he couldn't bear to be courted. From those who were taken with him he demanded affection and distance.

Nanni told Blum the itinerary of a splendid journey in Turkey.

His view of places was anything but academic. He gave specific information, which betrayed a great interest in classical culture, and he had a talent for narrating the most complicated things in an amusing way. It was only after lunch, when they were in the street, that Blum mentioned the incident at le Palace et du Golf. Nanni believed the shot was some kind of warning. Before saying good-bye, Blum asked him if he could offer any more precise details. Nanni, like all the others, knew that a little girl had claimed to see a woman in a raincoat.

A few days after the meeting with Belgioioso, Marc Blum received a phone call from Danesi, who wanted to know if he would come to Venice to meet his client. Naturally the journey and all expenses would be paid by Dennis. His curiosity aroused by this request, and by the proposed trip to Venice, Blum accepted.

Before leaving, he invited Vanessa Muller to tea at the Ritz.

"I realize Dennis's case is interesting for a criminologist like you. Why would they want to kill an intellectual?"

"I can't accept the notion that it was a mistake. Do you know Bosco?"

"Yes, I've known him for a long time. I know he's been working on a new novel for ten years, and Dennis says it's a great book."

"In your opinion, could that book possibly contain revelations that could motivate a crime?"

"I don't know what it's about, but I've never heard of anyone being killed because of a novel. Who cares enough about literature nowadays to think of committing a crime in its name?"

"I know, it seems unlikely to me, too. The strange thing is that so many people connected with the publisher were at the hotel at the same moment. It sounds like an Agatha Christie plot. You, for example, are a friend of Marina, the mother of the child who described the suspect. What makes me suspicious is the friendship that has developed between Bosco and Jean-Marie. Jean-Marie is a KGB spy and I'm wondering if Bosco isn't also somehow linked to the Soviets."

"I don't know Jean-Marie, but Bosco seems an unlikely spy. He's an artist. I'm not an admirer of his, but I know he's an artist."

"Is it true that Dennis has fallen in love with a very sexy woman who arrived some days after the shooting? They say she's a niece of Gustava von Traube, the writer. But what about you, Vanessa? What were you doing there?"

"I go there every year at the same time to rest and take the cure. The hotel is comfortable, the climate is bracing and it's relatively economical. I also found it odd, running into so many people who knew one another. It had never been like that before; that place was virtually a secret."

"Did you meet Dennis's new woman friend? They say she's an adventuress."

"No, I knew nothing about it. Unless she's a dark woman, a Slav I'd say, who arrived a few days later. She occurs to me because her children had been there and were shocked by the shooting. I learned that from their governess, a very likable Englishwoman. I'm glad Dennis has fallen in love. But if it's the woman I'm thinking of, I don't believe their affair will last very long. It's probably a sexual thing. It's curious that she should be the niece of Gustava von Traube. My friend Max, who unfortunately died years ago, could never bear Gustava von Traube. She wore too many jewels and hats with huge plumes. I haven't seen her for years."

2. Venice

With his doctors' permission Dennis left for Venice. Anna took her children to the Trentino so she wouldn't be far away from him.

Bosco and Duilio would join Dennis. Duilio was annoyed because an unhealthy situation had developed in the firm. Mario was acting more or less as editorial director, but he wasn't a real professional. He had installed himself in Dennis's office and had established an ambiguous relationship with Clara, who came to the office often and adopted a bossy tone. Mario did a lot of talking, but when it came to the point, he didn't know how to take risks. Duilio was jealous of the fact that Clara was being coy with Mario, and the two of them treated him as if they were the owners and he were an underling. If Dennis didn't take things in hand, Duilio was capable of quitting—he'd received important job offers from other firms. Dennis was not sorry that Mario was handling Clara, but he didn't want this to cost him his partnership with Duilio.

Because of his passionate affair with Marie-Françoise Marziano couldn't leave Paris and join the others in Venice. The two of them met furtively in bars or in little hotels. The fact that they had to see each other secretly and in haste made them aggressive. They didn't have enough time to give context to their relationship, but they didn't trust their feelings enough to break the established equilibrium of their lives.

When they saw each other they exchanged banalities or told each other their dreams. If they had a bit more time they made plans for a future life together, but they knew they didn't want it enough. As soon as Marziano mentioned Marina and Tatiana or his problems with Enrica, Marie-Françoise frowned and became edgy. She was very jealous and wanted to know nothing of Marziano's life beyond their meetings. If he asked her about Jean-Marie, she wouldn't say anything. While she considered it normal for her to be bound to Jean-Marie, she could not accept the fact of Marziano's having other women. So, frustrated by the lack of time, never able really to talk to each other, they would go to some hotel and make love. As soon as they finished, they knew they had to separate. They would part after a few minutes, taking the time only to wash and dress; they rarely made an appointment for the next time. A few hours after they had gone, one or the other would telephone.

MISGUIDED LIVES

At times Jean-Marie would answer, and Marziano would angrily slam down the receiver. Marie-Françoise would lose patience if she called the institute and they told her Marziano was speaking on another line and couldn't be interrupted.

Dennis had never understood why his mother had wanted him to consider men like Danesi his models. Virile, tall, impeccably dressed: officers in civilian clothing. One of the chief reasons for wanting to know his father's identity was his concern that he might be a man like Danesi. The idea of having such a father depressed him. He was irked by men who regularly used too much cologne and who, simply because they went to an office every day and earned a lot of money, were convinced that they were always right and knew everything. For Dennis nothing was more ridiculous than a man aware of his own good looks.

Marc Blum had asked that the meeting take place on Torcello. The island had a simplicity, an essential quality lacking in Venice, which had lately held less appeal for him. Since the death of Franco, Blum had neglected Italy and had gone to Spain a few times. During their Torcello lunch, no one let slip any personal opinions. After a generic conversation about Romanesque abbeys, a careful choice of wine and a digression about the Venetian sirocco, each stuck to his role. Dennis expressed the desire to have some light shed on his situation. And Danesi, without further hesitation, asked Blum if he was willing to stop writing his articles and help Dennis find the guilty parties.

The local crabs and the white wine had put Blum in a good mood. He said he could certainly understand Dennis's needs, but he wasn't sure he was the right person for this assignment. Furthermore, he was interested in finding things out, but only because he enjoyed telling his readers the story, reconstructing it for them. What had happened at le Palace et du Golf was interesting, with all those people who knew one another and who had turned up there together by chance. The story had a dramatic quality and was rich in events. It would represent a huge sacrifice for him to pledge silence and turn detective.

Danesi, after Blum's reply, felt that the moment had come to offer him a substantial sum. But Blum seemed to pay no attention. It apparently wasn't enough. Dennis couldn't bear the manner of an English gentleman, especially when, as with Blum, he suspected the gentleman of being bogus. So he became impatient, said good-bye to the others and took a motor launch back to the hotel. All those words, Blum's ambiguous talk and the rest of it had given him a terrible headache. He wanted only to resolve the case. If the Englishman chose to put on airs, so much the worse for him.

Dennis was already tired of the city, of Danesi and of the firm. He wanted Anna's warm body in his bed. He wanted to play with her beneath the sheets and say frivolous things. He couldn't wait for the whole business of the shooting to be done with so he could get away from Europe. He would collect Anna and take her around the world, then to America. If the children were jealous, he would find a way of coming to terms with them. In some cases it was necessary to buy complicity. As for Blum, it was best to let Danesi handle him. Dennis wanted to think only about Anna; if he neglected her too much, she might get away. She had been through too many experiences and had no patience for waiting.

3. Meanwhile

There were some misunderstandings between Dennis and Anna. After spending a few days with her Aunt Gustava and the children, Anna came to join him in Venice. She wanted to make love, be cherished, feel romantic. Instead, Dennis was constantly busy with the people who had to see him about business. He wanted to "tidy things up" so he could be free to marry Anna and go with her to the United States. Anna reasoned differently, without plans or specific destinations. She followed her moods, let herself live and, while making love, she said to Dennis, "We'll get married." It was a sentence that aroused her, but it had no precise meaning. Perhaps she would've liked Dennis to take her to a jeweler's and buy her an engagement ring, for the simple pleasure of celebrating.

She would have liked attention and sweetness, and then, euphoric and recharged, she would go back to Aunt Gustava's house. Instead, she remained alone in the hotel room for hours, waiting for Dennis to finish his appointments. She would lie languidly on the bed, talking with Maud on the phone. After waiting in vain for Dennis, Anna went to Harry's Bar, where she met Alessandro Campodifiori-Costagraphys, a businessman, playboy, half-Greek and half-Italian, whom she had known for years. Alessandro was involved in murky dealings, but he remained always afloat, always seen in the right places, with plenty of money to spend, many houses and young women who accompanied him on his travels. He used a little brilliantine on his salt-and-pepper hair, and his pencil moustache was always perfectly trimmed. He smiled constantly, and his manners were exquisite.

Anna and Alessandro had had a little fling many years earlier, and on this occasion, after drinking a couple of bellinis, pleased to have run into her old friend, Anna forgot about Dennis. Her need for amusement and idle conversation was satisfied. She wanted to eat well and have Alessandro tell her about Acapulco, Saint Tropez and other places, to listen to gossip and indulge in minor slander. She liked to lapse into certain conversations typical of a world to which she had belonged, marginally, a long time ago. They reminded her of her moment of greatest splendor, when she believed it was important to be among billionaires and go out in the evening to deluxe clubs in fast convertibles. Alessandro was a man who said simple, banal things, and he worshiped women. He gave expensive presents, showered her with compliments and suggested a thousand plans even though he knew they were never likely to see each other again. Alessandro was someone you came upon unexpectedly in bars, in nightclubs, at the airport.

That evening, in his motor launch, he said to Anna, "We should go back to Bali. I've been told there aren't so many tourists now and it's become beautiful again. I haven't been to Indonesia for years. You know, the Riviera is also magnificent this year. I was there on the boat last weekend, at Beaulieu, and there wasn't a soul. The Americans are afraid to come to Europe, the hotels are empty and the service is excellent." Anna felt good with Alessandro; she was amused, and he seemed a considerate friend. The only thing that seemed impossible for the two of them was any sentimental involvement.

At dinner that evening, Anna found Dennis pompous and wasn't the least entertained by his tales about Blum. At this point she had heard the shooting described too many times. Dennis had started talking and behaving like an elderly gentleman. So, thinking again about her afternoon with Alessandro and her former life, she suddenly wanted to go away. Dennis looked into her eyes and said, "Aren't you bored?" Without saying anything else, he downed three glasses of grappa, one after the other, and then, leading Anna by the hand, he went off along alleys and passages and led her into every kind of bar, dive and dance hall. Incredulous, Anna followed her man, who seemed perfectly at ease in these low haunts. Then, as they were dancing, he declared that he wanted to make love right away. So he made her come with him to the bathroom; he raised her skirt and tore a hole in her pantyhose. In a gambling den near the Rialto they stopped to play a bit and found some cocaine. A gypsy came over to read their palms. When they emerged it was dawn and they caught a motor launch to the Lido. First they took a walk, then Dennis dragged Anna to her hotel. In her room he undressed her, ripping off her clothes. Then he ordered some cold beef and chicken and forced her to eat. At this point he pulled a tube of cold cream from his jacket pocket. He smeared it on her and sodomized her, making her scream. Turning her on the bed, he made love in a delicate and conventional fashion but very slowly and without giving her an instant's respite. She submitted and whispered "I love you" into his ear many times. In the end he wearied of the theatrics and called a chambermaid. He gave her a hundred-thousand–lire tip and asked her to look after the signora. Anna was lying there, her head hanging to one side of the bed, her eyes dulled and staring. Dennis went out and walked towards the vaporetto station; in his head he felt a faint mist caused by the drugs. He climbed into the boat and got off at Riva degli Schiavoni. He went to his hotel at once, changed, and joined Duilio at the café where they had an appointment.

Anna slept all day, and when she woke up she realized that her room was scattered with roses; the perfume was heavy, nauseating. Beside the bed there was a large tin of caviar and a bucket with a bottle of pink champagne.

Outraged and amused, having regained some of her strength, she decided to go to a piano bar and look for Alessandro. She felt secretly wounded, enraged, but serene and happy. Before joining Alessandro, she couldn't resist the temptation to go by Dennis's hotel. It had been absurd and cowardly of him, leaving her like that. And then the insult of the flowers and caviar!

When told that Dennis had gone out, she was convinced that he was a man of many secrets. It was obvious from the way he moved his hands when he played cards or distributed tips in bars and hotels.

Alessandro was accompanied by a Nordic girl, a model who was young and very thin. Anna talked with him for a while and asked him to take her to Spain. He apologized, explaining that he had to go to Venezuela on business, then to the Arab Emirates.

Disappointed, Anna left. Alone in a dark, narrow street, she felt a sudden pain and realized that she missed Dennis. By his histrionic behavior, by making love to her with such intensity, he had tied himself to her much more strongly. Overcome by an irrational nostalgia for what had happened the night before, she fought the urge to scream as she walked along the street. Suddenly Bosco appeared. The moment she saw him, Anna tried to regain her composure, and she was briefly pleased to run into a friend. She stopped to talk with him. It was an excuse to stay on in Venice, not run like a madwoman to the station and climb onto a train in anguish. She wanted to see Dennis again before she left.

4. In Paris

In the waiting room Marziano convinced himself that this peremptory summons was the result of his behavior over the last few weeks. When he wasn't with Marie-Françoise he got shamelessly drunk, starting in the morning. As if his life weren't already complicated enough, he had suddenly been taken with Gloria, a girl in his office. Together they partied recklessly. At night, with Gloria, he began seeing a bunch of *clochards,* who gathered in a little square of the Latin Quarter, not far from the Seine. Marziano was drawn to those people no longer willing to face the obligations and ambitions of a so-called normal life oriented towards success, people who let themselves sink into increasingly empty days, clouded by alcohol, made up of highs, sleep, discomfort. For Gloria it was amusing folklore. Afterwards she went back to her apartment in Neuilly, where she would find mineral water in the fridge, and yogurt, fresh eggs, ham and, in the larder, crackers, canned goods, wheat germ, orange marmalade, packages of rice and pasta, various brands of mustard and herbs from Provence.

Marziano was thinking of Gloria's frantic consumerism when he saw Jean-Marie enter. There was no time to talk. An attendant showed them into the office of an official who, very politely, came to the point. He disapproved of their imprudent meeting at le Palace et du Golf at the very moment when a crime was committed. They had both gotten themselves interrogated by the police and, what's more, Marziano had actually gone to Italy for the wounded man. The most irritating and dangerous thing about the whole story was that a former expert on terrorism had written about it in the English newspapers. This ambiguous and shrewd reporter had been interested in ordinary crime for some time, but it would be easy for him to go back to writing about espionage. Moreover, Jean-Marie's wife had been seen too often at the casino and was leading a dissolute life. Winking at Marziano, he stressed the word "dissolute." He added that Marziano, in view of the responsibilities weighing on him, would be wise to get a grip on himself.

Because of the circumstances and their unworthy behavior, they were to take separate paths. Since Jean-Marie and Marie-Françoise were preparing to travel in the United States, as they did every year, it would be best for them to stay there longer than usual, until the investigation of the business at le Palace et du Golf had been shelved. As for Marziano, he had better go back to his wife and forget about Enrica and the child that was about to be born. Enrica was a dangerous woman, and it was preferable for him to keep well away from her. They would find a way to help Enrica through her pregnancy and then send her back to Italy.

Marziano came out of the meeting filled with bitterness. A grim, repressed anger made him all the more envious of those *clochards* he would have to stop seeing. He had gotten himself into a position where he could no longer command his own life, short of committing suicide. He could only hope that Blum would solve Dennis's case as quickly as possible. As they left the Soviet functionary's office, Marziano would have liked to take Jean-Marie aside and discuss with him their unacceptable situation. Instead, they had been shown out separately, under orders not to meet again. At this point who had the nerve to rebel? Now Marziano had been ordered to vegetate. How had he come to this, allowing a bureaucrat to prevent him from acknowledging his own son?

Jean-Marie found it intolerable to be told to leave for the United States. It seemed abominable to be placed in a situation where he was punished for having accidentally run into Marziano in a hotel and for having a wife whose behavior didn't meet Soviet standards. Ever since the AIDS nightmare had become so menacing he had abstained from certain of his habits. There was no telling what terrible punishments would have been inflicted if that had also come out. Still, it was mad to assume that he and Marie-Françoise would move without any hesitation to America. Everything had been said in a language all too familiar to him. It was a matter of life and death because in certain kinds of machinery personal situations are not important.

5. Unknown to Dennis

Anna and Bosco went into a bar to talk. "I ought to go home to my aunt's," she said, "but I don't feel like it. I'd rather be with Dennis a bit first. I never see him these days; he's too busy."

"Excuse me for interrupting, but that's the way he is. You know I'm here to go over the proofs of my novel with him. And what does he do? He avoids me."

"If we hadn't just spent a night of insane love, I'd say he'd fallen for another woman."

"I don't think he's the sort of person who abandons others. But it's difficult for him to break free of the women he's had. Dennis is a collector; he accumulates. No doubt this is his way of defending himself against marriage. He's afraid to marry because he's afraid it'll end badly, and besides he can't stand children. It's all tied up with his childhood and his relationship with his mother."

"I don't believe he hates children. He's so sweet with mine! They're the ones who reject him."

"You see? I'm right. Like all children, yours are very sensitive creatures and they realize his sweetness is due to the fact that he's captivated by you."

"That's possible. Have you known him a long time?"

"We don't know each other well. When he came to see me in Canada we talked about literature. In winter the days are short, it's cold, so you sit in front of the fire. He's a man who's afraid of stopping. I see him as a butterfly, lighting everywhere. This instability, if we want to call it that, is a rejection of the family, of family life. Luckily there was his mother behind him and now there's that Duilio. Otherwise Dennis would have ended up in taverns and gambling dens."

"Why? Did he drink heavily? Did he gamble a lot?" Anna was thrilled by this side of Dennis, which fitted in with his behavior of the night before.

"Yes, gambling is his vice—since he was a boy, I think."

"As soon as they find the criminal, and I believe a very clever man has been hired to do that, we're going to marry. Then, when Dennis has finished working with you on your novel and has the firm organized again, we'll go spend a year in the United States."

Bosco stiffened at Anna's unexpected matrimonial announcement. "I've never understood whether Mohammed should go to the mountain or the mountain should go to Mohammed. In any case, my dear Anna, if you like I can accompany you to the station."

"No, thank you. I'm not even sure I'll leave tonight. But come and see us one of these days. I know my Aunt Gustava would be happy to meet you."

"Thank you, Anna, but I'm hoping your future husband will decide to devote a bit of his time to me."

When Anna was alone once more, she set off briskly for the station. She was confused. She wept, then sang, huffed, talked to herself, smiled. She was in love with Dennis, had fallen in love the previous night; she was mad for him. What did it matter to know when or where they would marry or how the children would react? It was obvious that she wanted to go around with him at night and follow him in his life. She wanted to go to bed with him, but it was more rational to leave, to drag herself to the station and get on a train. How many times had her aunt tried to teach her that the best technique is to be unavailable. She was dying to wait for him at his hotel, but that would be the wrong course, a tramp's behavior, and he had no use for a tramp. She had realized that the very first time.

More than once she was tempted to go back, and at the station she couldn't resist the temptation to call him. They said he was out and she left no message. How boring it all was. It would've been so much simpler to be together at this moment, but maybe nothing was simple with Dennis. Maybe that's why she had fallen in love. She yearned for tenderness, and so there, at the station, she assumed a melancholy attitude. When she arrived at the house in the Trentino, everyone was asleep. In the mailbox she found a letter from Freya announcing her arrival. This news pleased and frightened her. Anna could already imagine that Freya would involve herself somehow in her affair with Dennis.

6. Wrong Choice Stricken with doubt, Dennis

preferred to escape the consequences of all he'd done with Anna and plunge into his work. That one night he had abandoned himself to instinct, to his true way of loving. More than complicity and friendship he sought in love the fulfillment of pleasure and imagination. That night he had wanted to make Anna know what he felt towards her. Loving involved a production that in some ways should resemble a pagan rite, a festival. In fact, his sincerity and abandon had won her love, but he didn't know that. Once he became sober again, his shyness prevailed. So, a little ashamed of what had happened, pretending to himself that it was only a dream, he set to work with Duilio. They went over accounts, and Dennis explained carefully what was to be done to keep Clara at a distance. He wanted to have nothing further to do with her. As for Mario, Dennis understood how irritating it could be to see him swagger around the office; obviously he had to be sent away. But this should be done cautiously. It was much better not to turn Mario against them, because with his twisted character he could create a good deal of trouble. Instead of dismissing him brusquely, it would be better to invent a project that would keep him far from Turin and yet make him feel busy and important.

Having delegated to Danesi the job of figuring out how to deal with Blum, Dennis had nothing to do but work with Bosco.

Dennis was convinced that the book was far superior to the many novels he had read in recent years, and it was also true that it was Bosco's most significant work. Yet there was something that kept him from believing that it was a great novel. But what were the criteria for judging whether or not it was a masterpiece? Bosco was fascinating; a man of genius. This didn't mean, however, that he was a great artist.

So Dennis decided to send the proofs to Marziano and ask him what he thought. Dennis's great activity was a pretext to disguise his anxiety. For three days he had had no news of Anna; he didn't dare send her flowers, much less telephone her.

Meanwhile, negotiations between Blum and Danesi were proceeding slowly. After the meeting on Torcello, Blum, offended by Dennis's sudden departure, had asked for two days to think things over. When the two days had gone by, Blum met the lawyer in a café. He was wearing a long, white Irish sweater and rough, unpressed trousers, which Danesi looked at with envy. The lawyer knew he was incapable of the true nonchalance that characterizes a certain class of Englishman.

Blum declared there was no call for an investigation since there were so few clues. He added that everything seemed torpid to him, from the climate of Venice to Dennis's absentminded behavior.

Danesi's response was specific and curt. "It's a question of time. The quicker the assailant is identified, the higher the reward will be. For the present you will be given all the funds necessary for conducting the inquiry, and all expenses will be reimbursed. I'm sure Dennis will take a great interest as soon as there are some results. If he seemed distracted the other day at lunch it's because it's hard for him to consider everything that's happened to him with the necessary detachment."

"But haste can be dangerous, though I understand your urgency."

Blum's attitude made Danesi nervous, but he forced himself not to betray his natural impatience. It was likely that Blum already had some clear ideas about the matter and was bluffing in order to raise his price. Danesi also needed to win Dennis's trust. Donna Ada had had absolute faith in him, giving him carte blanche, but this was not necessarily the case with her son. Danesi's concerns were of no interest to Blum; he was wondering if the money he could earn from this job would make it worth the trouble. By and large he knew who some of the chief characters in this story were, but he was almost sure that others were concealed.

Danesi didn't know it, but it was the literary aspect of this business, its crime-novel quality, that made Blum uneasy. He felt that the criminal, if sought in haste to satisfy Danesi, would not easily be found.

Part 10

Changes of Course

1. Padua

Mario's accident was a stern warning, a sign from destiny—but of what? Waiting to speak with the doctors, Dennis was leaning against the window of a corridor in the Padua hospital, and he felt guilty. What had happened?

The night before, walking along the Riva degli Schiavoni, he had felt for the first time since his arrival in Venice the absence of Vera. He would never again be able to go and stay at her place in Campo della Guerra; he would never see her laugh again or hear her horrible slanders. Had she been the woman of Mario's life? Mario's power of seduction lay in his hands, big and gnarled, with gnawed fingernails. Those hands had shot real pistols, handled a real submachine gun for a cause that had ended badly. But why was he so under Mario's influence? Why did Mario make him feel guilty, when Mario denigrated him and envied him at the same time? Even with women, there had been some ambiguity between them.

Mario began his affairs with passion, then he would regret having fallen in love and he would be afraid. At the outset, he gave women the sensation that he could protect them, but he proved incapable of that. His affairs always broke up sensationally, but Mario proceeded with pride, never learning from his mistakes, lacking any sense of humor. He acknowledged that he had been mistaken and soon began doing the same things again. Mario had his own way of shutting himself up in a room and reading. He would read, drink, smoke and lie in bed for days. It was these excesses that fascinated Dennis, the fact that Mario flung himself headlong into things.

He defied the world and confronted it because he hated it. He hated society. Thinking about him like this, Dennis had felt an urgent desire to see him. He telephoned him in Turin, and they talked about Vera, about Venice in those days. Finally Dennis had said, "Why don't you come and see me? We'll talk about ourselves and about the firm. It'll do us both good. I've seen Duilio, and I've told him I want to give you a new job, more prestigious."

Instead of showing up on the Zattere as agreed, Mario had crashed into a truck on the superhighway. But why Mario of all people? He was an excellent driver. Dennis talked with the doctors and was shown into a room where Mario was lying immobile on the bed, unconscious. This sight made a deep impression on him and reminded him of what had happened at the hotel. Looking at his injured friend, he again felt a great desire to have Anna by his side.

2. The Engagement

Dennis thought about becoming engaged to Anna all through the brief trip between Padua and Venice. He was a builder, and now he felt the moment had come to marry. Since it was such an important step and he had waited so many years, he wanted to organize everything properly.

Why Anna particularly? For the moment all he knew was that being with her, especially in bed, brought him a great tranquillity. But how would she manage to accustom herself to being a publisher's wife? Anna was possessed by a great inner fire, and her relationships were impassioned. If she was really in love with him, he knew she would succeed. Marrying Anna meant that, at the age of forty, he was becoming an adult.

3. Aunt Gustava

The sum Danesi suggested proved insufficient to persuade Blum to give up newspaper work for a while. Danesi didn't want to overdo the offer or to plead with Blum, so he went back to Rome without having obtained the desired result. From Turin, meanwhile, Duilio had informed Dennis that Clara had gone to Israel to work in a kibbutz. He would never have imagined Clara capable of a choice like that.

After the famous night in Venice, Anna had heard nothing from Dennis, and she was amazed to receive a formal, very polite letter in which he asked her to marry him, proposing an official engagement of six months. He also asked to meet Aunt Gustava to ask for her niece's hand. Anna's doubts vanished, along with the nerves that had been tormenting her for days. A letter was written, tangible proof. It wasn't just words, uttered idly in a moment of euphoria. This showed that Dennis meant it.

Anna was curious to see how Aunt Gustava would react, though she couldn't understand why Dennis wanted to meet her. She hadn't expected that he felt the need to become part of a new family. Ever since Anna had told him about Aunt Gustava and

MISGUIDED LIVES

Freya, he'd been fascinated by the idea of belonging to a family composed entirely of women and children. To meet her aunt, Anna and Dennis had to go to Paris.

Instead of going to a stately neoclassical villa to ask for Anna's hand from an elderly lady who would receive him in a drawing room and offer him tea, Dennis invited Gustava von Traube and Anna to lunch in a Montparnasse brasserie. He had imagined Aunt Gustava as a Virginia Woolf look-alike but found himself facing a huge woman who resembled a Russian general and spoke with a Spanish accent. She wore a gaudy dress that was too tight for her and big pieces of costume jewelry.

Heavily made-up, she smoked little cigars, which she extracted from a gold case. She addressed Anna in an authoritarian tone, calling her "darling." All through the meal Aunt Gustava tried to dissuade Dennis and Anna from being married.

"Nowadays everything is so short-lived—and when it comes to love! A man and a woman marry, to patch up the marriage they have a child, then they realize that the children of their previous marriages are unhappy and then the children of the new marriage become unhappy, too."

"Auntie, don't you think your view is too pessimistic?"

"No, darling. You two get along well together because you're infatuated, you attract each other physically, but you're not fond of each other in that calm, settled way that keeps good marriages going. People don't get married these days, they live together for a while, then they tire of it. Things end, they meet other people, have other episodes in their life."

"I wouldn't want to contradict you, but that calm, tried-and-true love you're talking about is a goal, not a starting point."

"I never married because I never wanted to be disappointed. These don't seem to me times for marriage. As for Anna, despite her many this-is-forever men, those kindred souls she's encountered in the course of her life, I see her come back every now and then to her children and to her aunt. Freya, too, another niece of

mine, is very fickle. She falls in love with great causes. I just saw
her here in Paris, back from one of her journeys, another shattered
love; she was going to some spa for a cure. I hate to say these things
when you've come here to announce your engagement. But why
should I lie? I've told you how I feel. The two of you will act as
you think best."

Dennis realized that Aunt Gustava was an elderly, embittered
lesbian. To him this woman's opinion meant nothing. He was sure
that he wanted to marry Anna. He could even imagine the morning
of the wedding. He would wait for her at the altar, and she would
arrive in her white dress with a train. A bridal gown, close fitting
and seductive. She would be in high spirits, her cheeks flushed.
Looking at Anna now, he enjoyed a foretaste of the ceremony; the
moment when he would slip a heavy gold ring onto Anna's soft
finger, and she in turn would slip a ring onto his finger, pronouncing the ritual words. He would then be a married man, a man who
wears a wedding ring. Then he would kiss her voluptuously, a
legitimate and sensual kiss in front of all present, in a church.
Anna's tongue would have a special taste. From that moment on,
speaking of Anna, he would say to others, "Yes, she's my wife."
Anna's children didn't represent a problem, as she thought they
did. They would be a little jealous, a little cold, spiteful, but he
didn't care; he would treat them like other children. Aunt Gustava
couldn't even imagine how stubborn and persevering Dennis could
be. He had decided he wanted to sate his sensual appetites making
love with Anna, his legitimate wife. They would cut the wedding
cake together.

At the end of lunch, Dennis, to irritate Aunt Gustava, ordered
a bottle of champagne and offered a toast to their engagement. She
didn't drink. Nothing would change her mind.

4. Encounter with Marziano

It wasn't easy to talk to Marziano without feeling slightly foolish. Dennis would have liked to discuss the radioactive cloud that was threatening Europe, but Marziano could easily have answered, "Who gives a shit? What can we do about it?" With his friends he didn't talk much. His long conversations took place in bed, with his women, after making love. "Have you read the novel?" Dennis asked finally.

"Yes. It's not bad, but it's too ambitious. Bosco's stay in America helped him find a new, simpler style. The content is interesting, but in some places it isn't developed. You can publish it. It would be useless to waste a lot of time revising it. It's better than lots of other books."

"Thank you for the opinion. But why don't you come and work with me? As soon as I've solved my case, I want to go and spend some time in America, and I need to entrust the firm to somebody I respect. Anna and I became engaged yesterday, and we're getting married in six months."

"Why in six months? There are some things that should be done promptly. If you wait six months . . . who knows?"

"I really need your help. Mario's had an accident—he's in a coma in the Padua hospital. I'm terribly sorry about it, but I have to find somebody to take his place in the firm, otherwise Duilio will quit. I thought of you because it has to be somebody who knows how to deal with books."

"It's incredible, the way you resemble Max in these things! The practical side doesn't count for you—you've always had money. How can I leave Paris and my job when I have to take care of Marina, Tatiana and now Enrica, who's expecting a child by me? I know I lead a sloppy life, that I don't have a cent and my health is lousy. At most I could be your consultant on Bosco's book."

"I don't want to insist, but I believe that sooner or later you should come back to Italy to live. I understand the fascination of exile and all the prejudices there can be even after you've been living for years in a city like Paris. But, believe me, in the past few years the quality of Italian life has changed a great deal."

"How did things end in Venice? What's Blum like?"

"A presumptuous snob. I didn't like him and I wouldn't trust him. Danesi insisted on continuing the discussions, but he couldn't settle anything. Blum won't give up his newspaper work, so we're back where we started. Ah, did you know Clara had gone off to a kibbutz?"

"Why, is she Jewish?"

"No. Duilio told me. I'd never have expected it."

"It's better for me not to come and work with you; we'd end up quarreling. We don't always have the same tastes. We think differently. For example, if I had to find my father, I'd see it through, stick with it to the end. That's why everything goes wrong for me. Nowadays nobody should see anything through to the end."

Dennis was aware that Marziano knew him well. True, he was too impatient, he always hurried on to the next thing.

5. The Marriage

Anna and Dennis stayed on in Paris, in a simple hotel opposite a pair of cafés very popular with artists and foreigners. Anna, by nature, preferred not to make engagements, not to have to think about tomorrow. She woke up late and liked to make love while the shutters were still closed. Generally it was already four o'clock by the time they went out to lunch. Towards midnight they would have supper and then dance in one of those clubs that open only late at night, where the customers are mostly rich Africans accompanied by very beautiful women. Anna was happy with her group of Brazilian and Chilean friends.

Dennis would have accepted this permanent party and Anna's nightly drunkenness if she'd been his wife. He would like having a wife who behaved badly.

"Let's get married right away," he suggested, following Marziano's advice. But this irked her. "Why right away, when we decided to be engaged for six months? Staying in Paris as an engaged couple and going dancing at night seems very romantic to me."

Dennis wasn't interested in that sort of life. If Anna didn't make up her mind soon, his desire for her could fade or change. As a lover, he felt that Anna was beginning to be boring. When she got drunk she talked obsessively, repeating herself, harping on one point. In nightclubs hours and hours were wasted in idiotic conversations, and she laughed hysterically at things that weren't amusing. Dennis couldn't stand Anna's raucous, forced laughter when she got to talking with strangers.

Dennis tried again. "I want to marry you right away because I have a presentiment and I wouldn't want us to lose this chance."

"If that's the case, it's better to give up the whole idea. The reason I wanted to marry you was the calm way you faced the thing. Six months of being officially engaged seemed a beautiful, unforgettable gift, but now you want something done in haste!"

"You're right, but for years I've been looking for the woman of my life."

"All right, but why this sudden impatience? You can't keep changing your mind. I've led a gypsy life, but finally I'm touched because I've met a serious man who takes me as I am and wants to marry me, to give my life and my children's a frame. I fall in love with his calm strength, and it turns out he's not like that, I've got it all wrong."

"No, no. It's just that I'd like to make you mine. I don't know how to explain."

"If you can't wait six months because you're afraid your love will die, that means you're not ready for marriage or even for love. Instead of always shutting up when we go out and making me feel how much you despise my friends, you should be glad to see me so happy. It's absurd for you to be jealous of the fact that I dance and have fun in nightclubs. If you don't know how to enjoy futilities, you'll never know how to spend a winter and feel at ease in the country, without friends, no proper heating, few books. You shouldn't find my Brazilian friends likable just to do me a favor; you should let yourself go, not be afraid. But now I'm hungry and dying for an ice-cold beer. To make me forgive you, buy me a present. Since you're so bored here, I've been thinking we could go to London for a few days and see the Belgioiosos. You don't know them, but I'm sure you'll become friends."

6. Marziano

Bosco arrived in Paris to discuss his novel with Dennis. When he discovered Dennis had gone, leaving the job to Marziano, he was seized by a fit of wrath and poured out his fury on Marziano.

"I can't understand how a man with Dennis's style and intelligence can lose his head over a faded little adventuress like Anna! Everything happens to me! I live for years like a hermit and then I get mixed up with a publisher who first gets himself shot and then, the minute he's well, loses his head over a woman who isn't worth it, forgetting all about his authors."

"What do you mean? Can't a man be in love and handle his authors at the same time?"

"Apparently not. We don't know each other well, and I wouldn't want to hurt your feelings, but do you consider it normal that an outsider—which is what you are as far as the firm goes—should be the one to tell me how my book will be published?"

"First of all, I'm a trusted consultant of the firm and not an outsider, and besides, what could flatter an author more than saying his book's fine as it is?"

"It's a matter of form. But you and he belong to a generation for whom these things no longer have any importance."

"Dennis asked me to read the proofs of your novel, to have a dispassionate opinion, the opinion of someone who isn't exclusively a reader of novels. I agree with Dennis: to me the novel seems finished. I don't believe anything more should be done with it. If you want to do something better, write another book."

* * *

During his enforced stay in Paris, Marziano was back with Marina, and in the evening he played the piano until he was in a daze. As he ran his fingers over the keyboard, playing by ear a senseless repertoire that ranged from Wagner to Neapolitan songs, he eluded the reproaches of each of his women. Enrica scolded him for disappearing after getting her pregnant, for not asserting his paternity. Marina scolded him for having allowed her to go off to California. Tatiana scolded him for many things, and so did Paola. Marie-Françoise had left. He had too many women around him, and none was really his.

In his most desperate moments he thought again of Adriana and their walk at Fregene. She was the only woman he could talk to without any obligation or guilt. He and Marina lived in the same house, but they didn't make love. Their amorous life had broken off over a question of stockings: he liked sheer stockings, and she considered them vulgar. It was their very vulgarity that aroused him. For him a woman was something to knead, to savor. It was probable that if there hadn't been women in his life he would have become an important scholar, but his sexuality had always distracted him from any discipline.

At times while he played he thought of the Soviet Union, about being ordered to stay in Paris and live a proper life. He considered Bosco's novel mediocre and commercial. He wasn't interested in commercial things. He had no money, would never have any, but this wasn't serious. At least he didn't lose any. Possessions were cumbersome and destroyed all spontaneity. He didn't want to slave away for a publisher. He had a very different view of culture. Really good things, sooner or later, got to be known and were never lost. But Dennis had the habit of possessing money. He had believed it was indispensable ever since the days when he played cards in bars to win some cash. Marziano was cheered observing the clouds: Paris was a city of clouds in motion.

7. Anna and Dennis

When they were seated in the taxi to the Gare du Nord, Dennis felt ill at ease. He knew he'd caused this sudden departure for England, but he was sorry to leave Paris. Anna didn't know this, and she was happy to be making a sacrifice for her man, whom she absolutely did not want to lose. The night before he'd proven his love: for the first time he had been cordial to the Brazilians.

This change in Dennis was due to an encounter the previous day that had upset him. As he was returning to the hotel, a woman with a full skirt had brushed past him on the sidewalk. As if by reflex, he had turned to look at her as she walked on. He couldn't get her out of his mind, and, as a reaction, he had been amiable with the Brazilians and extremely affectionate with Anna. He knew that the woman who grazed him on the sidewalk was the one who had shot him.

On the ferry from Calais to Dover, they stepped out on the deck. "We could get married in London," Dennis said, "but I feel you're afraid of losing your independence. You're afraid I want to dominate you financially. I understand, but for me money has no importance. I inherited it. I've always led a simple life. If money's a problem for you, when you marry me you'll have half, you understand what . . ."

Before he could finish the sentence, Anna slapped him. Outraged and in tears, she headed for the bar.

Dennis studied the cliffs of Dover in the distance and thought about the woman who grazed him on the Paris sidewalk. Assuming she was the one who had shot him, was she following him? Did she plan to shoot him again? Perhaps she was hidden on the boat. He remembered her perfume and wished she were there on the deck of the ferry. He would try to disarm her, talk to her of poetic things, tell her not to feel guilty. Actually, after he'd been shot, everything had changed, he'd been freed from his past. But if that woman wasn't following him, where would he meet her again?

Anna had just slapped him, but it wasn't anything serious. He joined her at the bar, where he saw her leaning on the counter, chatting gaily with Arnaldo, a Brazilian she'd met in Paris. They seemed to have many things to say to each other. Seeing her talking so easily made him jealous, and Dennis wondered if he should interrupt them. Should he instead consider himself offended and slip away at Dover? Wouldn't it be better for him to go and stay in Padua to be near Mario, whose life was in danger? What kind of man was he, what kind of friend? What was happening to him? He looked at Anna, who went on talking with Arnaldo, and he asked himself why he wanted to marry her so urgently when, after all, she was reluctant. When they reached Dover, Dennis and Anna got onto the train as if nothing had happened. Anna seemed to him beautiful, pale, Mediterranean against the background of the English countryside at sunset. There was no one else in the compartment, and he started kissing her and putting his hands inside her blouse.

8. Why?

In London, Anna grew daily more evasive about the marriage. If Dennis ventured to talk about it, she became insolent. Anna's attitude changed in the presence of the Belgioiosos. For her, Nanni and Maud were the perfect couple, her model. The Belgioiosos had a style, a way of talking that was contagious. Maud was serious, but she knew how to enjoy herself; she hated life to be heavy and bourgeois. Anna would have liked herself and Dennis to be a replica of the Belgioiosos, but Dennis wasn't the least bit fascinated by Maud. She talked too much and couldn't hold her liquor. She was accustomed to having her friends flatter her, the little queen of the group, and to having the last word, no matter what.

Since they'd been in London, Anna had completely identified with Maud and imitated her gestures and her way of speaking. But Dennis didn't much care. He found Anna irresistible, especially when she lounged on the sofa or the bed and stared into space. The folds of her body, her lips, eyes, her slight flush, made her very provocative. Then he would sit down beside her, begin to talk to her, stroke her, try to undress her. Often she would fend him off, but the distance she tried to establish, pleading a headache, hay fever or menstruation, vanished in Maud's presence.

Nanni was polite and smiling with both Anna and Dennis, but he was reserved. He concealed himself and his thoughts behind a well-tested patina and the role of good conversationalist and perfect host. When Dennis and Anna were alone in the hotel, she did nothing but compare their life with Maud and Nanni's, and she reproached Dennis for lacking a sense of humor, for not knowing how to talk to a woman.

Dennis felt ill at ease during those London days taken up with shopping, restaurants, theaters and nightclubs. He realized that if Anna was different from the Belgioiosos, her difference was accepted and complementary. Anna's sensuality, her desire for pleasure and amusement were irresistible to anyone. He grew bored listening to the same conversations, which the Belgioiosos considered entertaining. They spoke and behaved in terms of us and them, and Anna was neither in one category nor the other: she was the friend in town with a new lover. Among themselves they had an intimate manner, formulas like "chéri" and "mon amour," because their language was French. They talked only about people with whom they shared memories of travels, parties, binges. People met in Ireland, just back from Nepal, at present in Naples visiting churches, while other friends had gone to Marseilles for a wedding. Dennis was annoyed by the importance Maud and Nanni attached to the right addresses—for example, that place in Bangkok where you could find notebooks lined with crimson paper—and their insistence on labels. In Dennis's view, all this made them terribly conformist.

As they were leaving an Indian restaurant in the West End, Nanni greeted Marc Blum, who was dining alone. He would have skipped introductions but was amazed to see Blum stand up and say hello to Dennis with great politeness. Blum asked Dennis how long he would be staying in London and insisted they should all have dinner together one evening. Dennis was glad to see Blum again. He appreciated the fact that this mannered and disagreeable reporter had refused Danesi's proposal. Blum's presence made Dennis reflect about the encounter with the woman in Paris. Was it worth mentioning to Blum? The only person capable of recognizing that woman was Marziano's daughter. The encounter with Blum also altered relations with Nanni. Things became more friendly between him and Dennis.

9. Bosco's India
"Hello, Dennis. I've just called to say good-bye. I'm going to India. I want to go there to die."

"What! Surely you don't want to die just when your novel's coming out? Wait a little while, at least!"

"Your friend Marziano says the book is finished the way it is, and there's nothing more to do to it. He suggests I write another, if I want to do something. So I'm going away. I don't have the patience to live in society any more. There are too many things I'd rather not understand. An intellectual these days needs a great deal of strength, and I don't have any left. I want to find an ancient civilization and a place where nobody knows me."

"I understand. You're right to look for new inspiration, but it's very important for you to be present at the launching of your book. I know it's a bore, but considering all the time you devoted to writing it, it's worth consenting to interviews, radio and TV appearances, round-table discussions."

"Why should I stay here and be a puppet when you run off after a woman and leave my galleys to someone else? Obviously my publisher doesn't consider my book very important. Am I right?"

"What on earth are you talking about? Marziano's opinion has much more authority than mine."

"Yes, yes, but it's not only the book. The fact is that in Italy, in Florence, I've found everything unpleasant, and instead of ending up as a whining old bore haunting cafés and drawing rooms or harboring illusions encouraged by younger women who are interested only in my celebrity, I prefer to go far away."

"I understand, and I think you're right, but if you can wait a little it would be better. I'd be very sorry not to celebrate the publication of your book with you."

"Celebrate! I wonder why a book always has to be celebrated. Parties are the saddest things that exist: like an announcement of imminent death. It's not parties I need! I'm an old man, I feel drawn to a country with ancient traditions."

"I'm sorry about this decision of yours. I'll come and visit you in India."

"You know something? When Marziano told me the novel was finished as it is and nothing more had to be done, I felt ill. I was distressed to realize that the work of years of my life is about to become a commercial product that has to be launched with an advertising campaign. Don't think I missed the contempt for my book in Marziano's eyes. I recognize Max's ways in him. According to Max I was a writer who appealed to the female audience. The truth is that a real writer should be comic, like Rabelais."

"You're right, and I believe your novel is comic, in some of its aspects. Think some more before going away, and remember: your publisher would be very sorry."

Bosco had taken offense at Marziano's superior attitude. He had never learned how to behave with critics. Stern judgements hurt him, as if he were a novice.

Part 11

Spas

1. Marziano's Health

Marziano discovered that he weighed 205 pounds. For years he had known he was getting fat and was accustomed to buying new clothes as his old clothes became too tight. When his weight reached 190 his thighs began to give him trouble, even if he wore loose trousers. Whether he was sitting down or walking, his thighs touched, chafed and bothered him. He felt he was exploding in his suit, he became aware that his whole body was bloated. He was balding and every day it became harder for him to adjust his crotch decently. He had difficulty urinating, and when he made love, he felt a burning sensation afterwards and a strange heaviness in his testicles. His face had greatly changed. His cheeks were flaccid, sagging. There were deeper and deeper hollows under his eyes, which had turned yellow. His breathing had become labored, and in the morning, when he woke up, he coughed when he lighted his first cigarette. One afternoon, in the office, he had some kind of attack. His head swam; he couldn't breathe. When it was over an associate took him to the doctor, who examined him and then spoke to him sternly, saying things Marziano had been expecting. His blood pressure was high, his reflexes were slow and he had to lose at least thirty-five

191

pounds to ease the strain on his heart. Furthermore, his liver was swollen and his intestines were out of order. His condition was alarming.

Marziano reacted like a wounded animal. He stayed at home, lying on the sofa, then he decided to go and eat in a brasserie. He went out around six-thirty, taking the *Divine Comedy* along with him. He stopped at a kiosk in the rue de Rennes to buy the *Gazzetta dello Sport* and a pornographic magazine. When he arrived it was quarter past seven and the brasserie was empty. He ordered an aperitif and glanced at the headlines about the soccer games. Then, at random, he read the third canto of the *Paradiso* and ordered *choucroute* and a beer. He started leafing through the pornographic magazine, and when he was served he ate heartily. Then he ordered a baba and a cognac, then coffee and another cognac. It was eight in the evening, and people were beginning to come in, the tables were filling. Then Marziano took out a pen and began thinking, scrawling on the paper covering the table. He had been ordered to stay in Paris, and for this reason he couldn't go to America or accept the job Dennis was offering him in Turin. But now the doctor had told him he was ill. He had told him to go to Vichy for at least three weeks. Naturally he would have to stop smoking. All these treatments at once seemed to him an impassable mountain rising up before him. How could he explain his need to go to Vichy to the institute and to the Soviets?

Who would pay for it all, since he had no savings and cures at spas would be only partially covered by his health insurance? And, apart from the economic question, what would he do, alone, for three weeks in a spa? Total repose seemed terribly tiring.

It would be a good pretext for calmly spending some time with himself at last, working on his studies, but he felt too sluggish, and down there he wouldn't find the books he needed. If he were to follow his own nature, he would let himself drift. He no longer had any pride or will. But he wasn't alone in the world, he had a daughter and another child about to be born. Before going to Vichy he would do better to consult a doctor in Italy, but he couldn't. He had to submit to French jurisdiction. His bank account was in Paris, that was where he paid his taxes and had his health plan. So he would go to Vichy. Only a Paris bank would lend him the money. The only thing he could do to regain his health was borrow from the bank. He would pay the loan back in installments.

At the table next to his a bourgeois couple was seated, dressed in fashionable and casual new clothes. They were talking about a vacation. They seemed people who led a regular life, serious people. They probably considered life a constant exercise of good will, sacrifice and prudent moves that would lead them to greater comfort year by year. He felt they were people accustomed to giving up many things for the sake of their children, but this was a special evening. After a movie they were having dinner in a brasserie, where they couldn't stay past eleven-thirty because the baby-sitter had to leave by midnight. That summer they would spend two weeks at the sea in a simple but clean hotel on the Adriatic, in Yugoslavia, and afterwards they would stay another two weeks in the Haute-Savoie, with her parents. There, as they did every year, they would go on excursions, picnics, and would play tennis with the children and with the neighbors, who had children more or less the same age.

Marziano noted that the husband, in a yellow Shetland sweater, was not very handsome. Blond, thinning hair, neatly trimmed moustache, typical of certain Frenchmen. He wore gold-rimmed glasses. Marziano saw that the man was just developing a reddened nose, a double chin and a potbelly. But his appearance was totally normal, and in his black sealskin shoulderbag he probably kept his car keys, a wallet with some bills, his ID, driver's license and credit cards, a checkbook, a pack of low-nicotine cigarettes, a gold-plated lighter, a purse with enough change to pay the parking attendant or make a phone call, a designer ballpoint, a chlorophyll spray to freshen his breath. The wife was also blond, more or less the same age, and her face was tanned and deeply wrinkled. She wore a

MISGUIDED LIVES

windbreaker and slacks and was no longer thin, but she seemed in excellent health. She enjoyed the rosé they had ordered, and she was fond of her husband. You could tell they were still lovers by the way they said banal, very simple things to each other. Since it wasn't Saturday night, they were resigned to going straight home, without going dancing, and they would make love unless one of them had to get up too early the next morning; otherwise the alarm would ring as always at seven, in time for a shower, a quick breakfast with the children, then off to work. The couple at the next table were tranquil people who weighed less than two hundred pounds, who led a normal existence, who didn't need to go to Vichy and who, if they had needed to, had sufficient savings to do it without going into debt.

A profound despair invaded Marziano's spirit as he walked home along the rue de Rennes. He felt the burden of being a person without hope, with a body prematurely ruined by a mistaken way of life. The next morning he would have to get busy and organize the various things involved in his going to Vichy. Inwardly, he felt an enormous rage against the injustice of fate. The rage was part of his character. Over the years he had isolated himself to such an extent that he couldn't confide even in Marina. For that matter, he wasn't a man who confided his secrets. To Marina he was like a mountain: the solid, strong man she could rely on in case of need. How could he reverse their roles now and confess to her that he'd gone too far and was frightened by his illness? How could he ask her to come with him to Vichy? If she was with him, things would be different. And how could he justify the trip to Enrica? How could he decide to go off for treatment, to lose weight, just when he was about to become a father? But his life was in danger. He'd made the mistake of thinking himself young for too many years, and suddenly he realized he'd grown old and had ruined his own life. The fault didn't lie with fate, but with himself.

2. Towards Vichy

Despite his hateful destination, Marziano felt relieved when he took his seat in the train. Having to agree to this treatment had been a trauma. What could be worse than the city that had lodged Marshal Pétain and his fascist government? Before leaving Marziano had dragged himself around for days and days among bureaucrats, insurance doctors and the Soviet embassy. At the institute they had been understanding; the Soviets created greater difficulties and insisted that Marziano be examined by one of their physicians. Faced by the unequivocal medical report, they allowed him to absent himself from Paris for four weeks. The hardest thing to obtain was the bank loan to pay the hotel bills. Marina promised to come and see him; he and Enrica traded insults, but in any case the baby wouldn't be born before his return.

In the train he felt lighter. It had been an enormous effort, but he'd managed to get himself organized and leave. His capacity for reacting, for putting the pieces back together, had given him a bit of renewed hope. It was strange how he had been transformed into an exile, a spy. In spite of the fact that the train was ultramodern and superfast, emaciated and laden with books as he was, he thought he resembled Walter Benjamin fleeing Paris in '40 heading south, towards Spain, to emigrate to the States. Marziano felt he was in flight from everything, a feeling that wouldn't have come over him if he were going from Rome to Montecatini. Sometimes he felt homesick for his adolescence, the Roman days, the simplicity of his life then, free of practical and family responsibilities. For years he had felt made of air, without ballast. But now he was a bureaucrat with health insurance on his way to a spa for a cure. In the train he read a newspaper report on a murder in Corsica that reminded him of Marc Blum and the nonchalance with which the Dennis business had been kept quiet. Then he thought how fickle Dennis was, first obsessed to discover who his father was and then, the moment he met Anna, totally uninterested.

Bosco had telephoned to say he was leaving for India: a histrionic announcement. Perhaps he disguised his failings as a writer behind these dramatic scenes. After the long exile in Canada, the moment had come for a spiritual retirement in India. Though Bosco would've liked to be a prophet like Tolstoy, his novel was no *War and Peace*. To tell the truth, his novel wasn't bad at all. He was above the average, but he lacked something.

Vichy was not a spa that could satisfy the tastes of Marie-Françoise. She was in America with Jean-Marie, probably on some luxurious estate belonging to billionaire friends. Thinking of her, Marziano felt her absence, remembered her movements, her smell, the way she held on to him in bed. She couldn't have forgotten.

Would they meet again, or had they separated forever?

3. Vichy

The leaden sky, the filth of the hotel room and the nasty taste of the salty, heavy waters were stifling. Marziano kept thinking of what would happen to him after the cure, once his child was born. He would apply for a transfer. The time had come to go back to Italy and give up his career in order to work with Dennis. Marziano wondered how it could be healthful to be in Vichy, which was a sad place frequented only by elderly people. On all sides, under little marquees of rusting metal, strolled people plagued by ailments, each carrying a little straw basket that held a glass with decimal markings. The cure consisted of moving from one spring to another, drinking different kinds of water in certain amounts. Marziano had little tolerance for these regulations and for the prohibition against eating this or that. In his free moments between one session of the cure and the next, he was unable to concentrate on anything serious; the silent order of the place stirred listless desires and inner anarchy. It had been a long time since he'd been alone, concerned solely with himself. Overnight he had stopped smoking, had given up coffee and alcohol. As a matter of principle he was hostile to doctors and medicines; nevertheless he'd fallen into this trap. Everything around him was disgustingly liquefied. He felt done with, drowned; he looked on the plastic liter-and-a-half bottle of mineral water on his night table as something repellent. What had become of bottles made of glass, sealed with corks and filled with wine? What had become of him? He had landed in a health supermarket for poor old people, for women with varicose veins and bad circulation, for men with ruined livers and malfunctioning prostates, for people who looked at the past with nostalgia, people who would soon be dead. Having concluded the cycle of their active lives, they were prepared to vegetate for as long as possible. What was he, barely past forty, doing in here, drinking these fetid waters? Enrica had considered the whole idea ridiculous, pointing out that only young gentlemen of good families brooded about their health. The child that was about to be born would have a bellicose mother who would teach him to fight against compromise. But what was the use of Enrica's attitude, her systematic opposition to everything?

The hardest moment came one afternoon around four when Marziano obsessively saw Walter Benjamin's death unfold before him. Why had he killed himself before ·rossing the border? Presumably because everything had become too burdensome for him—his body, what he'd undergone in Germany, the exile in Paris, the racial persecutions. Despite Scholem's letters inviting him to Palestine—or those from Adorno, who wanted him in Amer-

MISGUIDED LIVES

ica—Benjamin hadn't found the courage to leave Europe and had killed himself. Mankind went on unperturbed in its massacres, heedless of Benjamin's supreme act of sacrifice. Marziano, on the other hand, couldn't go to America. He had no right to join a woman he was in love with. He had agreed, quite exceptionally, to leave Paris and follow a cure, and he was staying in a dreadful hotel staring at plastic mineral-water bottles. He was in Vichy, as if he had gone with his daughter on a holiday at Salò. For Tatiana, Salò would have meant nothing; she simply would have found the lake sad. For her, historical memory was of no importance. She wouldn't have felt Pétain's ghost or Mussolini's, much less Walter Benjamin's. Marziano was beginning to think once more that all of life was built on misunderstandings. In human relationships, only in the instant before orgasm is there something more than a misunderstanding.

On the second evening Marziano went to the casino to feel closer to Marie-Françoise. In spite of the exercises and three liters of water per day, he didn't think his suit was any less tight. When he sat down at the roulette table, he still had to unbutton his trousers to feel comfortable. After a while he noticed a woman with long, reddish hair on the other side of the table who was looking at him with interest. She had blue eyes, slightly speckled, and there was a suppressed smile in her gaze. Marziano, however, pretended not to be aware of this stranger. An absentminded gambler, he wasn't really enjoying himself and was afraid of losing more than a trifling sum. But the moment that woman's eyes lighted on him, he felt a desire to give her at least the impression that he was a nonchalant gambler. In a short time he lost nearly all his *fiches*. He would have liked to leave but didn't dare stand up and rebutton his trousers in front of her. So he staked the few *fiches* he had left, trying to pick his way between red and white, odd and even. It was only now and then that she dropped a single *fiche* on the table, with an expert and knowing gesture.

Marziano gambled his few remaining *fiches* on fourteen and won. Then he staked all his winnings on twenty-four, won again, and bet the whole sum on thirty-three; the number came up. In reply she bet on seven and seventeen and lost then gambled and lost again. Marziano staked all his winnings on red, won, bet them all again on black and won again. By this time the strange woman had lost all her *fiches*. Marziano kept on winning, and the tension and desire mounted between them. At a certain point, when she saw Marziano bet all his winnings on even, she approached him, frightened, but he won again. A whole mountain of *fiches* was set in front of him, and the few people present followed his furious winning streak with amazement. She slipped a ring from her finger and put it in his hand, asking "How much will you give me for this ring?"

"Whatever you say."

"Half your *fiches*. It's an antique ring, very valuable. I believe it's a man's ring."

"Thank you. I don't wear rings, but take what you want."

With a confident sweep of her hand she collected a pile of *fiches*, a few more than she'd lost, and gave him the ring. At this point, he calmly collected the other *fiches* that were left on the table, left a sizable tip for the croupier and buttoned up his pants without any qualms. "What would you say if we broke the rules of the cure and went to drink a glass of champagne?"

"With pleasure!"

Marziano put his arm around her shoulders and led her to a secluded corner, where he kissed her voluptuously; his pleasure increased when he felt her giving in to him. "It's amazing," he said, "how someone can fall in love in a second."

"I like the way you put your hands on my breasts. In Paris, on my way back from the Middle East, I met a man on the street I had loved and thought was dead. But I don't know why I'm telling you this."

"It's normal, the things we confess to taxi drivers. Your nipples are as tender as flowers. You're very beautiful."

"Don't make me blush. It's flowers that are as tender as nipples."

"I'm not exaggerating, but if I hadn't met you this evening, I'd have wanted to kill myself. What point is there in reducing your life to counting calories? The idea of being sick disgusts me. We know nothing of the meaning of our lives. I can't kill myself because I have small children, but I don't want to bore you. Perhaps you don't have any children."

"I have a cousin who has children. To tell the truth, years ago, after I'd spent a few nights with a man in Reggio Emilia, I was expecting a child. The man who got me pregnant never knew it, and I stupidly had an abortion. I tried to punish that man, years afterwards, but obviously I missed. He doesn't know it, but he is the man of my life."

"I'm not jealous. For the moment you're here with me, after all. What if we went and sat on one of those benches outside the gazebo?"

"Kiss me again, like before. Pretend to love me. What do you care if you're not the man of my life? You should laugh more, take yourself less seriously. You're sensual, and not everyone is."

Marziano kissed her, again holding her close, and she gave the impression of abandoning herself completely. When they walked off towards the river, clinging tightly to each other, they were free of gloomy thoughts. She had an elegant bearing, like an English sailboat with a hull of dark blue wood and orange sails. Was the story about the man in Reggio Emilia true, he wondered, or was she simply a lascivious woman who had looked with desire at his sagging belly in his unbuttoned trousers?

"Have you ever heard of Gustava von Traube?" Freya asked.

"The writer?"

"She's my aunt. I tell her about my travels, my encounters. She uses me as material for her novels. We met the other day in Paris. She had come there to meet the new fiancé of that cousin of mine who has all the children. In my family we always fall in love with Italians. But my aunt says Anna's crazy if she marries him."

"I've never read her novels, but I almost never read novels. I only read newspapers and, for some time now, chiefly the English ones. English journalists are good at informing the reader and amusing him at the same time. That's the truth. The tradition's different. I don't know if you follow Marc Blum's articles in the *Times*. He's investigating a series of crimes committed in French spas. Blum doesn't really know anything, and he invents hypotheses, keeping the reader in a state of enormous curiosity. You mustn't think I want to offend your aunt—I know very well she's an intelligent writer, without literary pretensions, read by millions of people all over the world. It's interesting to know she uses your stories to put her plots together. I don't know why, but it makes me think of quite a different story. In Paris, near the boulevard Haussmann, lived a Jewish gentleman, a man of good family, who suffered from asthma. He thought he was Proust, only he didn't know how to write."

"Your conversation is tiresome. Your inferiority complex is touching. Just because I told you I'm the niece of Gustava von Traube, you felt obliged to give me a lecture on literature. I forgive you because I've become more and more convinced that a real man has to be pedantic. Nowadays people seek only appearances. Instead, a real man must be a bit dull, slow in his actions, in his way of making love, in eating. That's why I like you and want you to come with me to Barcelona."

"I thank you for the invitation, but I can't leave France. I have to go back to Paris once I finish the cure."

"You can join me in Spain when you're able to. We can never do what we like! I told you: after all my training in Libya, I still wasn't able to kill the man of my life. A moment before wounding him, I thought of saying to him, 'Remember: I'm Freya,' but he wouldn't have been able to remember my name, because in Reggio Emilia I was called Tamara. But I'm sure, all the same, that at the moment I shot him, he did remember something. When we brushed past each other in Paris a few days ago, I realized it had affected him."

"If I could do what I like, I believe I would join my friend Marie-Françoise in the United States and run off to Mexico with her. We could find a comfortable house near a beach and lead a carefree life. You don't know how much I'd like to get high on mescal without its doing me any harm. Each of us has ghosts. You conceive an armed vendetta against an ungrateful man who raped you in your past. This is because you're a slave of the system and you're treating a case of hepatitis that you didn't catch in a Palestinian camp in Libya but by eating an oyster that wasn't fresh. You dream of being the niece of Gustava von Traube, and you've read all her books, but instead you're really a typist from Lyons or Dijon, working in a factory that produces domestic appliances."

"You've no idea how happy I am to seem a secretary to you, a simple person who has virtually no story to tell and who invents everything. Nobody saw me shoot the man; there are no witnesses. I'm not Marie-Françoise, but instead of going to Mexico we could go to Spain."

"Tomorrow morning we'll meet again with our measuring glasses, in a gazebo, to drink those disgusting waters, which should cure us of our liver ailments. And then in the evening, summoned again by fate, we'll go back to the casino to lose what we won tonight."

"It's not obligatory to follow the cure here. We could go off to Spain and do it on our own."

"Why does taking me to Spain mean so much to you?"

"You attracted me the very moment I saw you sit down at the roulette table. We both know what happened then. Since I'd like to be in your arms as much as possible, and since from here I have to go to Andalusia, it's natural for me to want you to come along. I had a very strong passion for the Palestinians and for their cause, but it wasn't my place. I was frightened, having shot the man I loved, and I'm glad I didn't kill him."

"Are you sure nobody saw you shoot him?"

"No, there was nobody there."

"Not even a little blond girl with glasses?"

"Why do you ask such a specific question?"

"Oh, no reason. For a moment I was thinking about a story. You know, the English reporter's story. For a second it occurred to me that, since we're at a spa, you could kill me. The motive, admittedly a bit weak, could be my reluctance to go with you to Spain. Getting killed would relieve me of many problems.

"It's getting late, and you mustn't worry. I'm not the murderess your English reporter is hunting for. My insistence on Spain was simply a sign of affection, but you missed the point. If I weren't obsessive, I would be indifferent to your kisses."

Marziano felt that Freya was a pure woman, and her smile was contagious. For this reason he trusted her. At the moment his trust was complete, he felt the blade of a knife. He hadn't the time to reflect on it; he was already dead. No one saw them, and it was easy for Freya to roll Marziano's body into the river. Pleased, she headed for the parking lot, got into her car and drove south at top speed towards the Spanish border.

The same night, Mario died in the Padua hospital.

Part 12

Without Points of Reference

1. The Commemoration Ceremony

In the lecture hall of the Italian Cultural Institute in Paris, a well-known medievalist was pronouncing Marziano's eulogy. Marina was seated in the front row with Tatiana and Vanessa Muller; Dennis was seated a few rows farther back. The funeral had taken place a week before at the Montparnasse cemetery. Dennis had lost his two dearest friends on the same day. What evil design was striking them all?

Marina listened with a suitable expression, very elegant in her black dress. Looking at her, Dennis realized he desired her. He hardly knew her, but he wanted to invite her to dinner, confess he'd fallen in love at first sight and ask her not to consider him superficial because of this declaration. He wasn't betraying the memory of Marziano. On the contrary, the fact that in this solemn place Dennis felt such a strong desire for Marina could be a sign. Looking at her, he felt his legs trembling, but there was an obstacle to the story he was developing in his imagination, an American boy seated a few places away from him.

Enrica was missing. A few days after Marziano's death she'd given birth to a boy. Tatiana was greatly upset by her father's death. The great sorrow of never seeing him again was balanced, however, by the fact of not having to share his memory with her little newborn brother. Her father had gone off, but he hadn't betrayed her. In one corner of the room, Dennis recognized Adriana Montefiore, leaning against a column and looking at the speaker with an expression of nostalgia. Had she been in love with Marziano?

2. To Daydream and Beat Your Head against the Wall

Dennis took a room in the hotel where he and Anna had stayed a few weeks before. He spent his days thinking about Marina and wore himself out trying to write her a letter declaring his love. He filled pages and pages, which he threw into the wastebasket, disheartened. Love letters were stupid and impossible to write. Still, he stubbornly refrained from calling her. Then he received a telegram from Bosco, who announced that, in view of the tragic events, he had postponed his trip to India until after the publication of his book. Bosco didn't dare confess that he felt relieved by Marziano's death. Marziano's influence over Dennis was strong, and with his cynicism he might've impeded the novel's success. Like Max, Marziano had believed that, after the nineteenth century, and with the sole exception of Proust, the novel as a literary form was dead.

When Dennis's frustration became too great he would fling himself on his bed like a corpse; he had the same vision every time. He bought a black and yellow Bugatti, packed a little black leather suitcase with a change of linen, a book and a toothbrush and went to pick up Marina in front of her house. She came out in a very tight black suit, wearing a lot of makeup, carrying a small red leather case. They drove off together along country roads, heading for Provence. Dennis thought of the black and yellow Bugatti, of Marina's perfume, the black suit, and a great desperation came over him. After the death of his friends he could no longer talk with anybody about certain things. He was bereft, alone in the world. When Anna, unaware of his moods, called from London to announce her arrival, he felt that his emotions had been upset, along with his habits: staying in the hotel, going down to the bar to drink a cognac, taking a walk, coming back to the hotel, trying to write a letter. There was a sense of pleasure in his deliberately desperate days.

When Anna arrived, he felt guilty and was rather contrary, disagreeable. He didn't know how to tell her he was taken with another woman, that he didn't love her any more. Their first two days together again were cold, but calm. Dennis thought constantly of Marina, reconstructed the tiniest details of how they had shaken hands on the day of the ceremony at the institute.

One day, while they were in a café in place Saint-Michel, Dennis went to the men's room and wondered if he could bribe Marina. He could send her expensive presents, which she would find vulgar and reject. But thanks to his insistence and to the number of packages, she would begin to open some of them out of curiosity. In the end she would become accustomed to the daily ritual of bouquets and luxurious boxes. He thought of something far more base and was immediately ashamed of himself: he would make Anna return the engagement ring so he could give it to Marina. Anna's children suddenly seemed an impediment to their plans. Why should he want to be accepted as a pseudofather by kids whose father he had never even met, only because he was going to bed with their mother? Besides, the whole family was outlandish. All those frustrated adventuresses! To say nothing of the ridiculous and servile friendship with that Maud Belgioioso. No, Anna wasn't the woman of his life. She had a kind of beauty that would fade badly and soon.

When he came out of the men's room, he wasted no time. "Your Aunt Gustava is right, we aren't made to be married." He didn't dare ask her to give him back the ring.

"What are you talking about?"

"We can't get married because we're not in love."

"Speak for yourself."

"Don't tell me you're in love with me!"

"Yes, as you know very well."

"Then why don't you make me feel it? Why do you always want to stay out late at night and be surrounded by so many people? Why don't you want to marry me right away?"

"You're the one who suggested being engaged for six months! Since your friends died you're out of your head, and I understand it."

Dennis had never liked place Saint-Michel, it always seemed squalid to him. He didn't want to discuss with Anna the question of how much his friends' deaths had distressed him. The only thing he knew was that he'd like to become engaged to Marina. Only with her could he put things in order. It meant finding his roots again, building something solid. He couldn't live with Anna any more; after London something had changed.

"We should both consider ourselves free from the engagement," he said. "We should be by ourselves for a while. I'll go to

210

Turin and deal with the firm. Now that Mario and Marziano are dead, I have to go back to work. I'll begin by handling Bosco's book."

"I realize you're upset, but it hurts me that you're trying to break our engagement. Fate is strange, but there's no point in my talking with you about it."

"What does that mean?"

"Nothing. It's all so ironic. I'm a week late. But don't be frightened, it's happened to me before."

"Have you had the test?"

"Not yet."

"It can be done after two days' delay."

"All right, I'll do it this week. But let's not talk about it now."

"Let's get out of this café. Ever since I was shot, I sometimes have the feeling that someone's following me."

"If we break up, I'll go to London, to Maud."

Dennis was no longer listening. Coming out of the café, he felt relieved. Anna would glide out of his life, and he would do everything he could to seduce Marina. He had gotten it into his head that she was the right woman for him. Marina was the sort of woman his mother would have liked. Only by marrying her would he be able to bear the void left by his friends.

The fact that Bosco had decided to return to Florence was a sign that flight was of no use, that at important moments you had to return to your point of departure. In life there were incomprehensible injustices. Mario had died leaving two orphaned children. Marziano left Tatiana, still a little girl; he would never know his son. What if the remedy for adverse circumstances was not to return to your roots but to escape? When he imagined flight, he began to envision old black-and-white photographs of Cairo and Jerusalem. He always saw a flight towards the desert, never towards the mountains. Or else he was in a port—Piraeus, for example—boarding a ship. He saw a flight in which he stripped himself of all his possessions, was poor and barefoot. Now he had broken his engagement. But what if she was pregnant?

Why, at the very moment they had regained their independence, did there have to be the suspicion that she was pregnant? Would she keep it, or would she decide on an abortion? Not an easy choice. He looked at Anna, walking ahead of him, her hands clasped behind her back. His gaze rested on the slow, rhythmic movement of Anna's small, firm behind. He had an unexpected erection. She sensed what was happening and slowed her pace, lingering to look at the shop windows. "I'm terribly thirsty," she said. "Would you mind if we stopped for a moment? I'd like a lemonade with lots and lots of ice. I don't know why I'm so thirsty—maybe bad news does it." The more Anna dawdled, the more urgent was Dennis's desire to take her to the hotel and hold her naked in his arms. They should go together to the station and leave. He could take her with him to Turin. Anna asked for a second lemonade then said, "What if we separated in this bar, without having to speak so many words?"

"And what if we didn't separate?"

"But you just said . . ."

"And what if I'd changed my mind? Come with me to the station. We'll go to Turin together and then we'll see."

3. The Sleeping Car

After so many dreams, had Dennis resigned himself to being with Anna? Was Marina no longer the woman of his life? The movement of Anna's behind had been enough to change his mind, and now they were together in a compartment of the sleeping car. They had made love first with their clothes on, then they had undressed, kissed and laughed; Anna had drunk a couple of little bottles of vodka, and afterwards had given him a long blow job. He had never had the courage to tell her that this didn't excite him. He preferred to stroke her hips and feel her belly beneath his. Anna sweated when she made love, becoming wet all over. Her belly was shiny and slippery. As they dripped sweat, their physical relationship became stronger. When they separated from each other, the berth was soaked. They remained a bit dazed. Anna smoked a cigarette. Then, flushed and in a good humor, they dried themselves and fell asleep. Anna was like his wife and his favorite mistress. The fact of her being with him changed things. He was seized by a great desire to print new books, imagine new lines, new dust jackets. Anna stimulated him, she was his muse. He should've asked her before to come work with him instead of criticizing her because she liked parties and Brazilians. But the firm imposed a demanding schedule, and in Turin there were none of the night-clubs and amusements of Paris or London.

At this moment he felt good with her, lulled by the movement of the train. Anna would adapt to life in Turin and would take an interest in the firm. She was a solid woman, with roots partly aristocratic and partly peasant. She loved pleasure, but she could also appreciate the duties of life. Anna's children would adjust in the end and come to live with them. After a trip to America they would all settle in Turin in a big apartment or else they'd rent a house in the hills.

When the train stopped at Modane and the customs men came aboard, Dennis woke with a start. He didn't want to go back to Turin. What did he care about continuing to prove he could survive while printing serious and important books? After Marziano's death he felt a void nothing could fill. What was the use of Anna's taking an interest in a publishing firm that had run its course? He no longer believed in it. The editorial programs for many years ahead had already been decided, they'd found a formula for success with a certain audience. Duilio was content. What they lacked was interlocutors, the intellectuals. A publishing house couldn't be satisfied just with printing books that sold well; they should run risks, look for new ideas, discover new writers. Dennis was in favor of the works of contemporary authors, and that was the reason for his interest in Bosco. He valued those who bore witness to their time. Marziano, on the other hand, would never have tolerated the work of living authors. He couldn't admit any interposition between life and the text. A page should not be bound to the emotions a living person aroused, someone who wrote day after day. Marziano wanted to read only finished works, detached from the reality of those who had written them.

But Dennis was interested in things that were still to happen, in the future. To go forward it was necessary to co-opt new forces quickly. The face of Italy was changing.

Anna went on sleeping peacefully in the berth, she hadn't heard the customs men go by. Her calm sleep reassured him. Women, when they make love well, fall in love and become more serene. The idea of having to spend time with Duilio bored him. For bookkeepers the supreme law is to balance their books. The firm had to make a good profit; everything had to be legal and this required a knowledge of laws and taxes, the arithmetic of finance. For an accountant the creative, human aspect was secondary. What mattered were facts and a kind of morality dictated by accounts and budget forecasts. The able and honest accountant feels he is always on the side of reason and is therefore faintly superior. Dennis had learned that this sort of person was indispensable to a business.

As he lay there, he began thinking about Marziano's murder. If Max's death in New York hadn't been natural, that meant someone had planned to do away with him, then eliminate his pupils. For the moment, Dennis thought, he had only been wounded, but if there was a conspiracy they would try again to kill him. But who? If his life was important to him, he'd better protect himself. It was a great nuisance having to think constantly about how to ward off unknown enemies who attacked with no motive. It seemed incredible that someone would be so fiercely opposed to a group of intellectuals who had never concerned themselves with anything but books and had played only a marginal role in politics, more than ten years ago. By now there was no hope of sleep for Dennis. He was in danger, and he had realized this the day before, in place Saint-Michel, when he thought he was being followed. He was afraid of dying and, if fate was against him, he wanted to elude it.

In Turin they got off at Porta Nuova Station and went to a nearby hotel. The newspapers were full of articles about a murder committed in the United States, a settling of scores among spies. Looking at the photograph of those killed, Anna recognized Jean-Marie, the man who had courted her at le Palace et du Golf.

Anna and Dennis spent the day together in the firm's office. Dennis allowed Duilio to express his complaints, desires and plans. Then, motivated by Anna's presence, he assumed the role of boss. He accepted some proposals and announced that he was leaving for Florence that same evening. There he would ask Bosco to become the firm's consultant for foreign fiction. He was going to invite Adriana Montefiore to join them. He would give her the job of handling public relations, the question of the firm's image, relations with the film world, television, politics.

In Florence Dennis wanted to meet a professor from Siena who had been recommended to him. This professor could assume some editorial duties. Dennis added that it was necessary to find a young person they could train as a future sales and marketing director, to reassure Duilio and allow him greater freedom to do his job as general director.

That evening, Anna uneasily read an article in the *Times* by Marc Blum entitled "Le Palace et du Golf." The wounding of Dennis and the deaths of Marziano and Jean-Marie were all linked. Blum suggested that there would be further surprises. Anna and Dennis considered Blum ambiguous, a sensationalist out to please his readers. He could easily be a spy and his newspaper job just a cover.

4. The Professor from Siena

There was an editorial meeting in a Florence hotel. The participants were Anna, Adriana, Bosco and Dennis. New roles were assigned to each of them, and then they talked about the launching of Bosco's book. The meeting was lively and stimulating for Dennis, who customarily worked alone. In the afternoon the professor from Siena came to see him. He was a taciturn man who made many notes with a thick fountain pen. He had a full, neatly trimmed beard and a bright, feline gaze. He would stare slowly at his interlocutor, half-closing his eyes, which became little slits; then he would smile. That he was a perceptive man was immediately obvious. He smoked slowly but constantly, ignoring the fact that no one else was smoking, and drank a mixture of tequila, champagne and ice that Anna also liked very much. The professor spoke only when asked a question, and he gave precise answers in a low, calm voice. He was both astute and affable, but Dennis couldn't make up his mind whether or not he liked the man. He knew, however, that he would trust this professor. He resembled neither Marziano nor Mario; he belonged to another generation, with another kind of culture.

Bosco, who was sensitive to power, immediately began swaggering in front of the newcomer. Perhaps with the arrival of the professor from Siena, the firm would change its outlook. It would address a younger audience and would have new ideas. To conclude the meeting fruitfully, they also discussed how to launch Bosco's book. From that first conversation the others realized that the professor had clear ideas about how to handle a writer's image. Bosco's new novel should be the literary event of the year. At the Frankfurt book fair the rights to the novel should be sold to all the foreign publishers so the book would become an international bestseller. Adriana Montefiore would have to sell the film rights to the right producer, who would make a major film with a famous director and an all-star cast. They talked about reissuing some of Bosco's previous books. The time had come to revive the complete works, for which Dennis had prudently acquired the rights.

The days that followed in Florence were relatively calm. Anna was at Dennis's side, and she encouraged him to make new plans and renew the firm. If they were to marry, they would have a new life but what was Dennis looking for in a woman? Did Anna still appeal to him? She, who had always needed parties, late nights, drinking bouts, now seemed to prefer cups of tea in Italian cafés with the man she loved. She liked the intellectual discussions

MISGUIDED LIVES

among Dennis's friends. If they were to stay on in Florence through the spring, they would take long walks in the country. The idea of Florence was a dream. Anna knew that Dennis wanted to leave for the United States once some things were settled. Then she began thinking of a little white house in Connecticut. Perhaps after so many Kasbahs, so many sleepless nights, so many journeys, her view of the world had changed. Windbreakers, leather pants and cowboy boots seemed things of the past. In Dennis she saw her teacher, the right person.

One evening Dennis walked Bosco home. Bosco was complaining of the way his city had changed, the way everything in the world had become more vulgar. At the same time, however, he explained to Dennis how important it was for him, the writer, to listen to his language spoken in the street, in cafés, on the phone, in the parks. Something had kept him in Florence, as if he had wanted to cling to the stones of his city and never leave it again. To him it was all the same, whether he sat in a café facing Santa Maria Novella, or went to the station to watch people arriving and leaving or took a walk towards San Miniato.

As he talked with Bosco about the professor from Siena, about Marziano's death and then commented on what had been decided for the launching of the book, Dennis felt a desire for Anna. He hadn't thought any further of Marina. The infatuation had been strong, but it had faded since he'd been with Anna in Italy. He would never have imagined Anna adjusting so naturally to his world, to his friends, to the publishing house. The books interested her and it was obvious that she felt at ease in Italy. Despite his fear of being killed, he had found a serenity here in Florence that had been lost for years. The pleasure of going to the café early in the morning to have a cappuccino, of buying the papers and reading manuscripts. It seemed to him that after hard, disjointed months in which he'd lost control of his life, he was now finding it again. As he returned home, he happened to wonder how he would die.

218

When he returned, Anna was looking out of the window. "It would be lovely to stay here for a while, don't you think?" she said to him.

"Yes, it really would. If only we could get to the bottom of this story!"

5. Following the Death of Bosco

Bosco was found in his room. Had he died of a heart attack in his sleep, or had he been poisoned? There would be an autopsy. Dennis had seen him home the previous evening, after a working day, and he had seemed fine. Marc Blum, when he heard the news, had no doubt. Someone was carrying out a very precise plan: to eliminate, one after the other, a group of guests who had stayed during the same period at le Palace et du Golf. The motive for this slaughter wasn't clear, nor was the identity of the killers. But even if the former vacationers at le Palace et du Golf were dropping like flies, the Italian papers spoke only of the exemplary end of a great writer: after a life of wandering, he'd died of old age in his native Florence.

As often happens when someone dies, in the days before the funeral or immediately afterwards, the relatives and friends who have met again, perhaps after a long while, experience a euphoric moment in which emotion and tenderness create a kind of intoxication.

Members of Bosco's family arrived in Florence, and so did

MISGUIDED LIVES

Father Wolfango, a priest and friend of his. Blum decided it was imperative to continue his investigation in the place where the latest victim had died. He didn't believe it had been a heart attack. Espionage was clearly involved, or else international crime. Blum learned the Belgioiosos were about to take a trip to Tuscany, and so, to be less conspicuous, he decided to join them.

Vanessa Muller, who happened to be in Florence, where she owned a little apartment in the San Frediano quarter, told Father Wolfango that she was frightened. She felt a dark cloud hanging over all of them, a great danger. The autopsy revealed no traces of poison, and Father Wolfango kept insisting that Bosco had died a natural death. Father Wolfango was curious, frivolous and proud of his collection of friends, which included artists, billionaires, princes. He knew how to mix wealth and intelligence, creativity, manners of high society, humility, reading, memories, concern for the future, travel plans. He spoke several languages, constantly switching from one to another. He tried to get Dennis to confess that Bosco had devoted a whole chapter of the novel to him. Dennis wasn't fond of this priest, and he told him that when the book was printed he'd send him a copy.

Dennis didn't believe Bosco had died of natural causes. When he learned Blum was coming to Florence, he realized that the reporter must be close to concluding his investigation. Bosco's death created a certain aura, as if he had been a great guru, a master. The obituaries of almost all the newspapers were full of praise, and certain critics, including the most severe, expressed interest in *Auto-da-fé*, Bosco's new book, which would appear posthumously. In Italy, anything posthumous becomes important.

As the newspapers and television were creating an actual "Bosco case," there was a meeting in the publishing house to expedite the novel's appearance. English-language scouts had already shown an interest in the book, and various British and

220

American publishers were in touch with Duilio. Vanessa Muller, terrified by events, was more and more in a state of shock and was clinging to Dennis, asking his advice. He suggested she go to Paris and see Marina. The moment he spoke Marina's name he was reminded of Marziano's memorial, of his days of suffering in Paris and the dream of the black and yellow Bugatti. He thought of Marina on the terrace of a café in Arles. As if in a Hemingway novel, he and Marina were arguing about how to get to Nîmes to see a corrida. Her head was in the shade and she had on dark glasses; her blouse was blue, faded, and her slacks were tan duck. They were eating fresh eggs *à la coque* with slices of buttered bread. There was a pot of coffee in front of them, that French coffee that tastes of chicory.

Dennis turned to Vanessa. "Why don't you have Marina and her American boyfriend come to Florence?"

"Their affair came to a bad end."

"No, no, they're together again. I saw him in Paris, at the ceremony for Marziano."

"I know, but they do nothing but quarrel. He's on drugs all the time, and he uses Marina as bait to attract boys. He forces her to put on makeup and dress like a hooker, and he takes her to clubs. But after Marziano's death, she can't bear those humiliations. Marina deserves much more. She should find herself a new husband, begin a new life. It's a good idea, I'll invite her to come here with Tatiana. I don't believe they'll want to kill Marziano's widow as well."

In Florence, Dennis thought often of Donna Ada. She had chosen Rome. She knew it was no longer one of the great cities of the world, but she was attached to it for that very reason. She was fascinated by the strata of things deposited by history, by the centuries, the closeness to Africa, the round sky, as intense as the desert's.

Then he remembered that Anna's children might have seen

221

certain things at le Palace et du Golf and thus might be in danger. Thinking about the children, he wondered if he should alert Aunt Gustava. But what if Aunt Gustava had set all these crimes in motion?

6. With Anna

Dennis was disturbed when he learned that Marina and Tatiana had accepted Vanessa's invitation and were about to arrive in Florence. In recent times his relationship with Anna had been strengthened. They had found their own rhythm. In the morning each went off on separate, solitary walks, and in the early afternoon they met at Giacosa's, the pastry shop in Via de'Tornabuoni. On waking, they dazed themselves by smoking a joint; it helped them forget what was happening. Anna had gone back to drinking margaritas. The two of them felt a need to be euphoric, especially in their lovemaking. Together, they made an effort to be high-spirited, to tell each other amusing things.

One day, while he was waiting in Giacosa's for Anna, Dennis saw Marina come in. Not knowing she was observed, she ordered a cappuccino, enthusiastically stirred sugar into the cup and ate a little sandwich. Then she realized that Dennis was watching her. They smiled at each other, and he motioned to her to sit at his table. Dennis couldn't believe it. To be in a café, alone with Marina, just as he had dreamed for so many days in Paris!

"Vanessa told me you were coming to Florence. You've done her a favor, because she's terrified by what's happening, and she needs company."

Blushing a little, Marina produced a package. "Do you like this blouse? It's the first thing I've bought myself since Marziano died. I couldn't resist it. As we get older, we become vain."

"You're right! I understand you so well. For example, yesterday I bought myself a Swatch. When they first came out, they seemed absurd to me, those plastic watches, so loud and chic, but the other day I saw a man wearing one I hadn't seen before, and I looked at him with envy. The watch suited him. Yesterday I saw the same kind in a window; I couldn't resist, so I bought it."

"I must say, I don't like them usually, but yours is very nice. I didn't know you were in Florence. Did you come because of Bosco?"

"Yes, and I've stayed on. I don't know why, but something's holding me prisoner in this city, which I've never liked. Walking through these streets has become indispensable to me. I feel protected, and I also manage to do some work for the firm."

"I know what you mean. I've never loved Florence, either, and I don't have good childhood memories of it. And yet, this morning, before coming here, I went up to San Miniato and the light was splendid. Tatiana isn't with me because she spends her days in the museums. She's already a cultural expert, exactly like her father. Tomorrow, if the weather's good, we're going to Volterra with Vanessa. Would you like to come along?"

"For the present I have to stay here. Are you going to be here long? I'm shy about saying this, since we hardly know each other, but you're very pretty. The little lines around your eyes are very appealing."

"You'll make me blush. Not everyone agrees with you."

"When you buy yourself something new, do you put it aside for a while, or do you wear it at once?"

"That depends."

"The new blouse?"

"I don't know."

"Why don't you go into the ladies' room and try it on?"

"What?"

"I'd like to see you with that blouse on."

Amused, Marina did as he asked. Dennis hoped Anna would be late. He wanted to be alone with Marina a little longer. When he saw her come back in the new blouse, she seemed less pretty than before.

"Well?" Marina asked, coyly.

"It enhances the line of your breasts, but that isn't the best color for you."

"Now I have to go and collect Tatiana at the Uffizi, and then we must meet Vanessa before she takes offense. You know what a mania she has for punctuality."

"I understand, but let's have a pastry together or drink something. You can't imagine how happy I am to be here with you. I've thought of you often since we saw each other in Paris."

"You say too many things at once, and I don't understand you. Now I have to go, but we'll see each other soon. Let us know if you can come to Volterra with us."

"Why won't you stay here a little longer? Are you offended?"

"We'll arrange about Volterra on the phone." She got up and left in haste, surprised and intimidated by Dennis's behavior.

It was strange that Anna hadn't yet arrived; she was at least an hour late. Dennis had been glad about her lateness, but after Marina left he began to grow impatient. He loathed waiting. It induced anxiety, deprived him of freedom. After a few minutes had gone by he got up and went to phone the hotel, to ask if she had come in. They told him they hadn't seen her. She could be lost or else she could also have run into somebody and gotten to talking. Dennis told the girl at the counter he was going out for a moment to buy a newspaper, he described Anna and asked her, if she saw Anna arrive, to say he'd be back in a few minutes. When he came back with the papers, Anna hadn't shown up. He sat down, ordered a Campari, got up again, called the hotel: they had no news. He looked anxiously at his Swatch and at the half-hours that passed. He shouldn't have bought that watch; it probably was bringing him bad luck. Finally, tired of waiting, he asked the cashier, if she saw Anna, to say he would be at the hotel. There he found a message from Duilio and one from the Siena professor. A call from Duilio meant trouble. There was also a message from the Belgioiosos, who were in a hotel outside Fiesole. Dennis immediately called Maud to ask if Anna was with them.

"No, I haven't heard from her. We got in yesterday evening. I called her this morning, but she was out. I can understand your being upset, the way things have been going. The best thing to do is inform the police, but you've probably done that already. We're staying here: call us as soon as you have news. Marc Blum is with us, and he'd like to come and talk with you tomorrow."

After that call, Dennis was certain that something nasty had happened. He was afraid to call the police, afraid they'd give him tragic news. Instead, when he called, they said they knew nothing and asked him to come by and file a report on this missing person.

The next morning there was still no news. Maud tried telephoning Gustava von Traube's house to see if Anna had gone to visit her children, but someone said that Miss von Traube was away. When Blum came to see Dennis at the hotel, Dennis asked him, forgetting his innate dislike of the reporter, "In your opinion, have they killed Anna?"

"I can't give you an answer. What I can say, for the moment, is that there's no word of her death. It could be an accident, but this long silence after someone has disappeared here in Tuscany— and I'm sorry to say it—suggests a kidnapping."

"But if she had been kidnapped, they would have gotten in touch by now to ask for ransom."

"Not necessarily. They might be having trouble."

"If it's a kidnapping, is it connected with Bosco's death, or Marziano's, or with the shot fired at me?"

MISGUIDED LIVES

"I wish I could answer you, but every time I think I have it figured out, something throws me off balance. I realize how agonizing it is to wait, but I believe there's nothing else to be done."

During the day many people came to see Dennis, and the only visit that brought him a bit of relief was Marina's. She was wearing the new blouse. She found Dennis attractive and shy. Marina appreciated shy people, they touched her.

Dennis realized that if it was a kidnapping, it was a way of striking him a double blow. They were using his woman as a weapon to wound his feelings and reduce his wealth. He was being punished for not being dead by being made to pay for being alive, being made to see the people dear to him die. They killed his most important author at the moment his new novel was about to appear; they killed his best friend . . .

When, after two days, there was still no news, Dennis began to wonder if it wasn't somehow connected with drugs: He didn't know if, on her morning walks, Anna hadn't taken to seeing dealers.

Vanessa Muller insisted on making her excursion to Volterra with Marina and Tatiana; Marina tried to postpone it and invented every sort of excuse to stay in Florence. She attached great importance to Tatiana's pedantic, scholarly passion and went with her to see the paintings of Pontormo. She also tolerated Tatiana's talk about the varying light in the landscape according to the hours of the day. For this reason they had gone several times, at different hours, to see the view from San Miniato.

For Dennis, Marina's furtive visits were a necessity. Even if, in this place, he felt he was locked in a vise growing steadily tighter, he felt a form of masochistic pleasure in staying on. During that exhausting wait, Dennis went every day to a bar near the station where he played pinball and drank Campari. After buying the Swatch he had begun to wonder if he had been right to choose the classic model or if he should have bought one of the colored ones. The wait for news of Anna was becoming surreal. Strangers kept arriving and leaving, bringing new elements and meaningless information.

Dennis, at night, half-asleep, hoped Anna would reappear. He dreamed he and Anna and Marina would have an affair together, all three of them in the same bed. He loved Anna and he passively allowed Marina to take a place in his life. Perhaps he wanted Anna and Marina to become lovers, for neither of them to be able to live without him. One blond, the other dark; one an intellectual, the other an adventuress; one Italian, the other not. He would have liked to lie calmly in bed, watching Anna as she unfastened Marina's new blouse. He imagined himself in a passive role, as voyeur, or else he would choose in turn his favorite for the night. But everything had to proceed in harmony, like a rite, without jealousy.

7. Bad Weather

Italy was struck by a wave of bad weather. In Florence they were afraid there might be another flood, and in other regions the damage was reaching catastrophic proportions. The newspapers spoke of nothing else, and the police were concentrating only on the disaster. The number of casualties was running into the hundreds.

At about three one afternoon Vanessa Muller had just stretched out for a siesta when the phone rang. A woman's unpleasant voice announced that Vanessa had been chosen to act as go-between. They would call her the next day at four-thirty to see if Anna's family was ready to pay five billion lire. If the reply was negative, they would start sending pieces of the victim to her fiancé and to her family. The woman's voice explained that she, Vanessa Muller, had been chosen as intermediary because of her intelligence and her poise. Then the line went dead.

Vanessa lay there, terrified, not knowing what to do. She was distraught. How had they discovered her telephone number? How had they known she was by herself in the house? It meant the kidnappers knew her habits and had shadowed her. A person close to her was acting as informer, playing a double game. But why choose her? She was anything but close to Anna. Now she had to convince Dennis that these people were serious, that the money should be paid as quickly as possible. Vanessa recalled stories of other kidnappings she had read about in the papers. She remembered a boy's ear being cut off and sent to his family when they had refused to pay. If Anna's ransom wasn't paid, they would accuse her of having failed to carry out the negotiations. Nevertheless, instead of facing her responsibilities, she lingered in bed and dozed off.

Waking, she thought of Dennis. Even if he was rich, he would never manage to put together that kind of money in cash. For that matter, why should he pay ransom for a woman he'd been engaged to for just a short time? Whose duty was it to pay? These were things to discuss with the police. Finally Vanessa went to Dennis and told him what had happened. He listened calmly and with a certain relief. After days of silence, this was the first solid news they had had. Dennis felt he should consult his lawyer Danesi, hoping that in spite of the bad weather and breakdown of communications the lawyer would manage to come to Florence immediately. Meanwhile, he decided to get in touch with the police and with Gustava von Traube, whom he asked to come at once. They could waste no time, because Vanessa Muller had to give a reply within twenty-four hours. They had to find a way to gain time while maintaining contact with the kidnappers. The most logical thing, and something the kidnappers couldn't refuse, was to demand proof that Anna was still alive and in good health: a Polaroid of her holding today's paper.

It would be interesting to consult Blum, but he was a journalist and the matter was too secret. Dennis realized that this whole maneuver had been set up to destroy him. He would have to pay, not so much because it was his responsibility, but rather because he obviously couldn't abandon his fiancée in such a situation. It remained to be seen if Gustava von Traube had some money she felt she could contribute. The one who was truly suffering in this whole business was Anna. God knows what they had done to her. Paying the ransom would be a way to rid himself of Donna Ada's inheritance, but his mother hadn't left him enough. Morally, wasn't paying them ignoble? Shouldn't he oppose this shameful black-mail? In a situation like this it was impossible to take a personal stand. Events would decide, the law, the police, the lawyers. He had only to clarify with Danesi if and how much he should pay. They would decide together what sum Vanessa Muller should propose.

When Dennis lay down between the sheets, he felt the heat of his body. He yearned for Anna and Marina in the bed, he felt a desire to rub himself against them. He remembered Anna's soft figure. Marina, too, must be soft and round, with thinner hips, slightly smaller breasts. He was greatly excited to think that he could have had those bodies, put his hands on their bellies. Instead, one had been kidnapped and he lacked the courage to declare himself to the other. And thus, dozing off and thinking of his women, he dreamed he was in front of a shop window, looking at the watches on display. Marziano used to wear a big black watch, waterproof, though he'd probably never gone in swimming. What use was a waterproof watch to him?

Marziano had been obsessed by objects, by shopping. He often bought rose water, cologne, lavender, bath salts and records. Obsessions were something he had in common with Max. Max had had a passion for picnics and wool blankets. Marziano had played chess well and gone to the movies in the afternoon. He had chewed chlorophyll gum because it dispelled the sensation of having bad breath. These last years he had abandoned Egypt, Islam and Nordic sagas in order to concentrate on Tibet and the Tibetan language. He knew that chaos had taken over the world, and mountains seemed less confounding than the desert. Moreover, something incredible had happened. He had always refused to have anything to do with doctors, and when he had finally made up his mind to go somewhere for treatment, he had been killed. Killed, no one knew by whom or in what circumstances, exactly as had happened with Max. Vanessa had always skipped over the circumstances of Max's death. What if she had been the one who killed him?

Dreaming, Dennis had the sensation the phone was ringing, but he didn't answer and wallowed under the covers. Anna had told him several times that a man should never be too handsome or too elegant. He shouldn't be a poet, either; better a thief or a tradesman. In any case he should know how to make money. According to Marina, though, a man should be cultivated, shy and well read. If possible, he should also be awkward when making love.

He woke up to the reality of Anna's kidnapping.

8. The Unraveling Begins

The morning before the kidnappers called was frantic. Danesi arrived at the last minute, but Gustava von Traube wouldn't get there till evening.

Vanessa Muller was authorized to offer one hundred fifty million, but she was worried. "Since they asked for five billion, they'll consider my offer an insult and take their revenge on me." The police inspector and Danesi, both of whom had some experience of kidnappings, explained to Vanessa that kidnappers always began by demaning exorbitant amounts, but everyone knew they would be satisfied with much less. Experience in this field was always tentative. Danesi himself, despite his sangfroid, had lost his temper with a *carabiniere* colonel, who made dramatic suggestions in order to look good in front of the assistant chief of police and the investigating magistrate. Everything was decided in an arbitrary way by people who had no connection with the victim. Vanessa was horrified by these professionals, who acted as if this were a theoretical problem. The human aspect was forgotten; those who had roles in this story played them like actors in a soap opera. Trial and error was the only possible procedure, and furthermore, no one knew how much Gustava von Traube was prepared to pay.

The kidnappers called at the appointed time. Vanessa expressed a desire to have some proof, a photograph for example. They asked if she had an offer to make and she answered yes but added that the assurance Anna was still alive had to come first. They hung up. Vanessa almost fainted. She had felt terrible distress giving precise answers to that voice at the other end of the line, and she was afraid the contact had been abruptly cut off because she'd done something wrong. All the others reassured her that she'd been splendid, very calm, and that the kidnappers would surely not be long in sending some proof.

Gustava von Traube arrived, and after she talked with Dennis and the lawyer it was agreed to offer a larger sum. The next morning Vanessa received a photograph of Anna, smiling and healthy, with that day's paper in her hand. Vanessa was given a telephone appointment: four in the afternoon at a bar in Fiesole. When Vanessa, on the phone, proposed three hundred million, they told her not to act like a dumb bitch. They were asking five billion, and human life wasn't something to haggle over.

Following the instructions she'd been given, she said that it wasn't possible to put together a larger amount in cash in such a short time. They warned her not to try any tricks and to say what the highest offer was. She answered that if they gave the family another two days and continued sending proof of Anna's good health, another one hundred million could be collected. She was told not to act smart. Those who were asking for five billion wanted the whole amount, not crumbs. In any case, considering the circumstances, they were obliged to stop using her as the contact, and she would regret it. The cause for which Anna had been seized was political, nothing to joke about. Their organization needed the sum that had been demanded.

Vanessa, terrified by this phone call, decided to leave immediately for London.

Meanwhile Marc Blum asked Gustava von Traube for an exclusive interview. He told her his readers would be interested to know what a famous writer of thrillers was thinking now that she was involved in a real-life crime. Gustava answered that she would grant no interviews. Since it was not a novel involved here but the life of her niece, she felt it was wrong, and she would not exploit this family misfortune for her own personal publicity.

The last telephone call to Vanessa Muller was followed by two wearing days of silence. The kidnappers weren't joking, and this was clear when Maud Belgioioso, in her hotel, received a package containing a letter, a photograph taken that same day and the tip of one of Anna's fingers wrapped in a handkerchief with a film of the mutilation. In the letter Maud was asked to be more scrupulous than Miss Muller in conducting the negotiations.

Marc Blum had already heard that Vanessa Muller had been hospitalized in London. Nobody yet knew why, but it turned out that she'd been poisoned.

After this series of events, all of them were terrified. Those people were merciless, and they would achieve their ends at any price. The police stubbornly went on saying that there could be no compromise and that they would discover the bandits' hideout in a few days. But in a situation like this there was no time; it was impossible to wait a few days.

Gustava von Traube and Dennis knew that, despite their most generous efforts, they could never raise five billion on their own. On the other hand, if they didn't come very close to the demand, those criminals wouldn't hesitate to eliminate them all, one after the other. But what was to be done?

The story of Anna's finger and the poisoning of Vanessa leaked out and was in all the newspapers. In a long article in the *Times,* Marc Blum expressed his concern at the accelerating pace of events. One after the other, people who had been acquaintances or guests at le Palace et du Golf were being mowed down. People connected with a Turin publishing house, a group of intellectuals, had become the target of a terrorist organization.

At the first call, Maud offered six hundred million, insisting to the hostile voice at the other end of the line that it had taken considerable effort to raise that amount. She asked them to bear in mind that Anna's family didn't have enough money to meet such a demand. Gustava von Traube received a letter and there was no doubt that the writing was Anna's. She said that if they wanted to save her life, or not see her returned to them horribly mutilated, they had to raise the amount asked. The kidnappers were not ready to compromise. They were working for a cause; they were militants. In the event their demand wasn't met, they would execute her. If it turned out that she didn't come home, Anna begged her aunt to provide for the children's education.

Clearly this letter had been dictated to Anna, but it had a horribly real ring. How could they put together that sum? Moreover the *carabinieri* and the police were getting nowhere with their investigations. Maud and Nanni offered a contribution; they also thought of approaching Anna's former husband. Maud informed the ban-

233

dits that everything possible was being done and the sum was growing. She asked if they could have daily reports of Anna's health.

The kidnappers told Maud they appreciated her efforts and would send a Polaroid every day of Anna holding the front page of the day's paper and wearing different clothes each time. They granted another week, but when that week was up, if they hadn't received all the money, they would kill her.

The respite granted by the criminals was welcomed with relief. In the past few days events had followed one another relentlessly. Dennis made a further attempt, with Danesi, to collect more money. Gustava von Traube calculated how much she could give, sacrificing all her savings. Together, they arrived at just under a billion. During the days of the truce, Dennis received a heartrending letter from Anna, obviously dictated to her, in which she begged him to pay up. She asked it in the name of her children. Once she was free, she would find a way to pay it all back to him.

The professor from Siena tried in every way to convince Dennis he shouldn't feel guilty. It was important for him not to feel responsible but rather to consider himself a victim of a criminal machine beyond his control. Dennis appreciated the professor's consoling talk; it kept him company. Unfortunately, Marina and Tatiana had gone to join Vanessa in London. He missed Marina's presence. Even though he'd seen very little of her and often with other people around, he had known she was there, close. But now when would they see each other again?

Meanwhile, the sun had returned to Florence. A strong westerly wind had swept away the bad weather, which left great devastation behind it. These days Gustava von Traube either remained in her room correcting the proofs of her new novel or met Marc Blum in a café near Santa Maria Novella. He had promised not to write about their meetings, but neither trusted the other, and they were very careful about what they said. It was a fact, however, that they got on well together, felt they were of the same class, and they both managed to observe with detachment everything that happened. They had tea and then happily moved on to white wine and, after some dutiful mention of the kidnapping, they would start talking about their travels in the Orient.

They exchanged countless opinions on hotels, restaurants, museums, and then they discovered some mutual acquaintances. They enjoyed talking about Italy. Gustava tried to convince Blum that it was still the only country where you could live among people who had a genuine intellectual vitality.

The horrible episode they were experiencing contradicted what Gustava said about how pleasant life was in Italy, but this was an anomalous event in the sense that at this point the great wave of violent kidnappings had passed. It was an unfortunate incident connected with a wider conspiracy that had nothing to do with Italy; Anna was only a pawn. It was truly a tragedy, just when she had found an intelligent, correct man who was suited to her. She had always had unhappy loves and now, on the eve of her marriage, this thing had happened to her, and God knew the shape she'd be in when it was over.

With Blum, Gustava let herself go enough to talk also about Freya. "I have another niece, very unusual. I saw her a few days ago in Paris. She is really independent. She has no children, isn't married and travels all the time. Every now and then she becomes passionate about some cause and flings herself into it headlong, then she changes her mind and goes somewhere else. Recently she lived in the Middle East for a long time, and something must have happened to her in Cairo . . . I suspect that the causes she becomes involved in are connected with the men she falls in love with, but I never ask her any questions. Both Freya and Anna write me about the people they meet, their way of talking, of dressing, the food they eat. The girls give me the names of streets, restaurants, movie theaters, nightclubs and smart hotels. Their descriptions are very useful to me when I am setting my stories. I'm too old to travel now."

MISGUIDED LIVES

"It must be amusing to have two nieces like yours. Are they sisters? Do they look alike?"

"No, they're cousins, and there's very little resemblance."

"Do you have any photographs with you?"

"Yes, and I also have some of Anna's children, my great-nephews and great-niece."

"What are they like?"

Proudly, Gustava showed Blum a photograph of Anna's children and another of Anna and Freya when they were little girls.

"You're right. The cousins don't look a thing like each other. But where is Freya now? Why isn't she here?"

"I'm so accustomed to Freya's absences that I hadn't given it any thought. She'll turn up, no doubt."

"Are the two cousins friends?"

"Yes, they are. But what do you think about the poisoning of Vanessa Muller?"

"It could be a vendetta. I know Miss Muller very slightly."

"Are you an opera lover?"

"Yes, rather."

"I ask because tomorrow night they're doing *Tales of Hoffmann,* and I'm going. If you'd like a ticket, I have one. But tell me sincerely what you think. Do you believe they'll accept the money, or will they kill Anna?"

"I don't know. I'm sorry I can't answer you, but I'm not a fortune-teller."

During these days, with the excuse that she was giving him news of Vanessa, Marina telephoned Dennis. She hinted at her home-sickness for the atmosphere of the days in Florence. She was affectionate; they both knew there was something between them, but they didn't allow their feeling to take shape. They were moved simply by talking with each other. Afterwards, Dennis often wanted to call her back, but he restrained himself. Two days before the end of the truce, the kidnappers, discarding Maud, informed Gustava von Traube that it was time to settle accounts. If the family wanted

Anna back, they had to pay as quickly as possible. Gustava said a huge sum had been gotten together, over a billion. The telephone voice declared that, under the circumstances, they were forced to take what was offered, but the others would be sorry. She wasn't given time to answer. A few hours later she received an envelope containing instructions and a precise, complex plan for the delivery of the money and the subsequent release of the victim. Events were precipitating and the conclusion was near, but no one could tell if the police would be able to capture the kidnappers at the moment of the delivery.

The evening before the exchange a terrible, macabre weight oppressed them all. What had happened? Why had things suddenly taken this turn, why this sudden haste to reach a conclusion? The police insisted there was a problem within the band, who felt threatened and close to being discovered. The family and the friends of the victim had other forebodings.

Part 13

Insane Destinies, Lost Serenity, Middle-Class Illusion Destroyed and Human Rights Trodden Underfoot

1. If You Had to Kill Someone, Whom Would You Choose: Your Father or Your Mother?

The kidnappers, at the last moment, informed Gustava von Traube that they had chosen to deliver Anna to the Belgioioso couple. She should give the Belgioiosos the instructions.

Dennis spent the hours before the liberation shut up in his room.

Gustava von Traube spent the time differently. She went to a café with Marc Blum, hoping to talk about other things. But she couldn't find a detached, conversational tone. Then she assailed him, talking about AIDS. Blum, in return, accused her of having exploited her nieces, of not allowing them to mature. She controlled them financially: an indispensable situation if she was to maintain her power.

There was affection between the two of them and they teased each other, a game of seeing who could be more treacherous. They also enjoyed anti-Semitic provocation. They knew that both of them had Jewish blood, though they denied it absolutely. Gustava had added her von, and Blum had changed the original spelling of Bloom.

It was Maud Belgioioso who told Gustava von Traube that Anna was back and was blind. Nanni agreed to give the news to Dennis. The kidnappers had written a letter in which they explained that they were not the sort of people you could joke with. In a war, rules were established; if one side failed to respect the rules, the other acted accordingly. The news, horrible beyond all expectation, caught both Gustava and Dennis unprepared. But at this point the chips were down, and they had to face the situation. Anna had begged them, she had warned them that the kidnappers meant what they said and would show no mercy.

Maud tried to reassure Gustava, saying that Anna looked very beautiful, only a little thinner.

2. A Need to Be Alone with Oneself

How do you behave with a fiancée who comes back to you more beautiful than before but blind? Do you love her in the same way and go on planning a life together, or does the relationship become embarrassing, pathetic, as love turns into pity? Both Dennis and Gustava von Traube were anxious, and they felt responsible for what had happened. From now on they would have to live with the reflected image of their guilty consciences. They had done their best, believing in the rules of common sense, not thinking those bandits could be so merciless. Now they could only face reality and go to embrace Anna.

Dennis entered her room first. He noticed at once that she was much thinner, her hair cut short. There was nothing intimidating about her appearance, but rather something ambiguous, provoking. She was seated, sipping a pastis, holding the glass in her hand in a frivolous pose, baring her legs. Dennis felt like stroking them. She was wearing sunglasses. Dennis felt awkward, he hardly dared move, but he said, "You must be exhausted! Welcome home. I'm happy to see you." As soon as he uttered these inopportune words, he felt ashamed of himself.

"I'm not tired. I'm happy to be here with you, glad it's over. To tell the truth, yesterday I enjoyed myself more than usual. They didn't take my picture and they didn't dictate any letters to me. Valeria and Luigi and I went on the merry-go-round longer than the other times. We went dancing; I think it was very late when we got to sleep. This morning somebody came to collect me, I didn't say good-bye to anybody, and then I got out of the car and Maud and Nanni were waiting for me."

"I don't dare think what this has been like for you. How much you must have suffered."

"It's true, I suffered very much, especially at the beginning when they couldn't find a regular hideout. But when we began going to amusement parks and dance halls, time went by faster. Emptiness is less frightening when you can't see it, that's why we tend to close our eyes. It seems obvious until you've experienced it. To plunge into the void without seeing produces a sensation of pleasure: it's hard to explain. You can't see, and so everything becomes light. I must say Luigi was always very sweet with me. He would caress me and tell me beautiful stories while Valeria played the guitar. In his own way, Luigi was very kind."

Anna's conversation had taken a turn that, instead of distressing

MISGUIDED LIVES

Dennis and making him feel uneasy, aroused him. He didn't know if the merry-go-round story was true or if Valeria played the guitar. And surely he'd forgotten how hoarse and provocative Anna's voice was. "It's true," he said foolishly, "in the dark the void isn't frightening."

"Especially if you feel protected by other bodies near you, lessening the fear of ending up in an abyss. I don't know why I've become so thin. We ate quite well, and we drank delicious wines. In the morning, when we woke up, we were already in that state of euphoria you feel with sparkling wine. Mimmo blinded me without causing me any pain. They gave me some tranquilizers, and I wasn't aware of a thing. Mimmo is a first-rate oculist. He really knew what he was doing! For example, to keep me calm and to make me sleep, he would massage me with a few drops of olive oil before I went to bed. He had soothing, sexy hands. I don't like massages, because they arouse me, but in Mimmo's case it was different. You know those very light massages that seem like caresses and make you feel good all over? Like something flowing in your bones. I don't think I'll ever be able to forget Mimmo's hands! He never came out dancing or to the amusement park; he waited for me at home, to prepare me for the night. At the beginning he was worried about my health, he thought I was run down, nervous, but he gave me some good advice about how to get over my complexes concerning Aunt Gustava and my cousin Freya.

"Every day they changed the flowers, very heavily scented flowers. Now it'll be hard to resume everyday life. When you've been so spoiled, catered to with such care, you get used to it. It's rare to be the center of everyone's attention. Then, you can imagine, when they tell you that your relatives don't care a thing about you, and they're forced to blind you because nobody wants to pay up, you feel like tarnished goods. You can't really believe that your man or your family has abandoned you, but, as I told you, since you've always been slightly euphoric . . . I thought a lot about you, about my children and Aunt Gustava. And Freya. If she'd heard

244

about my kidnapping she'd have been jealous: she's so twisted. An adventure she'd never had! When they cut off my finger, I couldn't believe it; it seemed impossible to me that they would mutilate me. There were times when I didn't believe I was the protagonist of the story. I thought it wasn't true, that I was playing a part in a movie. At the beginning it was terrible not being able to see. I wanted to yell, to slam myself against the wall, to rid myself of something that wasn't there but that blocked everything. Later, dancing with Massimo, a boy from Savona, I felt less sad. I flung myself into his arms, I loved him and I transformed everything into tactile pleasure. A bit like when you smoke grass and everything feels much more exposed, just beneath your skin. You understand?"

"The way you talk, you make it sound as if you enjoyed yourself, as if being kidnapped is a sensual experience," Dennis said, his jealousy aroused. It made him angry that she'd had, or had imagined, all those adventures, while he, filled with guilt, had been racking his brains to find the money. The awkwardness he felt with Anna in that hotel room was quite different from what he had expected. The truth was that he wanted to put his hands on her. He wanted her to go on telling him those stories and telling him in detail what that Luigi had done to her on the merry-go-round and what Mimmo and Massimo were like.

It was Anna who dispelled the embarrassment. "Dennis, be a darling. Have them bring up a bottle of sparkling wine and hang the do-not-disturb sign on the door. I want to make love, to be calmed down; I want you to make me happy, I want you inside me. Don't be afraid: our bodies will find each other the same as before, even better. That experience is past, and you'll help me forget. I'd like us to go off on a holiday and not think about it any more."

Dennis let Anna guide him; she had taken on a majestic, sublime manner. When they were in bed, naked, she said, "Don't worry, don't be nervous. I can smell how tired you are. You must have ruined your disposition." Anna was so sensual and feminine in her movements and in the way she stroked Dennis that he felt himself completely in her power. Something had changed, and it seemed as if their bodies were meeting for the first time. When Anna wasn't near him, he rarely missed her. And yet, the moment he saw her, something happened inside him that he couldn't withstand. He felt Anna really loved him.

3. Another Version

Aunt Gustava vacillated between a feeling of pity and compassion for her niece, who told her the bloodiest details of the kidnapping, and a physical desire to go away or to talk about something else. If it had been one of her usual stories, she would have felt differently; since this was reality, she felt suffocated. Naturally she didn't let it show, and she put on a benevolent smile, which alternated with a prim and occasionally horrified expression, the suitable demeanor. Anna was long-winded, reporting many particulars about how they tied her up, what the chains were like and the sort of pain they caused. She told how they'd held a pistol to her head, threatening to pull the trigger and told her they would mutilate and kill her because nobody in her family would pay the ransom for her. She was evasive, however, about the blinding, which aroused Gustava's curiosity because she couldn't understand why it had left no mark. "They must have been skilled and well equipped. There's not a sign!"

Anna changed the subject, replying that the cell where they kept her was damp and disgusting. Then, wearying of the subject herself, she went on, "All I want to know is how to disappear from

this place so I won't have to deal with the press and the police. I'd
like to consult an ophthalmologist. Maybe something can still be
done for my sight, and it would be a mistake to waste time. It's not
pleasant being blind. I was so happy when I felt the warm presence
of Maud's body, her hands! Then finding Dennis again, feeling a
woman once more. When I realized I was blind, you can't imagine
the despair I felt. I could never express it. Time and again I've
heard people say it's better to be blind than a deaf-mute, but I'm
not at all convinced. Being blind is frightful. Now I'll have to think
about how to face life again. As far as my children are concerned,
for the moment I'd rather they didn't know anything. Let them
think I'm traveling."

"Unfortunately that's not possible. They called this morning:
they saw you on television. That wretched TV is so indiscreet! I
tried to reassure them, and I told them a long story in the hope that
it would confuse them. I asked the governess to take them to the
amusement park to distract them and to keep them from looking
at television from now on. I said we'd come and see them again
soon. Children have no sense of time. I also said you'd bought them
some presents, and they wanted to know what they were; I kept
repeating that it was a surprise. Then I promised to take them to
Venice and let them ride in a gondola. Maud is so affectionate; she's
already telephoned from Zurich, where apparently there's an extraordinary specialist. If he doesn't find a solution they say there's
a clinic in Boston where they work miracles. Darling, don't worry.
It's all over now."

"The best thing would be for me to go into a convent. In any
case I want to leave Dennis. I don't want to be a burden for a man
his age, now that I'm blind. I don't want pity; I don't want to be
deadweight. He can't have a blind wife."

"What do you mean? You'll be cured, and he adores you. If you
only knew how worried he's been all this time, and how affectionate. How tireless he was in collecting the money. And the way he
quarreled with his lawyer, who didn't want him to pay more than

a certain amount and kept saying that, after all, the two of you weren't even married."

"And Freya?"

"What's Freya got to do with it? Poor child, who knows where she's ended up, what trouble she's gotten herself into. You can't imagine the state she was in when I saw her in Paris. In shreds. Adrift. She doesn't know anything about it; she probably hasn't read the papers."

"Of course not, poor little thing. Whenever there are problems, she's nowhere to be found. She never takes any responsibility. And now how are we going to manage with Dennis, who paid almost the whole ransom? How can we pay him back?"

"Don't exaggerate. We contributed a considerable amount, and some friends were also very generous. I didn't touch what little we have in Switzerland because I knew it wouldn't have helped you anyway."

"Not even to save an eye?"

"Do you think that pittance would have made any difference? Don't be unfair. How could I have known? I did it to protect us."

"If you'd given a little bit more, they'd have spared me at least one eye, and things would be very different. But let's not talk about it any more. Would you ask them to bring me up a glass of champagne and some *merghez?*"

"*Merghez?* In Florence? In this hotel? What an idea! And since when have you liked *merghez?*"

"They remind me of a certain smell in some North African places. Freya always talked to me about it. Just think how happy she'll be when she finds out she's rid of me at last. She didn't shell out a penny, and now she'll be the only one who travels and has things to tell you."

"I'm glad you're still so jealous of Freya: it means you're not as sick as all that. Actually, to be frank, with those sunglasses you look even more mysterious than before. You're more beautiful, my dear, slimmer. I know it sounds absurd, after everything that's happened to you, but you look like a woman in love. You know, when you have a new lover and make love all the time. You remember that Vanessa Muller? She died in a London hospital, poisoned. They turned her apartment inside out looking for papers. These atrocities are happening because somebody wants to hush up something very important that has very little to do with our lives. Maybe one of us is involved in some dangerous game of espionage or international crime, and we're used as a decoy to conceal some great plan. The only one who seems to come through every disaster intact, except for the symbolic wound, is Dennis. Can he have gotten himself shot to direct suspicion away from himself? Anyway, now he's found himself a successor for the firm. A young professor, ambitious and good looking. They say he's also efficient."

"How do you know?"

"Little things. I don't want to go into it now: this is no time to talk shop, but it's obvious he's trying to get me for the house, as one of his authors. I understand him. Whose mouth wouldn't water after a glance at my sales? During some idle conversation, he asked me what my favorite perfume is; I told him it's gardenia, and the next day he sent me a magnificent bouquet of gardenias. You understand?"

"You know what it means to become blind? It means not being able to read anymore, not being able to look at a landscape or a child, a picture, a friend. It means having to resign yourself to remembering forever the things you've already seen."

"Darling, how could we imagine? You've no idea how distressed I am. But now we'll go to Zurich. Just wait."

Outside the door of Anna's room, the reporters were insisting: they wanted interviews, statements. Anna realized she had become a heroine, but no one's solidarity or affection would ever restore her sight. Meanwhile her aunt went on talking, and Anna grew impatient, wanting to be taken to an amusement park, to the roller coasters.

4. Desire for a Metamorphosis

Marc Blum was enjoying days of great euphoria, creative days. He had been the first to take up a story that seemed endless. He felt as if he were in the shoes of Dickens; every day he sent the *Times* magnificent articles that were beginning to enthrall its readers. His latest piece was on the death of Vanessa Muller. Then Blum moved to Zurich, in the wake of Gustava von Traube and Anna, who had gone there to consult a famous opthalmologist. Blum was determined to interview them, but this would take time.

Dennis, for his part, had remained deeply shaken after the meeting with Anna. He decided, however, not to lose his equilibrium completely, to let her aunt accompany her to Zurich for the treatment while he would concentrate on his work. He had to concern himself with the launching of Bosco's book. Returning to Turin was the last thing he wanted to do, but he did it anyway. Working, for him, was a way of avoiding the incessant assaults of reporters and curiosity seekers. His life seemed a disaster, and he could no longer even say he was in anguish. He felt outside good and evil and could see no future beyond publishing the Bosco novel as successfully as possible; at this point it was the only thing that still seemed real to him. Was he guilty as far as Anna was concerned? This is what he was thinking as he drove between Florence and Turin. Would they tell her in Zurich that she could regain her sight? Danesi had suggested that Anna grant Marc Blum an exclusive interview, to be published in installments, so she could make some money and reimburse in part what he had paid out for her.

But the truth of the matter was that Dennis, as he drove along that stretch of superhighway full of curves and tunnels between Florence and Bologna, was formulating the desire that he cherished every now and then when he felt stifled. More than actual flight, he imagined a metamorphosis. It was something physical. He would like to change his face, change his way of dressing, go off to Volterra or any other city of central Italy, and disappear. Let his beard and his hair grow, wear only a pair of blue jeans and tennis shoes. He would like to be idle. Every now and then Anna or Marina would come to visit him. He wanted no responsibilities any more, wanted to live without feeling the weight of so many duties upon him, without any ambition for the important role his mother had brought him up to believe his due. He sought out small, cheap pleasures: a cigarette in a bar, a drink, a crossword puzzle, a pop song. But his responsibilities had been increasing with the change in his physique. His body had become different. It was no longer the sack of bones it had once been. He thought about it after that overwhelming night with Anna. She had come back blind, yes, but she had come back with the body of a girl, with a magical attraction that only a few very special women have, women for whom age doesn't exist. But who was he? He had already asked himself this question, God knows how many times. He would have liked to be handsome, intelligent; he would have liked everything to be easy for him. But he could no longer maintain an adolescent's body. What did he want, anyway—to become a monk? Or was he an epicure? Was he a traveler or a hermit? At forty, what sort of person was he? Was he an important publisher planning to set his firm on a new path, or was he an experimenter who had been part of an age that now had ended? Was he a tradesman? Was he afraid of being unable to survive without money? It seemed to him you had to make money in order to be a real man. But when would the moment come for him actually to turn over a new leaf? When would

251

he shift the course of the river that was his life? Until now external events had propelled him. He had always lived as a spectator. Until the shooting, he had found compromise comfortable. He had been relatively wise, moving with balance and prudence.

This wasn't his true nature but the way he had learned to face life, and it was the cause of his unhappiness. He didn't know if he was living, or especially if he had lived his life fully. He felt exhausted, his head swam. He would have liked a miracle to take place, for everything that had happened in the past few months to vanish. Going back would mean finding his routine life with Clara once more, and that was too much, that was worse than anything. Better this way. If at least he were to survive those dead friends, he would have the hope of encountering new ideas, new people, of reading different books, seeing the world change, making other discoveries. The life before him seemed a kind of spinning top, a kaleidoscope of possibilities. It wasn't true that he desired a monkish life. The life he imagined was the simplicity of Anna's body. Now she was blind, but she had lived through that atrocious experience in a sensual way. She had flung herself into the arms of young bandits who had raped her and taken her on roller coasters. She liked the bodies of young men, she liked riding on merry-go-rounds. She didn't care anything about tennis shoes, new writers, new trends. He would never be beautiful like Anna nor would he even have the same talent, the same vitality. She was naturally extraordinary.

5. Turin

In Turin Dennis went on long walks, wearing a new camel's hair overcoat. He had bought it thinking of the movie *Last Tango in Paris* and the scene where Marlon Brando crosses a bridge wearing the camel's hair coat, but now he regretted his purchase. The light color didn't become him, and he didn't look anything like Brando but rather resembled a Roman lawyer or doctor. He had bought the very coat that Danesi might have worn.

Bosco's book had been out for a few days, and the first articles had begun to appear. They were unanimous in saying that this was an important novel, the documentation of a world and of an epoch.

La Stampa had assigned the review to a somewhat academic, perhaps embittered, critic who had expressed himself in terms that were the opposite of what the others had said. He wrote that the book was ugly because it lacked spontaneity and the proper construction of a novel. Bosco had launched into a treatise that was an accusation of the political system and the function of the intellectual. It was an unsuccessful attempt to write his own *Divine Comedy.* The book did not lack interest, but Bosco remained a skilled man of letters and not the internationally important novelist he would have liked to be. This was the work of a man with great ambitions, unable to arrive at the poetry that was indispensable to a masterpiece. The conclusion was that "books are simply the mirror of their authors."

The article offended and upset Dennis, but it served to touch off a very heated debate. Some journalists began connecting Bosco with the shooting of Dennis and the kidnapping of Anna. All this newspaper fuss could have been useful publicity for the novel, but it had to be handled with care. It was decided to hold a press conference.

The professor from Siena spoke, underlining with conviction the importance of this *roman à clef.* Bosco bared the soul of his generation, introducing specific, clearly defined memories of the Fascist period. He admitted he had received subsidies from the party, as had the vast majority of Italian intellectuals under the regime. The novel, besides unmasking many people, was also a philippic against the philosophy of muddling through, which prevented the burgeoning of a serious nation. It also accused the ruling classes of being petty, reluctant to allow the cultural level of the country to be raised. In Italy the bourgeoisie barely existed, composed largely of shopkeepers who attached importance only to clothes and appearances, to what the neighbors would think.

6. Meeting

To launch Bosco's book, Dennis went with the professor from Siena to cities in the provinces. After ten years, after the period of student protest and terrorism, he rediscovered people he had known then, who were now changed. The idealists of May '68 had disappeared, had shed their old skins like lizards. They had gotten ahead, become rich. The former revolutionaries were prosperous homeowners. Italy had become a flourishing country where everybody wore the same jeans, the same shoes, the same fake cowboy jackets. Even the language had changed. In the new Italian some dialect inflections and local expressions remained, but in general people expressed themselves in the language of television.

Wherever he went, Dennis felt a homesickness for his past, for Mario, Vera, Marziano. Every evening he telephoned Anna for news. She was discouraged. Some of the tests were painful, and the results were uncertain. Perhaps it would have been more useful to go directly to Boston. It couldn't be said that Aunt Gustava was a great help in this situation, since she was unable to take a real interest in anyone outside herself. She couldn't offer Anna any support; on the contrary, she was a burden. All she did was complain because the hotel was expensive, the Swiss franc kept going up, the lake atmosphere put her to sleep, her brain was numb and she couldn't work well. Furthermore, the food in Switzerland was dreadful, and in particular she couldn't bear the seasonings; they even put bouillon powder on the salad. Anna was affectionate with Dennis over the phone, she tried to raise his spirits and make him laugh by describing the comic aspects of her medical examinations. She took an interest in the launching of Bosco's book. She asked if it was selling well, in which cities it had the biggest success, if the professor from Siena was really a help.

After a few days, Anna told him that, fortunately, Blum had left and Freya had arrived. For once she was behaving affectionately, concerning herself very efficiently with Anna's condition, accompanying her to the doctors. Moreover, since Freya hadn't been present during the kidnapping and hadn't been able to contribute financially, she now offered a considerable sum to defray the medical costs, now almost impossible for Anna and her aunt to meet.

Freya hadn't even tried to affirm her usual dominance. She actually volunteered to come with Anna to Boston and to pay for the trip, so that Aunt Gustava could go home and resume her habitual life. Aunt Gustava had been living for too many years in the atmosphere of her novels and was intolerant of reality, of true, everyday stories. Books were a system in themselves. She wrote them, then erased, cut or added, never having to apologize if she removed a character who suddenly seemed superfluous to her. With a stroke of the pencil she could alter a situation. For this reason she was edgy in Zurich and couldn't bear her own helplessness with the doctors. During the kidnapping she had felt stimulated by the exceptional events, as she had when Anna had come back blind. But then, when everything had become normal again, she had found herself in the role of the aunt accompanying her niece to the doctor, and she had begun to grow restless.

Dennis wanted to know every detail of what Freya said or did because he was jealous of the protective role she had assumed with Anna and he felt left out. After all, traveling around Italy to launch a book had become a bore. So he suggested to Anna that he accompany her to Boston. Anna was shy on the phone; she didn't know what to say. She was sad, desperate, because she loved him and she knew that, short of a miracle, things between them would have to end. One evening, after a ritual call, Dennis decided he would leave the next day for Zurich. Something told him the moment had come.

7. In the Train

In the train taking him to Switzerland, seated in a crowded compartment and indifferent to the other travelers, Dennis felt the inner serenity that at certain moments makes you understand why some especially sensitive individuals have composed music. Passing the lakes and mountains filled him with a great private tranquillity; since his boyhood he had found peace in train compartments. As a rule he read or jotted things in his black notebooks, but that day he felt no need to be occupied, and he savored the pleasure of traveling among the mountains, imagining the fresh smell of the valleys, looking at the snow lying on the peaks and on the pines.

He had just finished a trip through the cities where he had been as a young man, where he and his friends had thought they would change the world. Now he was going to Switzerland to solve a problem concerning the life of his woman. He saw the conductor move along the passage with a bright red leather bag over his shoulder. Switzerland was a country unlike any other, everything seemed made of marzipan: the cows, the streams, the fountains, the Alpine lakes, the music boxes, the flower clocks and the chalets. It was as if all those ingredients, plus some chocolate bars and a Swiss army knife with the white cross, were kept inside the conductor's red bag. Dennis suddenly felt himself a child seated opposite Donna Ada in the compartment of the same train. These were the only moments of his childhood he could remember spending alone with his mother. She would accompany him to boarding school and would come and collect him. During those journeys, his mother belonged entirely to him. She would tell him long stories, and she tried to console him because he was sad at having to return to school. The things Donna Ada taught him in those few hours on the train were far more important than what he learned during the tedious days of school, where dull and not very cultivated professors were charged with his education. During those journeys, Donna Ada didn't tell him fairy tales but true stories that gave him courage. The recollection of his mother's deep, blue eyes—expressive and smiling but also threatening—reminded him of the tragedy of Anna, who had magic, stupendous eyes and had been condemned never to see again. No doctor could give her back her sight. She who had always loved lakes, forests, birches, sea and sunset was now reduced to living in darkness. Was it his fault? They had all been so ingenuous. When the finger arrived, they should have realized the sort of people they were up against. Instead, it had gone otherwise; their mistakes had been paid for by another, by the woman he was about to marry.

As Dennis watched the landscape pass before his eyes, he was no longer the shy boy enthusiastically listening to his mother's stories; he was a man of forty who had done certain things, had rejected others and was in trouble. Once again he had proved that he knew how to be a publisher; Bosco's book had been a big success. But what about everything else?

He had no children, he wasn't able to tie himself to a woman and now he didn't even know where to live. He was no longer sure of his work. He pretended to carry on a normal life while around him only terrible things happened. With those grim thoughts the views of Switzerland and the vision of his childhood faded; the train pulled into the Zurich station. He didn't know why he had come here. Organizing Anna's journey to America seemed a way of keeping alive a futile hope. But it is said that the seriously ill, like betrayed husbands, often don't know their situation and have faith. For the mortally wounded there is an indulgence, an innocence that as a rule belongs to children. What's more he would have to meet—as if they were his family—Aunt Gustava and a niece he didn't know, a woman involved in Islamic revolutionary movements. He had left the professor from Siena behind in Reggio Emilia, set off on a whim, out of jealousy, the desire to be a protagonist.

Part 14

Zurich

1. Pêches Melba

Gustava, Anna and Freya were dining. Gustava welcomed him politely and introduced Freya; he embraced Anna then sat down with them. His hands were sweating. Anna was wearing sunglasses with tortoiseshell frames, and she seemed more beautiful than when they had parted in Florence, more perverse and more feminine. At first glance, he felt a shudder run down his spine; he recognized Freya as the one who had shot him, who had grazed past him on the Paris sidewalk. He recognized her voice, her gestures. She had reddish hair and blue eyes, the look of an Anglo-Saxon woman. Freya, who was an expert in the art of lying, did not betray her feelings in any way. She barely spoke, as if to play down her presence; she allowed her aunt and her cousin to do the talking and answered only when it was necessary to avoid arousing suspicion. Dennis pretended to be absorbed in the conversation, and at the same time he made an effort not to reveal his agitation. He was thinking that his story was becoming more and more unreal.

How was it possible for his would-be murderer to be Anna's cousin? Was she the one who had killed Marziano? Had she killed Bosco and Vanessa Muller? Had she organized Anna's kidnapping—had she, finally, been the one to decide that her cousin should be blinded? How was it possible for this shy and polite

MISGUIDED LIVES

woman to be a dangerous killer? Probably she was here, in Zurich, to shoot him again. To kill him this time.

Dennis began to look at Freya in a different light when she started eating the peach Melba she had ordered for dessert. She ate the peach and the ice cream greedily, chewing slowly and moving her tongue from one side of her mouth to the other, and then she moistened her lips. Through an association of ideas, while he was watching Freya chew her peach Melba, Dennis had the impression that before his eyes a metamorphosis was taking place and she was becoming brunette, undulant, lying on a bed of reeds and leaves on a Polynesian island. In his mind Freya had turned into Anna in Polynesian costume, like a Gauguin model. That woman, half-Polynesian and half-Anna, moving her tongue almost disgustingly, was a nymphomaniac who would make love with anyone who asked her. Freya, eating her peach Melba, was distracted, and her face changed from that of an English traveler of bygone days to that of a lascivious, frustrated woman who wanted nothing but a man who would desire her. Freya ate the peach in that provocative way to let him know that she wanted him at this moment, but surely not in order to kill him. He felt the same sensation growing, but he would have liked to bring Anna into it. As had happened to him before with Marina, he wanted to have Anna as well. Together, the two women would have been very beautiful. The fact that Anna was blind would have given Freya more confidence, for she surely had a complex about her cousin.

Dennis began to desire them together as he observed Anna's different attitude towards her own peach Melba. She ate listlessly, knowing that in the afternoon they would make plans for the future in which she didn't believe and which mattered very little to her. She had never cared a great deal, even before, about her future. For her, life proceeded from day to day. Aunt Gustava, on the other hand, ate her peach calmly, glad to have her nieces with her and pleased by the arrival of Dennis, of whom, during the period of the kidnapping, she had begun to be very fond.

2. Conversations

They went to have coffee in one of the public rooms of the hotel, and with scant enthusiasm they began talking. At a certain point Freya said, "A friend of mine, a woman I met years ago in Katmandu, who's living in Paris now, gave me the name of an extraordinary doctor who gets miraculous results with acupuncture. I was wondering if, before going to Boston, it wouldn't be worth stopping in Paris to try this Chinese. You never know. It can't do any harm. I don't mean you shouldn't go to America. Not at all. It's just an added suggestion."

Anna smiled. "All I remember of America is bars, hotels, nightclubs. I remember some cocktails you drink in one gulp and they go straight to your head. Then you feel a sparkling drunk. I'd go to America just to taste one of those sublime cocktails again."

"All joking aside," Freya went on, a bit annoyed by the interruption, "if you want to give that a try before you end up in the hands of an American surgeon, I suggest you come with me to Paris. It doesn't cost anything to try."

"Anyway, it costs less to go to Paris than to Boston," Anna said, "so let's go ahead and try. Here they've made it obvious to me that they can't do anything, and I don't see why they should be able to work a miracle in America. Maybe you're right, after all, about the Chinese and their cure. Especially if it's cheaper, given what the kidnapping cost all of you!"

"Excuse me, Anna," Freya said, "don't misunderstand me. It's not a question of money."

"We're here because we love you, darling," Aunt Gustava said. "You mustn't think it's a financial matter. Freya mentioned Chinese medicine only because it's said to be less painful and more effective. You understand, darling, everyone has their own ideas. Personally, I'm not at all sure I believe in acupuncture. But you mustn't misunderstand me either, Freya dear; I know how it helped you in the past. But perhaps Dennis has a different view, another course to suggest."

Exhausted, Anna felt that her blindness was the object of a conversation in which everyone tried to underline his own knowledge. "What if we talk about it later? I'm grateful to you all for your concern. I know you love me, and I appreciate your kindness, but I'm tired. I feel slightly dizzy, and I'd rather not have to decide anything in haste. I'd like to take a walk with Dennis."

Dennis stood up, took Anna's arm, and they left the hotel, heading for the lake. Close together, they walked in silence. Dennis felt the warmth and the shape of Anna's body beside him, and he thought again of Freya, who aroused him and frightened him. He knew that in her purse she had a loaded pistol fitted with a silencer, that she was only waiting for the right moment. She wanted to kill him as she had killed Marziano and God knows how many others, for reasons Dennis didn't know. And yet he couldn't deny his attraction to this murderess who concealed behind an exemplary calm a feverish sensitivity, a megalomaniac desire to be loved and to control every situation.

Her features and sharp profile, as well as certain glances, suggested she was not a normal person. For example, when she said acupuncture was a less expensive cure and Anna was hurt, Freya's gaze betrayed a flash of hatred towards herself for having said something wrong; that hatred was then directed at Anna. For something only a bit more serious, she was probably capable of killing. Her gaze was truly hypnotic. Now she had returned to the family, with affectionate and childlike manners, but her purpose was to kill Dennis and close the circle. What if he were to try to seduce Freya? If he declared his love, what effect would that produce? Would she despise him because of her cousin? Would she be indifferent? She would surely consider any act of seduction ignoble in view of the situation and the fact that he was engaged to Anna. It was also possible that she had nothing to do with her cousin's kidnapping and was here only to shoot him. Why not discuss it with Anna, say to her frankly, "What shall I do? Freya is the woman who shot me at le Palace et du Golf." What would happen to the firm if Freya killed him that very evening? Was he so sure, after all, that he could trust the professor from Siena? Would that young intellectual be capable of resisting Duilio's pressure and maintaining an editorial line, a prestigious program? Why not? Both the professor and Duilio were endowed with common sense.

Anna interrupted Dennis's thoughts. "What if I vanished? What if I went off by myself, far away? I can't stand any more of this talk about treatments, treatments in Boston, unconventional treatments, less-expensive treatments, Chinese needles and God knows what. Being blind isn't a disease! Since my blindness people have been treating me like some rare animal. Instead of wasting so many words on how to treat me, where it costs more and where less, today I'd like to go on the merry-go-round, the roller coasters, then in a few days I'd leave for Hong Kong or Singapore to be a prostitute, and then when I'm too old to be a prostitute I'll ask the last of my customers to give me a handsome Alsatian dog and I'll go to a big city and beg for alms outside a deluxe shop. Rio de Janeiro or New York, I don't know. While the rest of you were talking about which treatments would be best, I felt a strong desire, right between my legs, and I had to ask you to take me out for a walk. A desire to go and prostitute myself in a street in the old city of Zurich. I'd like you to take me to a hotel where they rent rooms by the hour. I read in a picture magazine, years ago, that Zurich has a very high percentage of whores and night spots."

Dennis sometimes was surprised and intimidated by Anna. He forgot what kind of woman she was. She wouldn't accept her blindness with common sense.

MISGUIDED LIVES

Once they were in a hotel in the old part of downtown Zurich, Dennis felt like a rag doll caught between the madness of the two cousins. He was there with Anna to satisfy her sexual desires, while he risked being killed by Freya at any street corner. "I'd be very jealous if you wanted to prostitute yourself," he said to Anna, "even though I realize that, beautiful and blind, you'd be a treat for any brothel. If you want my advice, go to New York. They'll pay you very well."

"I think they'd pay more in Japan, where a white woman is much more valuable. Imagine: European and blind."

"Yes, but then you ought to be blond as well."

"In that case, I only have to dye my hair. Do you think Catherine Deneuve is really blond? But my problem is different. Money doesn't interest me; I'd like to sell myself cheap in a brothel patronized only by yellow men in a city of the Far East. I'd like to be accepted by the Chinese or Indian women. I should go to Calcutta or Benares. I'd like to give myself to poor, undernourished men, like a prostitute of the lowest level. I'd like them to pay me less because of my blindness, not more. I'd like the fact of being blind and hence less attractive to force me to learn special tricks to keep from being sent away. It pleases me to think that I'll be old then and undesirable, and I can beg for alms. I prefer poor customers because I think the rich men who come to deluxe brothels are disgusting."

While Anna talked, Dennis was thinking that Freya had followed them, perhaps had taken a room next to theirs, and would soon come in and kill the two of them together, in the bed. If Freya had been there and had listened to what Anna was saying, she would have had a fit of devastating jealousy. Now it was clear where the erotic scenes in Gustava von Traube's books came from. Anna had an exceptional way of living and of narrating her life. She knew the oblivion and tumult of the night instinctively; it was a part of her. The margaritas, the Brazilians, the Zurich hotel, the roller coasters and the lower depths of Calcutta were all part of the same way of looking at things. Anna had the taste of a whore, and after a certain hour of the night she would let herself be taken by the first comer, she would go anywhere with him, waking the next morning as if nothing had happened.

Anna went on. "Maybe I could tell Freya I'd rather be examined by Chinese doctors in Hong Kong. She could accompany me there, not suspecting a thing, and keep me company for a few days then go away again. While I diligently went through with useless therapies, I could at my leisure find the job I want in a brothel. This idea cheers me up. After what's happened, I want only to enjoy myself. I need absence, a period of rest. I tell you, life's a mess. A woman gets herself kidnapped, causes her family to appear in all the newspapers and bankrupts them, she comes back blind on the eve of her wedding and then she's supposed to act like a good, honest citizen, go and sit in front of a judge who never stops smoking and submit to hours of questioning, which all gets written down and becomes property of the state."

Later, back at the hotel, they found Freya waiting for them. She was elegantly made up and had slightly changed the way she did her hair. Dennis continued to find her seductive.

"Where's Aunt Gustava?" Anna asked.

"She's talking with an English journalist she met in Florence; he's trying to interview her."

They all went out to supper, and Marc Blum came with them. His arrival had restored Gustava's good humor. She enjoyed herself with Blum, finding him cultivated, intelligent, able to tell interesting anecdotes. Anna, immersed in her Hong Kong fantasy, began to talk about a trip to Asia, and Blum proved well informed. Freya remained silent; she realized Blum was dangerous. As soon as the conversation allowed him to, he turned to her and asked, in a nonchalant tone, "Where were you during your cousin's kidnapping, when all of us were in Florence? To get our minds off things, in moments of panic, we talked about your absence, and your aunt insisted you never know what's going on because you don't read the papers. Since I'm a newspaper man, I couldn't help but ask myself, with amazement, why not? As if it were a sin not to read the papers!"

"That's right!" Gustava added promptly. "She's always been like that. She never read the papers as a child, either. They irritated her; she considered them rubbish. We all have our unlikely phobias!"

"It's very simple. Buying newspapers seems to me a useless expense. You can always learn the news anyway from other people or by listening to the car radio," Freya answered.

"Do you often travel by car?" Blum pressed her.

"Less than I used to. Now I like to travel by train. I feel more protected."

"I understand you. I also greatly prefer the train. You can read the papers peacefully. Ah, but of course! You listen to the car radio."

The conversation was interrupted when Anna inadvertently upset a bottle of wine on the table. This reminder of her blindness embarrassed everyone. But Anna laughed and said that spilling wine brings good luck, and so the talk turned to wine, California wines and a trip Freya had to take to California. Freya suggested that Anna might come with her. Anna replied that, since she was to try out Chinese medicine, she wanted to go to the Orient, not to Paris and not to California. The cousins' tone became shrill. Dennis was bored and couldn't figure out why he was here, in this famous Zurich restaurant, listening to the word games of a group of snobs who took pleasure in showing one another how intelligent they were, how clever, how up-to-date on everything. This conversation bored him just as, in childhood, he was bored listening to the men talk about football.

"You still haven't told us where you were during Anna's kidnapping," Blum repeated unexpectedly.

"Only because you were all talking about other things! You seemed so amazed that I don't read the newspapers. I don't read them because, thank God, we are all free to do as we choose. I don't buy newspapers because they're badly written, and besides I'm not interested in knowing what's happening. I admit that when Anna was kidnapped I would've done better to read them; I could've come earlier to help Aunt Gustava. But no one has to feel obliged to read the newspapers just in case some close relative's been kidnapped! Still, I understand your curiosity about why someone doesn't read the newspapers. But you're here with us this evening, no doubt because of your undeniable fondness for Aunt Gustava—but chiefly to collect as many indiscretions and as much news as possible so you can write an article about Anna. If it weren't for your friendship with Aunt Gustava, which forces me to be particularly indulgent towards you, I'd ask you to leave us alone."

"Freya, why do you have to be rude to Mr. Blum?" Aunt Gustava said. "Darling, has anyone reproached you in any way? The fact that you don't read the papers is only one of your acts of rejection of the society we live in, and I'm the first to respect your way of thinking."

"Forgive me, I'm tired and therefore pointlessly argumentative. But I don't believe journalists should be given so much importance. I think it's a sickness of our time."

"You surely have a grudge against us," Blum couldn't help adding.

"I don't want to inflict too many details on our friends to explain why I'm not particularly fond of journalists. I believe that giving such power, as is done nowadays, to people who almost never tell the truth, because the truth isn't fun to read and doesn't sell, is one of the causes of the many disasters in this world. My rejection of newspapers is a way of saying no thanks to a society that believes it has a bit of power because of the bits of news it absorbs from the mass media. I believe power lies in silence, in meditation. I think, for example, of a verse in the Book of Job that says something like 'let him who has a headache study the Torah.' "

Listening to this conversation, Dennis was convinced she had wanted to kill him. In Freya's gaze there was a glacial impersonality. He knew for certain that she could handle weapons and that she had the nerve to behave, in society, like a woman of the world, though she had committed countless crimes and was on the verge of committing another. Clearly, for her, killing was the only possible and definitive way of getting rid of a person who was hostile to her. She made her own justice, according to her fanatical criteria. That night in Zurich, Dennis felt saved, because he saw that Freya's murderous desire had shifted to Blum.

3. More Deaths

Nothing special happened that night. The next morning Freya took the train to Paris, and Aunt Gustava accompanied her to the station. In the afternoon Marc Blum caught the London plane. The next day, Dennis, who had remained in Zurich with Anna and Gustava, read in the newspaper that Blum had been found dead in his London home. That same night, in Zurich, Anna committed suicide.

Anna was lying lifeless on the bed in her room, and in the adjoining sitting room Dennis and Aunt Gustava looked at each other in silence. From time to time, just to stir the air, one of them would say, "Poor Anna!"

Awaiting the return of Freya, to whom she'd telephoned the news, Gustava, for all her vast imagination, couldn't even remotely suspect that Freya settled her scores with a pistol or a dagger.

Dennis was dumbfounded by Freya's behavior. He envied her. How many times had he wanted to be rid of that slimy and presumptuous Englishman!

Blum had been murdered because he knew too much. It was becoming obvious that they would all be exterminated, one after the other. Poor Anna had been wise to kill herself without waiting for the ghostly assassin to execute her.

The distraught Belgioiosos arrived before Freya. In a voice tense and choked with emotion, Gustava said, "I admire my niece Anna very much, and if I were religious I would go and pray beside her corpse. She didn't want to go back to her children defeated, disfigured. That's why she killed herself, I'm sure of it. She wanted them to retain the memory of a beautiful mother, different from anyone else. She didn't want to become pathetic in their eyes. Anna wouldn't drag herself from doctor to doctor, looking for a miracle. Poor darling, what a difficult life! I have very bright memories of her as a child. She always wanted to go on the roller coasters when there was a fair, and her passion for roller coasters remained with her as a grown-up. She loved ices and ate them all the time, in secret. She was a woman the world corrupted very little. She reasoned simply, became happy then sad, then jealous of Freya, then she got over it. Those two girls always adored each other, and at the same time they never stopped quarreling. You could say they were sisters! Freya should arrive at any moment, and I can't think what state she must be in, poor darling! For her Anna's death is a tremendous disaster; I can feel that already."

After unburdening herself, Gustava was silent. The others were also quiet, staring into the void as if it might offer an answer to this death. Gustava didn't seem concerned about Blum's death; she was too distraught over what had happened to Anna. All her life Gustava had played niece against niece, for a while leading Anna to believe she was the favorite, then Freya. Now that Anna was gone, it was clear she would remain the favorite forever. Only Dennis knew Blum had been killed by Freya. Freya knew that he knew because she was aware he'd recognized her; both had put up a good pretense, as if they were accomplices. It was incredible that this woman had left such a trail of crimes, all unpunished. But where had Freya hidden during Anna's kidnapping? The truth was that Dennis had to try to prevent more murders, find genuine evidence and report Freya to the police. It was necessary to put an end to the monstrous chain of crimes. Dennis showed them Anna's letter in which she expressed her final wishes:

Dear Dennis,

I know you will consider this act of mine cowardly, but it is the only thing I can do. I'm going away, at peace because I have felt your nearness and affection. If it is possible, please have me cremated and scatter my ashes in Venice. It was in Venice, that night, that you won me. So I would like to be taken there, a small, not very cumbersome package. I've never liked corpses, coffins, death rites. After life, nothing. Ashes scattered on the water like incense. Even this seems presumptuous to me. A sublime, slightly theatrical gesture. Forgive me if I'm vain and ask this of you, but I'm a woman. I love you.

Anna

P.S. I think you won't die. Keep on with your work as publisher and trust the professor from Siena.

4. Marcello Bresci

When Freya arrived at the hotel in the late afternoon, she looked different. She was dressed in black leather, with a red and white polka-dot scarf knotted around her neck, and she had cut her hair. Short, it seemed more vital; her lips were very red. She made a great impression on the Belgioiosos, who didn't know her and behaved affectionately to her aunt and tried to say light things that would relieve some of the grimness gathering in the room. Then Freya went alone into her dead cousin's bedroom. Later that evening it was decided that Aunt Gustava was too weak to accompany Dennis to Italy, so Freya would go to Venice to represent the family. Scattering the ashes was against the law, so they would carry out Anna's wishes at night. She had mentioned no specific place in her note. Which was better: the Rialto Bridge and the Grand Canal or a little back canal? It was incredible how they could discuss the problem of Anna's ashes as if it were an ordinary practical question, when the day before she had been there, alive and sensual.

In her will Anna had expressed a precise wish for Dennis to scatter her ashes in Venice, and Freya would go with him. But he wasn't afraid, because Freya seemed to have changed—not only her way of dressing, but also the expression on her face. Anna's suicide had arrested her way of thinking. Freya wasn't accustomed to life without Anna, and even if she had been an accomplice in the kidnapping and had somehow contributed to her cousin's blinding, she surely hadn't foreseen her death.

273

MISGUIDED LIVES

During the cremation and on the plane that took them from Zurich to Venice, Freya was taciturn. Grieving, she hid her feelings behind her sunglasses. Freya's presence was less disturbing for Dennis because at the last minute Maud had joined them. Nanni had gone back to London. Maud's presence made a murder more difficult. When Maud left after the scattering of the ashes, either Freya would kill him immediately or they would make a bargain and he wouldn't report her. The only person he had left was Marina. He didn't feel up to calling her at that moment; his feelings had become confused. The most frightful events were overlapping before he even had time to reflect. So he dismissed the thought of Marina and imagined himself going back to Turin, to work. In her letter, Anna had asked him to do that. In the space of a few months Anna had gained a huge influence on his life.

Freya, Maud and Dennis threw Anna's ashes into a secluded little canal near the Salute—a discreet place, in accord with what Maud felt was Anna's true nature. Dennis and Freya didn't agree, but it would have been out of place to quarrel. The ceremony was cold, rapid. Afterwards, they remained taciturn, and they withdrew alone to their rooms. Things could have gone differently. They could have invented a festive ritual, but it hadn't been possible.

The next morning, after a night of gloomy thoughts and tormented sleep, Dennis rose early and went out. He had arranged to meet Freya later in the morning at a café in Campo Santo Stefano to say good-bye. Maud had already left for London. On his way to the café Dennis stopped at the window of a bookshop and saw a number of copies of Bosco's book, prominently displayed. Out of professional habit, he went inside to speak to the bookseller, to ask how the novel was selling and how the firm's other books were doing. Then, nearly forgetting all that was happening to him, he lingered to talk about future publishing plans and about the young collaborator he had taken on, a man interested in new talent. Coming out of the shop, Dennis thought how for months he had kept himself away from really good people. But that characteristic guilt towards those who held regular jobs and led ordinary lives was something he'd felt since he was a boy. He bought the papers, then he sat down at a café table to wait for Freya. On the first page he recognized the photograph of Nanni Belgioioso. The headlines read: "Marcello Bresci, the London strangler."

Marcello Bresci, who passed himself off as Nanni Belgioioso, had strangled, the day before, in a London apartment, an Italian woman whose photograph was also reproduced. Dennis recognized her as Marina. His confusion and bewilderment were absolute. It seemed impossible that this could be his reality, his life and his story. He had just thought of Marina, of getting in touch with her in a little while. And Nanni Belgioioso—who'd been in Zurich two days ago, so cordial and so polite! And what of Maud—did she know her husband was a murderer? Were they accomplices? And were Freya and Belgioioso-Bresci accomplices? Were they part of the same organization, or did they work on their own? Were they rivals? It occurred to him that it could all be a plot directed by Clara, from her hiding-place in a kibbutz. In any case there was something suspicious about her having withdrawn to Israel, to a kibbutz, to forget. She wasn't capable, however, of organizing all these crimes. But whoever was responsible, it was a monstrous and surreal business. By now, of that group, only a few were still alive, and each of them could be either victim or murderer: Enrica, Tatiana, Gustava von Traube, Freya, Maud, the professor from Siena, Duilio, Danesi . . . But would they all die? He couldn't manage to feel sad over Marina's death, events had outstripped it. The evening before, he'd thrown his fiancée's ashes into a Venetian canal, and now he learned that a woman he was fond of had been strangled by a man he knew, and he was about to have a coffee with another person he knew to be a murderer, who had wounded him only a few months ago. His head was swimming; if he went to the police to report Freya and tell the whole story, they would take him for a madman. When Freya arrived, what would he say? Until this moment they had pretended to know nothing about each other, but how could he talk about one murderer with another?

Dennis saw Freya in the distance. The best thing would be to act as if nothing had happened, to be as cordial as possible and separate quickly. Seeing her arrive, he was touched, noticing for the first time a family resemblance between Freya and Anna, in their way of moving. It was amazing how, after Anna's death, Freya had assumed certain poses of hers, even her way of speaking. When she sat down at the table, she greeted him with a dazzling smile. Again he found her sexy. Her lips were painted with a bright red lipstick, and as she drank her coffee she moved her mouth and her tongue just as she had a few days ago in Zurich, when he had watched her eat the peach Melba.

She wore a fresh perfume whose scent suggested childhood and a very strong sensuality. But what was Freya thinking at that moment? What did she feel towards him? Did she know about Belgioioso and the crime in London? Would she kill him here in Campo Santo Stefano? Unable to restrain himself, Dennis said, "Life is becoming unbearable! They've strangled a friend of mine in London, the wife of my dearest friend! It's mad. And you know who strangled her?"

"No, who?"

"Look: it's written in all the papers. You remember him, the day before yesterday, in Zurich? Nanni Belgioioso, Maud's husband? Well, he was the one. While Maud was here in Venice with us. His name isn't even Belgioioso. That's a fake. His real name is Bresci. The whole story seems crazy to me!"

"I can understand your being so nervous. May I see the papers, please?"

"Of course. Read them!"

Freya read without displaying any special reaction; her hands were not large, but slender, nervous. She held the paper expertly and, without removing her attention from it, she took a cigarette from her purse and lighted it. Dennis felt a yearning for a cigarette, then a desire to kiss her on the mouth and stain his lips. His life depended on that woman, and he had just spoken to her in a friendly tone, seeking her solidarity. As Freya went on reading carefully, he asked impatiently, "Is it really possible that Belgioioso-Bresci is a murderer?"

"If you ask me, he's an amateur, and it's some sentimental thing."

"Was Maud his accomplice?"

"She'll feel betrayed by the fact that her husband strangled a woman for love."

"Why for love?"

"I don't know. I just said that. How should I know?"

"If Maud hadn't been so damn serious about Anna's ashes, I'd have thrown them into the Arno."

"But Anna wrote that she wanted them scattered in Venice! And anyway, can't we talk about something else? Conversations about cities make me think of those rich bourgeois I despise, or the English. When I was a little girl I used to hate it when Aunt Gustava and her friends would start talking about Aden, Cairo, Bombay and so on . . . In her books, too, she talks about cities and hotels, as if that society of sleeping cars and ocean liners still existed!"

There was a silence, and both pretended to read the papers. Dennis thought that, in hating conversations about cities, Freya was like Marziano. But Marziano had been a city man, whereas Freya was a traveler. Dennis noticed the weather was turning bad and, looking from time to time at Freya, he became uneasy. It occurred to him that if he was the only one who knew she was a criminal, and assuming the Belgioiosos didn't turn her in, then little Tatiana was the only person who could implicate her. Basically, Freya was a checkers player who, on the board of life, consumed the pieces that got in her way. He imagined seeking refuge with Freya in Volterra. But why would he consider protecting her? It was her way of sitting at the café, her way of showing her legs while skillfully hiding her ankles that attracted him.

Freya wasn't really reading the paper. She was thinking about Dennis. She knew he had recognized her in Zurich and had caught on to everything, but she suspected he had absolutely no recollection of the Reggio Emilia days. She had gone by the name Tamara then, she had been much younger and had worn her hair differently. At that time everything was free love, they lived in a group, and in the heart of the night they all traded women. If she were to talk about it, he would remember; but what was the use of digging up things buried for years? Freya would like to bury everything and start over. She hoped to experience that love story she had waited for all these years. She wanted Dennis to kiss her, but she had to be patient and wait for the right moment. Men don't realize. They don't understand how important it is for a woman to make someone make love to her.

5. Tatiana

As if they were a couple, Dennis and Freya decided to go to Florence together. Dennis had to meet the professor from Siena to discuss work, then they would go on to Rome to Marina's funeral. In the train they did nothing but read books and newspapers, occasionally speaking to each other in monosyllables. In that train Freya was different from any other woman. Every now and then she left the compartment to go and smoke a cigarette, leaving her handbag on her seat. Dennis wondered if there was a pistol with a silencer in the bag, the way other women carry a key ring, a compact, a lipstick.

Freya would have liked Dennis to know nothing about her, just to notice a foreign woman smoking in the passage of the train and try to strike up a conversation. "You're going to Florence?"

"Yes."

"Is this the first time you've been in Italy?"

"I came once as a little girl with my parents."

After a pause he would say, "If you don't know Italy well, don't go to Florence immediately. It's an austere city. Come with me to Rome. I'll take you to dinner in Piazza Navona. You'll see how beautiful and languid the squares and fountains of Rome are."

In Florence they went to the same hotel and took separate rooms. They chose a slow game, in which everything remained suspended.

All the newspapers were filled with articles about the Belgioioso-Bresci case, and the police had provisionally arrested the wife, a Frenchwoman who worked in fashion. The papers reported that the inquiring magistrate had questioned the daughter of the strangled woman. There was a question as to whether the same Belgioioso-Bresci had murdered the girl's father, the spy killed a few months ago in Vichy.

Reading about Tatiana, Dennis felt he would have to muster the courage to confess to Freya that Tatiana had seen her and might be able to identify her. For that matter, from the way Freya read the papers in Venice, he had realized her claim to pay no attention to the press was a pose. Almost certainly she had read Blum's articles, which said several times that Tatiana had seen a woman with a scarf around her head and a long raincoat. But that description no longer tallied with the person who was in Florence these days. He himself, though he remembered very well the appearance of the woman who shot him, wouldn't have recognized Freya now. She was a great actress, capable of genuine metamorphoses. But it was normal for a murderer to be skilled in disguise, in changing identity.

The truth was that Freya had changed inside. She was someone trained to live in the present, in a concentrated fashion, quickly draining herself of anything that had happened before. She had become the only niece of Gustava von Traube. She had money, she was here as the friend, companion and imminent mistress of a neurotic and versatile Italian. In the past, she and that man had already been lovers. Now her chief occupation was shopping. She roamed through the streets of Florence in search of a present to give Dennis. She wanted to find something personal, special. Hour after hour she searched for an object that might please him. In the boutiques she bought herself dresses, costume jewelry, perfumes, bath salts, cosmetics. She changed her clothes often, prettied herself, was different at every meal. She wanted to be a sexy, striking woman but also mysterious and elegant in every detail. Day after day she tried to replace Anna in Dennis's life without his noticing. She never spoke of the past, there was no past, only the two of them remained. Freya had interpreted Anna's suicide as a testament, a bequest. In every sense she had inherited Anna's place, so she was therefore Dennis's fiancée. She wanted him to be constantly aware of her seduction, her presence. She wanted him to need to have her near, and when she wasn't there she wanted him to miss her physically, even though they hadn't yet made love.

Freya realized that the professor from Siena was taken with her, an idea that didn't displease her. As an added element, to heighten Dennis's attention, she let him suspect there might be a mutual attraction. When they went out together and the talk was about books or about the firm, Freya would participate, assuming polemical attitudes to show she didn't intend to flatter anyone. Dennis was far from insensitive to Freya's slow seduction. He hoped Tatiana would reveal nothing compromising and that there would be no new turn of events. Perhaps Dennis didn't see Freya as Anna's heiress, as she imagined, but he desired her presence and liked to savor the slow development of their feelings. At times, alone in his room, he imagined what it would be like to live with her. Then he called himself a madman, a masochist, well knowing that Freya was playing this slow game of seduction to reassure him, to wait for the opportune moment to kill him. And yet, at certain moments, he had the illusion she was sincere. Undeniably, she knew how to protect herself. For example, she waited for him in Florence, hadn't tried to accompany him when he went to Rome to Marina's funeral. Thus she had avoided encountering Tatiana.

Dennis was working with the professor from Siena to perfect the editorial programs, and in the evenings, when they went out to supper, Gianna Galbiati, who was there on tour, often came along with them. Dennis and Gianna had known each other for many years; she had been a friend of Mario's. Freya had met her in other circumstances. The only things that mattered for Gianna were the theater and Russian literature. She wasn't a famous actress, but she was good. She was high-spirited, witty and, most of all, not involved with the publishing firm or the Belgioioso-Bresci case, which the newspapers went on writing about.

In the restaurant Gianna Galbiati flirted a bit with the professor from Siena, who had eyes only for Freya and hadn't yet lost all hope.

Meanwhile, in London, according to the papers, Tatiana told the police about the woman she'd seen at le Palace et du Golf. Tatiana, Dennis thought, would recognize Freya in any case. It wouldn't be possible to change her vocal cords, and Freya's guttural and slightly hoarse voice was unforgettable. On the other hand, Tatiana might not have heard her speak.

Freya was prepared to defend herself. She hadn't had anything to do with Nanni Belgioioso's strangling of Marina. She hadn't taken part in Anna's kidnapping, though she'd known about it. As for the blinding, that was a foolish error on the part of one of the kidnappers, who had thought he was acting for the best. He was an idiot, and the organization had arranged for him to be eliminated. She had killed Marziano, who had come to realize too many things. And she had also suggested the murder of Blum, who had frightened her that evening in Zurich and made her aware that he

281

represented a great risk. Blum's death had probably been attributed to Bresci-Belgioioso, and the same went for Bosco and for Vanessa Muller. Only Blum had realized, belatedly, that there had been two different kinds of murders after Dennis was shot.

Unlike Bresci-Belgioioso, Freya wasn't connected with international espionage. She was protected by a terrorist organization aimed at destabilizing the Western countries. Dennis was afraid that if they weren't somehow able to get Tatiana out of the way there was always the risk that Freya would be unmasked.

But Freya was busy. Watching Gianna Galbiati act, she was learning how to become another character. Freya wanted only to put an end to this business and marry Dennis. Once married, they would build a normal life for themselves. Nothing in her past mattered anymore. She was sure Aunt Gustava would approve of their marriage, which, after a reasonable period of mourning for Anna, would seem natural.

Dennis hadn't the remotest suspicion of Freya's thoughts. Though he was growing fond of her, he didn't show it, and he preferred everything to remain vague. Gianna Galbiati announced one evening that she was leaving; she had to go to Todi and then to Montepulciano. She invited the professor from Siena, Freya and Dennis to come and see her.

Part 15

Montepulciano

1. Which Side to Be On?

Freya left with Gianna Galbiati for Todi, the professor from Siena went to Turin and Dennis remained in Florence. Tatiana had called, saying she wanted to come see him.

Since she was Marziano and Marina's daughter, he looked on her as a relative. It touched him to see this girl, and he felt intimidated by her presence. She bore a surprising resemblance to both her father and her mother. Her eyes and her speech recalled Marziano's intellectual precocity, and her movements had something of Marina about them. As soon as she saw Dennis, she said, "I came in order to know you. I want to help the police unmask the woman who shot you. I told the judge I saw her. I'd recognize her anywhere. Only it's not easy to find a person when you don't know anything about her."

"It's sweet of you to be concerned for me, with all the misfortunes you've had. Your thoughtfulness makes me happy because I was a close friend of your father, the person I respected most in the world. He knew everything; with him I could talk about everything. When he was gone I had the sensation that I had lost a fundamental part of my life, and from that moment on I would have to learn how to remain silent. I met your mother late, but I was very fond of her. You mustn't worry too much about the person who shot me, it could've been a mistake. Now, though it will be hard, you must think about studying and try to construct a normal life. You must go ahead, and I promise I'll come to visit you at your school."

"The police want me to help trace that person. It's dangerous to allow a criminal to remain free and unpunished, isn't it?"

"Did they show you photographs? Were you able to recognize her?"

"I didn't see any photographs."

Tatiana was curious to know certain things about her parents, and they talked for a long time about Marziano and Marina. Then they discussed her future. Tatiana said she would stay on in the same school, trying to finish as soon as possible, then she hoped to win a grant and go to an American university. They spent the whole day together, conversing like old friends as they walked through the streets of Florence. Tatiana and Dennis parted with a certain emotion.

Left alone, Dennis realized his apprehensions were not unfounded. He felt very close to this girl, who had come to see him so spontaneously and had talked with him as if she were a daughter. An orphan, she was alone in the world. She hadn't even mentioned the name of Enrica's child, her little brother. The girl could hardly imagine that Dennis knew Freya. But if Freya wanted to live peacefully it was obvious that sooner or later she would have to kill Tatiana. But how could he wish, as he had so often, for the murder of the child of his best friend and of a woman he had loved in order to save a woman who had tried to kill him? Why didn't he call the police and give them the name of the hotel in Todi where Freya was staying? Tatiana would identify her, and with Dennis's testimony that would be enough to have Freya arrested. Why had she gone off with Gianna Galbiati, not even suspecting Tatiana's arrival? She was unbalanced, you had only to look into her eyes. Her speckled gaze betrayed her instability. Assuming that Freya, through a miracle or a radical change, were to give up the idea of further murders, could they lead a life together? Tatiana wasn't on every street corner, she was a little girl in boarding school and therefore didn't represent an imminent danger. But to live together, he and Freya would have to go off, far away. He would have to abandon the firm, forget his work.

It was a pity Freya had such a notorious past; he was convinced that she really loved him. Nobody had ever shot him for love. In their case the roles were reversed: he was the man of Freya's life. He didn't recall exactly where or how, but he realized that, in the remote past, there had been something between them. Freya had had to shoot him, and all the rest, to win him back. He didn't dare begin something because he didn't want it to end tragically, as his affairs always had before. He couldn't explain it, but he trusted Freya. It was incredible how she had conceived such a complicated plan to gain his attention! This was her greatest weakness: wanting all the attention for herself. As a child she had demanded all of Aunt Gustava's affection, while her aunt had created a constant rivalry between Freya and her cousin. Dennis realized that he'd said nothing to Tatiana because he absolutely didn't want to sever his tie with Freya. He was moved by the unbelievable efforts she had made to bring their love story into existence. But was what he felt for Freya true love or gratitude? Was he capable of turning his whole life inside out and devoting himself to a love story? In lying to Tatiana he had deliberately made himself Freya's accomplice. Undoubtedly it was a dangerous game, living with a woman who had a pistol in her handbag.

2. Montepulciano

Dennis and Freya had agreed to meet in Montepulciano, but not in any specific, binding way. What had led Freya to go off with the actress? She wanted to create a bit of distance and also to go on learning the tricks of the profession. She noticed that actors, in their manner, succeed in creating a permanent ambiguity, even when they're not performing. Something of their characters always rubs off on them. You only have to think of when you're in love and the way you tend to copy your beloved: you move, talk and dress a bit like the other. You assume similar attitudes or political positions. Or else, on the contrary, you take a polemical stance, become a rival. After you have been in love, you bear memories with you, habits and phrases that have settled inside you by a kind of chemical process. Similarly, the actor, even when he changes roles, carries with him roles from the past, certain gestures or tones of voice. Freya was studying how to change and yet remain herself. It wasn't a question of altering her voice or having plastic surgery. She had to alter something inside herself so that she would become unrecognizable. While remaining the same person, she was transforming herself into the sole, favorite niece of Aunt Gustava, without other, more beautiful cousins; into the heiress of Anna; and into an English-woman she had met and admired in Cairo; into the woman of an Italian publisher and into a young theater actress. She was still Freya, but those ingredients, mixed with the fact that she had taken to speaking Italian, were already giving her a different look. She and Dennis telephoned each other on the pretext of discussing Gianna Galbiati's performances. "If you come," Freya said, "and

288

the professor also comes, Gianna will be pleased. In Todi the play's going well, but you know what these small theaters are like. In any case, it's a great pleasure for an actress on tour if friends take the trouble to come and see the performance. It would be wonderful if the two of you came Saturday to Montepulciano. If not, we'll see each other later, in Florence."

The professor stayed in Turin with Duilio, and Dennis went to Montepulciano alone. He met Freya and Gianna Galbiati at the café near the square, then they walked him to a little, modern hotel where he could leave his bag. The rooms were simple. Bed, closet, night table, chair, crucifix on the white wall. The bath was in the corridor. He had a single. Freya and Gianna were sharing a double.

After lunch, Gianna had to see a reporter and then go straight to the theater. Dennis and Freya were left alone. They took a short walk and came back to the hotel for a siesta before changing for the performance. They withdrew to their separate rooms, and a moment later they ran into each other in the corridor. They smiled, barely touching hands. Dennis grazed her breast with his fingers and realized her nipples were hard. Without saying anything, they went into Dennis's room, shut the door, and kissed. Freya's kiss was overwhelming. Long, hot, a kiss she had always wanted to give him, an impassioned kiss. Dennis was moved. The kiss didn't end, couldn't end. They were unable to separate. After so many years and so many tortuous events, they had finally found each other. That embrace was the confession and, at the same time, the absolution of everything. Finally they undressed each other, slowly, clumsily. They didn't dare look at each other naked, they felt their bodies with their hands. Tentatively, Freya put her hand on Dennis's sex and he stroked her small, hard nipples. She was a tiny creature, with a subtle shape and a childlike smile, her gums red, almost purple, with small, white teeth. In her eyes there was gaiety and a vague sadness.

MISGUIDED LIVES

They made love for a long time: with tenderness, with timidity, with passion, with lasciviousness. In that embrace they wanted to find each other expert, tender, enamored. It blended spontaneity with the wish not to disappoint. When they separated, the bed was soaked, and they didn't dare look at each other. Then they kissed again impatiently, as if they didn't want to part. As they started to dress to go to the theater, they remained silent, dazed, then pulled each other onto the bed and embraced again. They loved madly, with strength. Their bodies were very close. It was as if neither of them had known or made love before that moment. When Freya moved to go to the bath and get ready, Dennis felt alone. He followed her and began kissing her again, then he looked at her and couldn't help smiling. Their hearts were pounding and they didn't know whether to speak or cry or laugh.

Finally they went to the theater. During the brief walk they held hands. Freya was flushed, happy. Her features were relaxed. Dennis felt light, he still had Freya's smell on him. In the street, he blurted, "You and Anna haven't the same body or the same smell."

Freya acted as if she hadn't heard.

"Who would ever have said you two were cousins? Anna so voluptuous, and you so thin!"

Freya said nothing, but she turned pale.

3. The Box

The theater was like many little eighteenth-century Italian theaters, with rows of boxes. Some theaters are deep red, others white. This one, recently restored, was white. Dennis and Freya entered their box a few minutes after the play began, and Gianna Galbiati was already on stage. Dressed all in white, she was playing the part of Anya in *The Cherry Orchard.* The theater was dark and almost empty. Dennis and Freya were clinging to each other.

Dennis didn't have time to scream; he died at once. Without his noticing, Freya had drawn a knife from her handbag, a knife similar to the one she had used with Marziano.

Carefully resting Dennis's chest on the velvet railing of the box, Freya wrapped the knife in a handkerchief, replaced it in her bag and left without making any noise. In the lobby, with an amiable smile, she said good night to the uniformed usher, and with tiny steps she headed for the square. She saw a trash receptacle and dropped the handkerchief and knife into it.

In the square she climbed into a taxi and asked the driver to take her to the Chiusi station. There she would catch the first train for Venice. As the car left Montepulciano behind, Freya lit a cigarette and heard Dennis's voice say, as if in an echo, "Who would ever have said you two were cousins? Anna so voluptuous, and you so thin!"

Cloudwalk, November 1987

Ex Libris